Scaring Crows

The Joanna Piercy series:

Winding Up the Serpent
Catch the Fallen Sparrow
A Wreath for my Sister
And None Shall Sleep

Also by the same author:

Night Visit

Priscilla Masters

Scaring Crows

This edition published in Great Britain in 2001 by
Allison & Busby Limited
Suite 111, Bon Marche Centre
241-251 Ferndale Road
Brixton, London SW9 8BJ
http://www.allisonandbusby.ltd.uk

Copyright © 1999 by Priscilla Masters
First published in 1999 by Macmillan Publishers Ltd

A catalogue record for this book is available from
the British Library.

ISBN 0 7490 0358 8

Printed and bound in Spain by
Liberduplex, s.l. Barcelona.

This book is dedicated to Robert and Margaret and their splendid herd of Friesian cows who give me so much pleasure as I watch them from my kitchen window, and to Marilyn Liu who made an admirable Detective Inspector Joanna Piercy – just when I needed her most. And, of course, not forgetting Kerith.

Chapter One

A mischievous starling had learnt to mimic the farmer's whistle and lure the cows to the gate. So while he sat on a high branch of the hawthorn tree, his head cocked to one side, beak open, the animals stood, foolishly, waiting to be led to the cowshed.

Milk leaked from their bloated udders and dampened the cracked mud. And impatient for the relief of the milking parlour the cows trampled the dusty clods and jostled for prime position while the starling continued to tease, repeating the call at intervals.

It was a good enough impersonation to fool the cows.

But they were stupid animals anyway.

Ahead of them, air shimmering with buzzing swarms of flies, gaped the empty lane, with its baking cow pats and the hawthorn tree with the taunting starling, its tiny eyes bright with intelligence, trilling its deceitful tune.

A few of them lifted their heads, absorbed the familiar sounds and were vaguely aware that one thing was missing. Perhaps the familiar stamp of farmers' boots?

By seven fifteen the cows were desperate. Full udders are painful and the hormones given to stimulate their milk production meant their udders were filled to bursting point. They widened their stance and bellowed for help. A few at the back of the herd shoved forward, increasing the pressure on the leader so she was forced against the gate. The hasp holding it was old and rusty, the nails pinned into wood weak with damp rot. Under the pressure of the cows, goaded by the cheeky starling, it suddenly broke and swung open. They were free. They could have wandered at will. Without the farmer's switch they could have waddled up the road or down the hill to other pastures. But they were cows, simple animals without imagination or direction. A few of them grazed half-heartedly at the verges yellowing in the summer's heat but the burden of milk was heavy. The instinct to drain their load overcame any sense of liberty. As though the farmer and his dog were behind them they stamped and snorted, flicked their tails against the flies and moved along the dusty track, towards the milking parlour, passing the yawning door of the farmhouse. As they drew level with the house a huge black and white Friesian with a number 79 stamped on her rump lifted her head to stare. But cows are incurious creatures. The open door meant nothing to her. So she bent her head again, swayed her boney hips and walked steadily to the milking parlour.

But once outside the disorganized herd remained there.

10.00 a.m.

They said you could set your clock by him he was so punctual. At precisely ten o'clock every morning Dave Shackleton swung the milk tanker round the tight corner and drove along the lane towards the farm. It was his job to suck the milk out of the tank and drive it to the Milk Marque headquarters. He honked his horn, as he did every morning, to warn the farmer to be ready. He had another collection to make and was anxious to sun himself at home. The job necessitated an early start and he was tired and a touch more impatient than usual. So when no one came to greet him and a couple of the stray cows crowded round his cab he was annoyed, slapping his hand on the horn again. He scanned the entire dusty yard, the cowsheds, the stone farmhouse, even back along the lane. But instead of being met by the farmer, a cow jostled the tanker. In the distance a dog roamed the lane. Puzzled he scanned the chaotic yard and honked his horn for the third time.

It was then that the absence of humans began to trouble him and he started to notice other things. The tractors were still and the ancient Landrover was neatly backed up against the wall. The door to the farmhouse stood open, as usual, but this morning no one appeared in it. Shackleton's hand left the horn and found the cab door handle instead. He threw the door wide open and jumped down, elbowing a path through the needy cows who were pushing towards him desperately, perhaps connecting a human form with deliverance. One or two pushed against him roughly. Shackleton ignored them after a soft, 'Hay-up.'

Shouting now, he peered first inside the milking parlour, straining for the familiar sight, the thin, bent old man in his dungarees and the square, bovine son who worked so tirelessly alongside him. Maybe even Ruthie.

But it was empty apart from two or three heifers who optimistically stood in their usual stalls. And now a new sound joined the mooing of the cows and the droning of insects. Noah, the old dog, sensing something, was barking and rattling his chain.

Shackleton glanced uneasily towards the house. The door was open. Maybe they had overslept and were finishing their breakfast. He started towards it, already mentally pulling their legs about being lie-a-beds.

But even as he formed the thought he knew he was mistaken. Aaron and Jack Summers *never* overslept. Like him they were reliable, industrious. In all the years he had been calling at the farm the cows had always been milked every day. This family, for all their strangeness and segregation, were steady people, the three of them, father, daughter and son.

Shackleton scratched his wiry curls and took two reluctant steps towards the open door of the farmhouse.

It was not like them to neglect their herd. Other farmers, maybe, and his head gave an involuntary jerk towards the neighbouring farm. He called out and listened for an answer before resolutely climbing the steps. But even then he didn't walk straight in but knocked and called again only to be met by the same ominous silence. Apprehensively he stepped inside the stifling glass porch before pushing the door wider, shouting as he went.

'Hello. Hello there. Aaron. Jack. Hello.'

Later when he recalled it he would remember the shout as a scream. But then there was nothing to warn

4

him except maybe the buzzing flies which had been attracted by the jewelled lights of the porch.

And the scent.

Ahead of him the stout door was also standing ajar. And Shackleton caught a waft of the scent that had attracted the flies. Not toast or tea. Not souring milk or fresh cow dung. All these were part of the background, normal, everyday smells for Hardacre Farm. This was a new smell, sweet and sickly like the scent in a cowshed when the afterbirth had finally been dragged from an exhausted cow.

Nervously he stayed behind the door, letting the sun cook his back as he contrasted the ominous quiet within the house with the noisy jostling of the cows in the yard.

It felt wrong.

Searching for clues he looked at the jumble in the small porch, the waxed jackets hanging up, the pairs of wellies, the double barrelled gun that stood against the three-legged stool. He was certain something was very wrong.

The gun was missing.

The door yawned in front of him. He took one small step forward. This gave him a limited view of the room, dark, still. A heavy, Victorian sideboard, dust. The scent was overpowering now. Dave Shackleton lifted his hand to knock. A month ago he would not have knocked. He would have walked straight in. But something had happened.

It had been in early June, a month ago. He had been desperate to see Ruthie again and had used a parcel handed to him by the postman who resented the long drive to the farm as an excuse to see her. Calling out casually he had walked straight into the sitting room to see three faces staring at him with the blank hostility they would only have given a complete stranger. And for the first time in the fifteen years since he had started calling at Hardacre Farm, a youth of nineteen, he had felt an intruder. He had known then that the family had a secret. And they didn't want him – or anyone else – to know. At first he had felt hurt, then curious while he had stood, awkwardly, on the muddy coconut mat, scanning the three faces: the thin, crusty old man, hands gnarled from years of farming, the simple, honest features of the lad who never quite understood. And Ruthie, her face pale with shock, her eyes dark and deceitful, almost unrecognizable in their hostility. He had been dismayed by her expression and his face burnt. This was not the Ruthie he adored but someone else, someone strange. And she had known it, flushing with awkwardness; but it had been Aaron who spoke in a hostile, gravelly voice. 'What do you want, Shackleton?'

So this morning Shackleton knocked for a third time.

Matthew was watching her anxiously. 'Well, Joanna, what do you think of it?'

He was like a small boy, showing a half-decent report to his parents, trying to ignite some enthusiasm yet knowing, in his heart, that he would receive none.

Joanna slowly moved her head a full 180 degrees to take in the wide sweep of the barren slope with its one redeeming feature, a stream at its base crossed by a stone bridge. At last she turned to look unenthusiastically at the derelict cottage Matthew had wanted to show her.

He dropped his arm around her shoulders and tried again. 'Beautiful, isn't it?'

Without speaking she absorbed other details: the breached wall, stones fallen and left; the grey stone, mossy and damp even in the middle of a heatwave; the slates missing from the roof; the sagging gutters; broken, cracked filthy windows, rotting frames. On the hottest day of the year here was a chilling air of damp, decay and neglect.

She turned her head again to look at Matthew. He was giving her an anxious grin, still making the effort to coax her to like it. But her face must have displayed her mood and eventually he gave a wry smile. 'Look, I'm not saying it doesn't want a bit of work . . .'

She couldn't resist it. 'That's an understatement.'

'She was an old lady. Probably hadn't touched it for years.'

She said nothing.

'It can easily be done up.' He narrowed his eyes as though picturing the industry. 'A lick of paint here, the wall rebuilt, new window frames, a stove in the kitchen. Just think of the peace, Joanna. The utter, blissful peace. Please. Don't be a wet blanket.' His green eyes were wide open now and shining with enthusiasm. That same enthusiasm which made him careless with his next statement. 'These places can so easily be done up. You should have seen our old farm before Jane and I attacked it.'

It was an unfortunate remark.

Matthew tried again. 'Let's look inside.'

The gate fell off its hinges as they pushed it open. Joanna let it clatter on to the path. It was just another symptom of decay. The key was heavy and old

7

fashioned, the lock almost too stiff to turn the ancient mortice and tenon. It took all Joanna's strength to rotate it and force the door open.

Inside was, if anything, worse. Dark and poky with a musty, damp smell, peeling cream paint, meat hooks ominously embedded in the ceiling. There were mouse droppings and bird droppings, spiders webs and bits of nests. In the corner was a heap of rags, a makeshift bed. Had it recently been home to a tramp? She stood in the centre of the room and sighed. On a day when the sun dazzled outside, indoors was dingy, dull and depressing.

She could not live here. Not even with Matthew. She turned to him and tried to communicate her sense of foreboding. 'What on earth must this place be like in winter?'

Typically he shrugged. 'I know you think it's a bit dismal, Jo.' And his defence was repeated. 'But honestly, as I said, a lick of paint, patch the roof up, put in an Aga and . . .' His voice trailed away. At last he had stopped peering round the cottage and was facing her. 'It needs more than that.' She peeled away a strip of the paint and watched the plaster behind turn to sand and spill on to the floor. The eternal emblem of time running out. 'I wouldn't mind if it was a bit of cosmetics but this needs structural gutting. It's a shell.'

'All right. But.'

'Besides that, Matthew.' She wiped a peephole in the window to peer along the empty valley. 'It's just too isolated.'

He stood behind her, criss-crossing his arms around her body. 'I know. That's what makes it so wonderful.

The whole valley, all to ourselves.' He spoke into her thick, dark hair.

She was still facing the window, watching how the dusty glass blotted out the sun. 'And in the snow?'

She felt him squirm. 'I know it'll be a bit tricky in the winter but in the summer . . .'

'A bit tricky?' She moved away, crossed the room and shoved the kitchen door open. 'We'd be cut off down here, stuck, in the valley. The snow will drift and lie for weeks.' Her voice was a hollow echo rolling around the room. It sounded disapproving, dismissive.

Matthew gave a brave smile. 'Four-wheel drive?'

'Even with a four-wheel drive we'd be stuck. You know as well as I do these isolated homes need helicopter drops for their groceries in a really bad winter.'

'Great.' He followed her into the kitchen. 'Four days, log fires. Steamy sex by the fire.'

'Yes,' she said, exasperated now at his complete lack of practicality. 'We could play snowballs or go sledging, make love until the snow melted. What might be a bit more difficult is your work as a pathologist and mine as a Detective Inspector. You think they'd send a chopper out for me every morning or for you for every urgent post mortem?' She didn't allow her eyes to rest on the cracked sink, the leaking tap, the horrible poky smallness of the place.

He was beginning to look disappointed so she modified her disapproval. 'Maybe we could manage it if we were nine to five but we're not. We could be called in at any time of the day or night. Matthew,' she appealed to his reason, 'we have to be available.'

He lounged against the door, a shaft of sunlight

catching the thick, honey blond hair and she knew he had yet to concede defeat.

Matthew could be stubborn. He found her hand. 'Let's go upstairs.'

But the first floor proved even more of a mistake. Once they had negotiated the steep, narrow staircase with a couple of slats missing, they found a tiny bedroom painted navy blue and another one pink. Just two rooms and no bathroom. Empty except for a white china potty standing in the middle of the floor underneath a blast of sky blue where both roofing slates and plaster board were missing.

Joanna had an overwhelming desire to escape. 'I've seen nicer cells in Her Majesty's Prisons.'

Matthew looked disappointed but he tucked the details back into his trouser pocket. 'All these little cottages with land are getting snapped up,' he said, 'if they come on the market at all. The families hang on to them for generations. Handed down from father to son. You know what farming people are like. They never let go of property or land. It's like a superstition with them. And if they do have to sell their farms they get bought by speculators who wave their magic wands and hey presto one small, isolated cottage becomes valuable prop. with barn conversions, holiday flats and rural setting. And then they're unaffordable.'

But however right he was she had no desire to live here. It was a relief to clatter down the stairs and walk back out through the door into the blaze of sunshine. Staffordshire, this summer, was as hot as the south of Spain. Joanna took a deep gulp of the air and raised her face to the sun, glad to leave behind the fustiness of the derelict cottage.

Shackleton had pushed the door open a little wider and was staring into the room as though it was the set of a horror-film.

But not all the bloodthirsty movies spewed out of America, or the clever effects of make-up artists or contortions of stuntmen could ever have prepared him for the sight that met his eyes.

Death is much uglier than the filmmakers dare to portray.

It took him a fraction of a second to back out of the door, through the porch, down the steps, carve a way through the distressed cows and into his tanker. Too panicked to manage his usual three point turn he reversed all the way back down the lane to the neighbouring farm half a mile away.

She knew the time had come for her to be brutally honest or Matthew would continue to hope.

She didn't want to live here.

She found his hand and pressed it to her cheek. 'It isn't for me, Matthew. I don't want to live so far from civilization.'

He smiled at her and for the first time she knew he did understand her misgivings. His smile was warm. 'Not even with this nice little stream?'

She shook her head.

'There'll be kingfishers,' he said, 'ducks and wagtails.'

She smiled back at him, knowing he was teasing her now. 'Well, the only birds I can see at the moment are a couple of magpies and a hedge sparrow.'

'You're hopeless,' he said. 'Where is your soul, your poetry, your imagination?'

'Waiting for a nice little house on the edge of a village,' she said, 'within walking distance of the local pub, cycling distance of work and not too far from the main road in the event of snow.' Matthew closed his eyes for a moment. She knew he was disappointed and she felt the familiar guilt that she had let him down, again. 'We'll find somewhere soon. I promise.'

'Will we?' There was more than a simple question in his face. There was doubt too. 'It's taking longer than I thought. It's been two years since I left Jane. And we're still not really together, are we? I'm sick of being on the top floor of Alan and Becky's. I want a home, Jo.'

Shackleton had managed to pull the milk tanker on to the yard of Fallowfield and sat, too dazed to move, until finally he acknowledged the hum of the milking machine. Here was one farmer whose daily habits were not disturbed. Pinkers was late with the milking again.

Shackleton staggered into the milking parlour and ran the gauntlet of swinging tails until Martin Pinkers saw him, straightened slowly and pushed a cow out of the way. 'Hello, Dave. Anything the matter?' In response to Shackleton's dazed terror he put a hand on his shoulder. 'Dave,' he said. 'What the hell is it?'

'Get the police,' Shackleton mouthed hoarsely. 'Get the police.' Panic was making him breathless.

'Dave?' Pinkers tried again. 'What's up?'

'Hardacre,' Shackleton gasped. 'Aaron and Jack. Lying in the sitting room. Martin,' he said. 'Somebody's shot them.'

They were heading back to the car when Matthew stopped her. 'You do want to be with me, don't you?'

'Of course.'

'Only everytime we look at somewhere you find fault with it.'

A light breeze stirred the leaves and a tiny, wispy cloud blotted out the sun for a brief second. The magpies began a chorus of harsh, scolding squawks. 'Because I'm beginning to wonder,' Matthew continued quietly, 'if it isn't the house that there's something wrong with.'

And in a flash of perception he added, 'Could it possibly be that to share a home with me might sometimes mean sharing it with Eloise too?'

Matthew could be so perceptive but she could never afford to be a hundred per cent honest with him. So she evaded the issue, glanced at her watch again. 'I have to go.' She started towards the car, ignoring Matthew waving a sheaf of estate agents' details. 'There are others you know.'

Right on cue her radio phone crackled and with a feeling of relief she held it up to her ear.

'Detective Inspector Piercy.'

'Sorry to interrupt your search for paradise.'

She recognized the voice at once. 'That's all right, Mike. Was it anything special?'

'There's been a shooting at one of the moorland

farms. First reports suggest two people dead. The bloke that phoned said it was the farmer and his son.'

She recognized the familiar surge of excitement even while she gathered the early details.

'Whereabouts?'

'Hardacre Farm. Just off the Buxton road towards Flash. And while you're at it I suppose you'd better bring Leek's answer to Bernard Spilsbury with you.'

She took the jibe on the chin. 'I certainly will.'

'I'll see you there then.' And he gave her brief directions.

Matthew was watching her. 'What did Korpanski want?'

She was always uncomfortably aware of the antagonism between the two men, at the same time powerless to do anything about it. 'There's been a double shooting at one of the remote farms.'

Already she could sense his excitement as he slipped the maroon BMW into gear. 'Fill me in on the details of the case, I'll drive if you can give directions.'

He bumped the car up the unmade track, wincing as it struck a stone. She caught his eye and smiled but said nothing. At the top of the valley they travelled along the high ridge, across the moor until they came to the Mermaid Inn then they dropped down towards the town, turning right along the main road to Buxton.

'What details have we got?'

'He just said a double shooting, sounded like father and son.'

Matthew jumped to the same conclusion she had. 'Murder and then suicide?'

She bit back a smile. 'Give Korpanski a chance,' she

said. 'He's just on his way over there now. Even Tarzan can't solve crimes until he's been to the scene.'

She was quiet for a moment, thinking private thoughts. Murder was always like this, a tightening of the stomach, a combination of excitement, exhilaration – and nausea. And then there was the further worry, of getting it right.

Glancing across to Matthew she knew his mind was moving along the same tracks. He too would have his role to play.

They turned off the main road and approached the remotest part of the moor, high farmland. Full of secrets.

Chapter Two

They could have found the farm without Mike's directions, merely by following the police car screaming along the ridge until it turned off along a narrow lane.

Matthew made a face. 'How they do love the drama and the noise. And what's the point? The poor sods are dead anyway and all the police cars in the world aren't going to bring them back to life.' He took his eyes off the flashing blue light for a moment to give her a wry smile. 'Almost certainly some poor, isolated chap has flipped his lid and blown his son's head off then realized what he's done. Or the other way round,' he added.

'You're prejudging. And you're being unfair.'

He shook his head. 'No. I just prefer to play things down, rather than up. It isn't drama. It's just life and a rather sad end to a life at that.'

She said nothing but watched his long fingers wrapped around the wheel, steady; yet she knew inside he was excited. As a forensic pathologist, this unravelling of a person's last hours was his obsession. It brought him alive, as her work did to her. They might see the case from different angles, his from tangible evidence yielded by the body and hers from that of the killer and the evidence left behind at the scene of

16

the crime. But underneath the flow of adrenalin was the same and she knew had they not been lovers they would still have worked twin-close to solve cases. Their relationship merely made it easier – sometimes.

Abruptly Matthew twisted the wheel to follow the police car which had turned left and disappeared behind clouds of dust and flies.

And then they were forced to stop.

A milk tanker was partly blocking the way, slewed half across the lane, drunkenly parked. Already the crime was creating visible evidence. Matthew pulled the BMW up and they climbed out and walked between the clusters of still flashing cars to the clumps of people; uniformed officers plus a couple of casually dressed men who Joanna took to be the tanker driver and possibly a neighbour. She picked Mike Korpanski out easily, blocking the doorway to the farmhouse, built like a gladiator and a couple of inches taller than the rest. She walked briskly towards him and registered the relief on his face when he saw her.

'It's a bit of a mess in there, Jo, what with the heat and all that.' He was staring across the fields as though to abstract himself from what she knew must be carnage inside. It had to be that to have made his face so fish-green.

She gave him a quick, sympathetic nod. 'Two bodies, you said?'

He grimaced his answer.

'Father and son?'

'Looks like it.'

'So what's your first impression, Mike, a murder followed by suicide? A crime of isolation? A quarrel?'

His eyes still held that haunted, abstracted look

even though he spoke casually. 'I dunno. At least I wouldn't like to say, not yet.' And some of the old Mike peeped out. 'It isn't something you can guess at, Joanna, but the furniture's not tipped. There's no sign of a struggle.'

He moved aside and she glanced ahead at the porch.

It was a Victorian addition to the stone farmhouse, perhaps intended to sweeten the plain facade, or merely to bring it up to date. Inside was both hot and brightly coloured, the sun streaming through blue and red-leaded glass, turning it to sapphires and rubies, stirring old memories of church singing, chanted psalms, windows peopled with the Saints. Had it not been for the clouds of buzzing flies she might even have been tempted to linger and postpone the moment of entry. But one landed on her arm. Huge, fat, iridescent blue. She shook it off in disgust and spoke to the nearest uniformed constable.

'Get some fly spray, Scott, for goodness sake. Get rid of these damned flies.'

Maybe it was apprehension. Perhaps a portent of certain things to come or even more probably it was a natural loathing for the flies and their lack of respect for dead bodies. But they repulsed her to an extent which she knew even then was unreasonable.

She led the way into the room beyond.

It was a small, dark living room, square, with a couple of doors off, a window opposite and a chill, damp atmosphere, even on a blistering hot day. At first sight it seemed dark shadows striped the walls, the floor, the furniture. It took her eyes a moment of adjustment to realize the stripes were from splattered blood – and worse.

There were two bodies, both dressed in navy, cotton overalls. One lay almost at her feet, the other on the right side of the room. The nearer one appeared older, about fifty, thin, with straggle-grey hair, feet pointing towards the door from where the force had blasted him backwards. He lay on his back, his arms outflung, dirty work-roughened hands, calloused palms lying uppermost. There was a hole in his chest. A big hole. A quick glance showed exposed flesh and bone, red gore. It had been an accurate shot. Fighting her rising nausea Joanna took note of the radiating splashes. He must have been standing very near the door, facing the intruder when the shot had been fired. She took two steps forward to make a closer study of his face, grey with a poorly shaven chin, spiked bristles and the mouth gaping open to expose a few blackened teeth. She breathed in deeply to steady herself before allowing her eyes to pass down the thin legs to the man's feet, one wearing a muck-spattered wellington boot, the other pathetically covered in a matted grey-woollen sock, the big toe tidily darned.

It lacked dignity as well as life.

Without moving her feet she shifted her attention to the second body.

He was younger, probably in his late twenties, and stockily built. The blast had caught him standing too but the door had supported him as he had collapsed so he was slumped against it, pinning it shut. His hands were crossed over his chest as though to staunch the blood. So he had not died instantly but had frozen in this position, head dropped, to peer at his wound. Mike shifted his weight behind her and she turned to see him staring at what had caught her eye, the blood-stained hands.

Finally she moved her head slightly to the left and saw a double barrelled shotgun lying where it had been dropped, its butt towards the door, the barrel still pointing into the room, covering both bodies.

It completed the picture. But what picture?

The sequence of events lay here, in this room. Like the creases in a palm they only needed interpreting. But it must be an accurate reading.

Murder by person or persons unknown meant a full-blown sealing off of the area, large-scale investigations, enquiries, suspicion and with a bit of luck a court case followed by a conviction. But a murder and then a suicide? That was a cheap affair. A coroner's court, only needing a watertight motive. And there would be plenty: depression, anxiety, psychosis. Already she could imagine the coroner's speech. These had been hard times for farmers. BSE, the delayed cow cull, a drop in the milk quota. All these were motives strong enough for the lethal use of a shotgun even without dragging in the old story of social isolation and strange, old fashioned standards. Guns were readily available on most farms and the farmers prepared to use them on rabbits, crows, sick animals. But a son? Or a father?

So which was it?

Matthew had already snapped on a pair of latex gloves and was giving each body a more detailed examination, taking notes, drawing sketches. She left him to it. He would not be hurried towards his verdict so she and Mike started their work, trying out the various scenarios. If their verdict fitted with Matthew's – good. If not . . .

'I think we can rule out the son,' she observed, glancing towards the door on the right hand side of the room. 'The gun is too far away and surely his wound is too severe for him to have moved. Would you agree with that, Matthew?'

He looked up briefly. 'Absolutely.'

'And the father was in the middle of putting his wellingtons on.'

'Getting ready to do the milking,' Mike suggested.

'Y-e-es,' she answered cautiously. 'So halfway through that would he have picked up the gun and taken a pot shot at his son before turning it on himself? It isn't either possible or plausible, is it?'

Matthew shook his head. Mike was looking far more unconvinced.

'It isn't easy,' she said, 'to shoot yourself with a shotgun. The barrel is too long. Besides . . .' She knew Matthew would know the answer. 'Don't they almost always hold the gun against the head?'

'Usually,' he said. 'I think I'd rather back that with my observation that it looks as though the gun was fired at a range of about a foot.'

He knew she would want his reasoning and watched as he fingered the coarse navy-blue cloth around the chest wound. 'I would have expected more scorching had it been a contact wound.'

Both Mike and Joanna were listening intently.

'Anyway,' he carried on, 'a man contemplating suicide or going slowly off his rocker doesn't make his mind up to do the dreadful act halfway through putting his wellies on to do the milking.'

'Not even if he suddenly flips his lid?'

There was some fault in Mike's suggestion but she couldn't quite find it. She looked first at Korpanski before meeting Matthew's eyes. 'So they were both murdered by our old friend?' she said. 'Person or persons unknown.'

They both nodded.

Matthew straightened up. 'I'll be able to tell you more at post mortem.'

'I know you're going to hate this, Matt, but . . .'

They had worked on enough murder cases for him to anticipate her next question. 'I won't be able to be very accurate,' he said, 'but judging by rectal temperature I would think about five hours. The weather's warm. It could be more. Not less. There has been definite cooling of the bodies.'

'So we're left with collecting statements,' she said, 'to find out when they were last seen alive.'

Matthew nodded. 'Basically we're looking at somewhere around six a.m. I don't suppose many people were around so early.'

'This is a rural community,' Mike put in helpfully. 'Early risers.'

'Well I suppose it'll help to know at what time they usually milked.'

'Precisely.'

'So let's get the scene of crime officers started then,' she said. 'The less evidence disturbed the more chance we have of a sound conviction. When do you think you'll get around to doing the post mortems, Matthew?'

'The sooner the better,' he said. 'But I'd like them formally identified first. How about tomorrow morning?'

'Fine.'

It was not fine and he knew it. She hated post mortems, finding the smell, the sights and the sheer butchery nauseating. In fact it was anything *but* fine but it was her duty. Matthew would uncover plenty of pointers that would help solve the case. She could not afford to renege on her responsibility.

She was distracted by PC Scott arriving back with two large aerosols of Vapona and generously squirting the fly spray around the room. For a while the buzz of dying flies was the loudest sound.

Mike was frowning, toying with ideas. 'Do you think,' he said, 'that the old chap was shot first and the blast brought junior in through the door so he got it too?'

'Rather than the alternative, that the younger man was shot and the older man was trying to wrestle the gun from the assailant?'

'In the middle of putting his boots on?'

'No. It has to be the way you described it. Old man gets it first. But then why the hell did the younger one come in? Why didn't he stay put?' Her eyes were drawn to the door. 'Do we know where that leads?'

PC Phil Scott supplied the answer. 'According to Mr Shackleton, the tanker driver, it leads upstairs.'

'And the killer,' Matthew said, 'didn't even need to move. Judging from their wounds I think both were shot from the same position.'

'Presumably having entered through the porch. I don't suppose there were any signs of forced entry, Mike?'

'Shackleton claims there wouldn't have been any

need for anyone to break and enter. The door was always left standing open.'

'You mean the porch door?'

'Both doors. I particularly asked him that. Both the front door and the porch door were always unlocked. They only closed both doors when they were all going out. Otherwise, even through the winter, just the porch door was closed and the wooden door was open. Anyone could walk in.'

'And the gun?'

'Says he's seen it plenty of times. It used to stand in the porch.'

'Loaded?'

'He *says* he didn't know but I suppose he wouldn't, would he, unless he checked.'

'Or put the cartridges in himself.'

'But he wasn't here until nearly ten.'

'And they'd already been dead for around four hours by then, I know,' she said irritably. 'Like you, I'm just thinking aloud. Where does that door lead?'

'The kitchen, then the back door and out into the courtyard.'

'Also left unlocked?'

'Yes.'

Matthew was still kneeling beside the younger man's body.

'Do we know their names?'

'Well Shackleton's more or less done us the honours.'

Picking up the truculent note in Mike's voice she gave him a sharp glance of reproval which made him modify his manner.

'We have here Aaron and Jack Summers, both farmers.'

'Which one is Aaron?'

'The father. Jack the son.'

For the briefest of moments she studied the expressions on the dead men's faces. Aaron's mouth open to scream, an imprint of shock still on his body, arms outflung, legs slightly buckled. By contrast the younger man's position held less shock, hands across his chest, head bent, an almost calm expression of acceptance on his face, mouth and eyes both closed. It seemed to express a different emotion, puzzled surprise. Why me?

No trauma here and no shock. Unlike his father. Even though he must have caught sight of his father's body as he emerged from upstairs. And he had not died instantly but had had time to finger the open wound. She turned to Korpanski.

'Their faces, Mike.'

'Yeah?' He had missed it.

Matthew had not. 'I noticed that,' he said. 'The old man was terrified. He must have seen what was coming. But he didn't warn his son.'

Why not? Because even though his killer had picked up the gun and pointed it at him he had felt no threat?

'And if he did warn his son it had no effect.'

'So we assume Aaron Summers was shot first?'

They both nodded. But it was still bothering her. 'I don't understand. Why did Jack run downstairs to the sound of gunshot? Why wasn't he more cautious? He could have hidden or simply stayed upstairs. I don't understand it.'

She carried on fishing – for anything. 'I suppose the gun definitely is theirs?'

Again Mike supplied the answer. 'They've got a licence for a Winchester .22.'

'Not to leave propped up in an unlocked porch.'

'They hadn't been checked for a while.'

'Have we got anything else, Mike?'

'Just something that doesn't quite seem to fit.'

'Yes?'

'Shackleton says they usually milk somewhere between six and seven, OK?'

She nodded.

'And father, here, is wearing one wellington boot. Right?'

'Yes.'

'But Shackleton says it looks as though Aaron Summers had already let the cows out of the field and must have been leading them up here when for some reason he called back to the farmhouse.'

She eyed the one wellington boot; the other, she had noticed, was standing upright in the porch.

'Maybe he called in to shout for Jack to come and help him.'

'He'd have just stuck his head round the door, surely? He wouldn't have taken his boots off.'

'Shackleton's sure the cows were let out of the field?'

'It's what he says. He says the gate was open and the cows were wandering around the yard and the milking parlour. They weren't in the field. So although Jack was still upstairs he was dressed ready to start work when the killer came. So did our killer walk back *with* Aaron as he came to get Jack or was he hiding

26

somewhere round here? If so, how could he know that Aaron would return? Do you think it might have been Jack he was after?'

'Who knows?'

She included Matthew in her next question. 'So we're all agreed that they died sometime around six a.m.'

'Yes.' His answer was, as usual, both brisk and precise.

She left the room to speak to the group of officers outside. 'It's a double murder,' she said briefly. 'We'll need Sergeant Barraclough's team of SOCOs and an incident room set up. You can start by taking statements from near neighbours and the milk tanker driver.' To Mike she added, 'And I suppose I'd better speak to Superintendent Colclough. It'll make his day. A double murder in the middle of a heatwave.'

Chapter Three

She watched Matthew stride back down the garden path and moments later heard his car start. Then she turned back to Korpanski. She was about to use him – and not for the first time – as a sounding board.

'I can't be convinced,' she said, 'that Aaron went alone to get the cows and then came back.'

'To get Jack,' Mike said patiently.

'All right,' she said. 'Even if he *had* left him in bed and wanted him to help. Surely once they'd fetched the cows from the field they would have taken them straight to the milking parlour and started the milking. Otherwise the animals would just have wandered all over the place. So how far did he get with the cows and why did he come back?'

'Well not as far as the cowshed. Shackleton said not one cleat had been fixed.'

She tried to suppress her amusement but Mike had seen the ghost of a smile. 'The things they stick on the udders.'

'I guessed that.'

'So our killer probably approached the farm through a herd of cows?'

Mike nodded. 'He'll have muck all over him.'

'Let's try this. They get the cows in somewhere

28

between six and seven. Someone drives here, or walks, interrupts their trip from the field. Aaron's in the doorway, pulling his wellingtons off. Jack's upstairs. No.' She shook her head decidedly. 'It doesn't fit, Mike. They were disturbed *before* they got to the cows.'

'But Shackleton said . . .' Mike objected.

'Whatever Shackleton said they were disturbed here before they went out.'

Mike scowled at her. 'Are you trying to say it was the killer who let the cows out?'

'Maybe.'

'Then why? *They* can't give him an alibi.'

'I don't know, Mike. I'm simply thinking. That's all. It could have been to destroy footprints – or tyre marks – or something. But I am certain that if they'd both started to lead the cows in from the field to be milked they wouldn't have come back, leaving the cows to wander around. And if Jack had come back he wouldn't have gone upstairs unless he was going to fetch something. Let's just have a look at . . .' She picked up the boot that paired with the one on the dead man's foot. It was dusty and dry. 'As I thought,' she said. 'He hasn't worn them this morning.'

'The weather's hot,' Mike pointed out.

'Have you had a look out there in the lane? Cow pats everywhere. And a farmer wouldn't pick his way around them. He'd walk straight through.' She picked up another, larger pair. 'And I assume these are Jack's.' She turned them over. 'He hasn't been out this morning either. So our killer . . .' She frowned. 'Why he let the cows out of the field is beyond me—' She was silent for just a moment. 'What else did Shackleton say?'

'Only that the cows are usually back in the fields by the time he gets here at ten.'

'This Shackleton, Mike. He would have known the family well.'

'What are you trying to say?'

'Nothing. I'm just collecting facts. Did he know straight away that something was wrong?'

'Pretty soon. At first he just thought they were a bit late with the milking, that they'd overslept.'

'Was that usual?'

Korpanski shook his head. 'But he thought it all the same.'

'So when was he sure something was up?'

'Almost at once. As soon as he turned into the drive. The cows were causing havoc, wandering around the yard. They hadn't been milked. So he comes round to the door to find out what's going on. And he sees this.'

'Then what did he do?'

'Backs the tanker all the way down the lane to the neighbouring farm and telephones us.'

A swift vision of the milk tanker blocking the lane reinforced the story.

She glanced at a green plastic phone standing on the window sill. 'He didn't use this phone?'

'Nope. I can understand the man. He panicked. He just wanted to get the hell out of here. And I can't blame him.'

She looked at him sharply. 'He claims he didn't enter the room?'

'No. He could see it all from the doorway.'

She thought for a moment then startled Mike by asking, 'What's happened to them?'

'Sorry?'

'The cows, Mike. I didn't see the cows when we drove up.'

'Oh. The next door farmer came back with him and offered to do the milking.'

'A good neighbourly act.'

'Yeah. A good neighbourly act.' But they were both police officers. Nothing could be taken at face value. Korpanski's eyes darkened.

She pressed her point home. 'Someone who knew the door would be open, that the gun was not kept in a locked cabinet, someone who had the opportunity to make sure it would be loaded. Someone who knew the doors would be unlocked and where both father and son would be at that time of the morning.'

'But why?'

'I don't know. And in my book, blasting a couple of farmers with their own shotgun doesn't exactly comply with the Neighbourhood Watch scheme.'

He picked up on that. 'Neighbourhood Watch,' he said. 'What exactly are you suggesting?'

There was an angry light in her blue eyes. 'I'll be looking at the locals first,' she said slowly. 'Shackleton knew about the gun. The point is who else knew and who loaded it because don't try and tell me person or persons unknown arrives at the porch, picks up the gun, presses the trigger and, Hey Presto, what a bit of luck, it's even loaded. And even I can't believe the Summers were quite so careless as to leave a *loaded* gun lying around in an unlocked porch. No. I think it's more likely that someone primed the gun. But why?'

The two bodies lay motionless. 'Look at them, Mike. From the way they're dressed I'd bet they had nothing more exciting planned than a morning in the cowshed. So why slaughter them? Robbery? A thief could have slipped in at any time and pinched stuff without going to the bother of murder. So why? And who? And because I have to start somewhere we'll start next door with our friendly neighbour. How far away is he?'

Mike relaxed. He preferred facts to questions. 'About half a mile. Three fields away. The farm's called Fallowfield.'

'And this friendly neighbour's name?'

'Pinkers. Martin Pinkers.'

'Right . . ' She thought for a moment. 'We'll start there and gradually widen our circle. We'll need a good map of the area. I want to know everyone who lives within a two-mile radius. If we get no joy the circle grows.'

'From what I know so far a two-mile radius covers about four homesteads.'

'Good. That makes the job distinctly easier.' She gave Mike one of her wide smiles. 'I suppose it's a bit soon to know anything about bad blood between the two farms?'

'Yeah. Far too soon.'

She moved back into the bright, brave colours of the glazed porch and studied the Victorian panels of red and blue glass.

'The SOCOs might get some decent prints off this as well as the gun but I'm not too optimistic. Uugh.' She gave an expression of disgust as a fly landed on her hand. 'Where's that bloody flyspray?'

Like the genie of the lamp PC Scott appeared in the doorway and gave a prolonged squirt. She coughed. 'Let's go outside.'

The heat met them as they stopped on top of the three steps and surveyed the country, the wide expanse of fields, huge trees, cows sheltering beneath them, swallows darting in and out of the barns. Straight across the field, to the right, she could see dark-blue slates through the trees. That must be Fallowfield.

The silence was almost tangible, the air crystal clear and sharp with the scent of pure oxygen. This bright, pretty scene seemed miles away from the dark claustrophobia behind them. Murder seemed too ugly an act for this perfect summer's day. For a moment she closed her eyes in order to blot it out, leaving the scented tranquillity to imprint on her mind. It failed.

Even with her eyes tightly shut she could still see the two bodies.

It must have been no more than a second later that she felt a tap on her shoulder. 'Excuse me.' It was a solid, country burr. 'Don't mind me asking but are you the lady detective they said was in charge?'

He was tall with curly brown hair, a pale, sweating face and troubled brown eyes.

'Yes, I'm Detective Inspector Piercy.'

'Dave.' He introduced himself. 'Dave Shackleton. It was me that found them.' He hesitated before asking quietly, 'Was it Jack? Did he finally flip?'

Confused she managed, 'We can't say, yet.' Then curiosity got the better of her caution. 'You think Jack murdered his father before turning the gun on himself?'

The eyes were far too honest. 'Well, what else?'

'Why would he kill his father? Had they quarrelled?'

Shackleton blinked and looked even more troubled. 'No, but I thought—' he said awkwardly.

'It isn't what we think, Mr Shackleton.' She didn't know whether she was consoling him or not, telling him something he wanted to hear.

'We think both were shot by a third person.'

Shackleton looked stunned. 'You mean . . .?'

She eyed him curiously. 'You knew them well?'

He nodded jerkily.

'Then you've had a shock.'

Shackleton's eyes were bright. 'Known the family for years, I have. I just can't believe . . .' He wiped beads of sweat from his forehead with the back of his hand. 'Of all the families I know,' he said softly, 'I would have sworn they would have ended their lives peacefully. Not like this.' An expression of misery descended on his face like fog. 'If you say it wasn't Jack . . .' he began.

'It wasn't Jack. It was someone else.'

Shackleton gave a start. 'Ruthie,' he said hoarsely. 'Is Ruthie in there too?'

Joanna felt chilled. 'There was a daughter?'

'Yes.' There was a desperate tone in his voice. 'Little Ruthie.'

And Joanna made a natural assumption. 'She was younger than her brother?'

'No,' Shackleton said impatiently as though the girl's age was the least important thing about her. 'She was five years older than Jack.' His eyes were focused fearfully on the door behind her. 'Is she in there too?' He switched his gaze back to Joanna. 'Have you found Ruthie in there?' There was a desperate, almost violent note in the tanker driver's voice.

'No,' she said dully.

But now she had another, more urgent charge. Forget Fallowfield. There might be a third body, lying somewhere around the farm, in the barns or upstairs.

Shackleton was shaking. His muddy-brown eyes fixed on Joanna and he knew exactly what she feared. 'You think she's in there too, don't you?'

'A constable's already checked upstairs.'

There was an aura of deep grief around Shackleton. He had been shocked by the two bodies. But at the talk of Ruthie that had changed to this abject, miserable, uncontrolled grief. It didn't take much imagination to connect the two.

'We'll conduct a thorough search of both the house and the barns,' she said.

'Do you want me to help?'

She shook her head, almost ashamed of her suspicions. 'The police prefer to do it themselves. Don't worry, please. If Ruthie is here we'll find her.'

Shackleton looked away. 'So he got her too.'

'He?'

'It's just a way of sayin' it.' His voice was choked with emotion. 'You can't imagine a woman doin' that.' The shock had made his face so white she thought he might faint. 'Not that.'

'I'm afraid,' Joanna said wearily, 'there's nothing in there that excludes a woman. *Anyone* could have pulled that trigger, Mr Shackleton. Anyone.'

They stood in silence for a moment, then Joanna asked, 'The three of them lived here?'

He nodded. 'Yeah. Old Aaron, Ruthie and Jack.'

'No other women?'

Shackleton shook his head. 'No, Mrs Summers had cancer. She died when Jack was just a baby. He were only ten months old. Ruthie brought him up.' He made an attempt at a smile. 'Proper little mother she were to him.' But then some old memory must have moved through his mind and his face assumed a pained expression. It seemed to Joanna that for some reason this recollection compelled him to defend Ruthie. 'She really did love Jack. She did. I know. She was devoted to her brother. People can say what they like.'

And Joanna's mind was instantly on the alert, as though pricked by a pin. Shackleton stayed silent for a long time.

'Do you have any idea who could have done this, Mr Shackleton? Had the family any enemies?'

Dave Shackleton shook his head. 'Must have been a robbery that went wrong.'

But Joanna didn't think so. 'We will, of course, be searching the house but so far we have seen no sign of . . .' She paused. In this house of open doors there would have been no need for forced entry. Anyone could have simply walked in.

Shackleton must have picked up on her train of thoughts. 'Exactly,' he said. 'No one would have needed to break a window or force a lock. It was so easy. Like I told the big guy.'

'Detective Sergeant Korpanski.'

'You could walk into Hardacre any time of the day or night.' He looked away, embarrassed.

'That makes it all the more difficult for us to work out who did.' Joanna hesitated before plunging in with her next question. 'Tell me, Mr Shackleton. How did they get on with their neighbours?'

There was a movement in front of them, a snorting and bellowing. A herd of cows was careering along the lane towards them. She watched them pass. Behind them a thin, bent figure dressed in navy dungarees was slapping the cows backsides, forcing them into a brisk trot. For that one moment she had a vision of Aaron and Jack Summers doing the identical manoeuvre.

The farmer waved a hand as he passed.

Shackleton nodded briefly and Joanna took up her cue. 'So that's Martin Pinkers?'

'That's him,' he said, looking uncomfortable. 'He offered to do the milkin' and . . .' He scratched his head. 'They needed doin'. They was goin' wild.' He eyed Joanna dubiously. 'It might seem hard and uncaring gettin' him over here but they need the milk takin' off. Cows' udders fill murder or no murder. Besides Aaron would have wanted it.'

Hard and uncaring getting him over here. Had she imagined the emphasis on the *him*?

And if she had not imagined it what vague hostility lay behind it?

She glanced again at the thin man with his hard, boney face and then turned her attention back to Shackleton, knowing one thing was for sure. Shackleton would provide no more answers now. He flushed, hunched his shoulders and dug his hands deep into his pockets, staring at a point somewhere behind her right shoulder, leaving her to watch the diminishing figure of the neighbouring farmer.

Hostility there may have been. But it had still been to Fallowfield, Martin Pinkers' farm, that Shackleton had headed when he had discovered the bodies.

Yet looking at the wide, empty panorama where else could he have gone?

Something else had struck Joanna. He had not

mentioned Ruthie Summers until she had started questioning him about the family. But if Ruthie had been the female pivot of the farm what would be more natural than that she would have been standing in the kitchen, preparing breakfast, when the assailant had blasted her father and brother with the gun? And if Ruthie had been the one to call them in from the yard what would be more natural than that they would come? *So where was she now?*

Her mind was working furiously. If they found Ruthie inside the farmhouse their theory would not fit. They had assumed the assailant had not crossed the threshold but had fired two blasts from the doorway without entering the room. Besides . . . the weapon was a double barrelled shotgun. A third shot would mean reloading, a lengthy, cumbersome process. And already she was moving forward. If Ruthie Summers was not in the house or the barns or the milking parlour or anywhere else on the farm . . .

Shackleton broke into her thoughts with a sharp exclamation. 'The old woman,' he said. 'She'll have to be told. Someone will 'ave to tell 'er.'

'What old woman?'

'Miss Lockley.' He sounded surprised she didn't know. 'Miss Hannah Lockley. She will have to be told. She'll be the next of kin. Close to the family she was. And if anythin's happened to Ruthie she'll go fair mad. Devoted to 'er she was.'

'And where does she . . .?'

Shackleton jerked his head. 'She lives in the cottage along the way. Brooms, it's called. She was Mrs Summers' older sister, aunt to Ruthie and Jack.'

Joanna craned her neck to peer along the track but it bent too far to the left. 'Where is the cottage?'

'You can't see it from here but if you'd carried on up the road instead of turning in you'd have come to it. Small, pretty place it is. Stone built with two trees at the front. You can't miss it. The name's on the gate.'

'Thank you, Mr Shackleton.' She paused for a moment, anxious to set the facts straight in her mind. 'Can I just get something clear?'

'Sure.'

'Miss Hannah Lockley was sister-in-law to Mr Aaron Summers?'

'That's right. And special fond of little Ruthie she was. Loved 'er, she did, like she was her own daughter. She will be destroyed by all this.'

Joanna noted he had used the past tense to speak about Ruthie.

Wearily she moved to go back into the house.

'We'll want a formal statement from you at some point.'

'No problem,' he said. 'You can get in touch with me through the depot.'

'And I suppose we'll have to ask Miss Lockley to identify the bodies. Although if she's elderly . . .'

Shackleton gave a dry, mirthless laugh. 'She ain't the traditional old lady,' he said. 'Tough as old boots she is. Still 'elps get the hay-bales in.'

Delaying the moment when she would have to go back into the house she followed him with her eyes as he climbed back into the tanker and swung it out of the farmyard, raising clouds of dust. It might be interesting to study the tyre tracks at some point. Had he really left in such a hurry? Seconds later further clouds were raised by the arrival of the police mobile incident unit. Joanna turned around. It was time to return to the abattoir.

Maybe she would even need to recall Matthew to look at a third body.

The SOCOs were a pleasure to watch, she decided, moving carefully around the room, already using grid maps to indicate where each specimen had been taken from. A couple were lifting fingerprints from the glass porch, two others bagging up the furniture covers, the rug from in front of the grate. Even the telephone was being shuffled into a plastic bag. But her work wasn't in here but outside where the officers were assembled, waiting for their primary briefing.

She stood on the steps of the Incident Unit and spoke quietly to Mike. 'Change of plan, Korpanski. The sister is missing and there's a next-of-kin living almost next door. We'd better visit her before she gets wind of this from elsewhere.'

Then she faced the waiting officers. 'The farmer, Aaron Summers and his son, Jack, were found just after ten o'clock this morning by the milk-tanker driver. Both had died of gunshot wounds at some time around six a.m. A shotgun, owned by Mr Summers, was found nearby. Also resident here is Ruthie Summers, daughter and sister of the deceased. This is a big farm with a lot of land to cover. We have to search every inch of it for any evidence linking the killer to the crime. Detective Sergeant Korpanski and I will start in the house. OK, Mike . . .?'

He nodded.

'DC Brown, I want you to take a team and go through the barns, the sheds and all the other out-houses. We'll start there. If we do not find Ruthie Summers we'll have to widen our search to include the surrounding fields and hedgerows. I, um.' She swallowed. 'I very much want her found.'

There was no need to underline the implications.

'I don't have to remind you this is a double murder already. Be vigilant and don't miss anything, please.'

Someone had to ask it. 'What if she isn't in the house or in the barns or anywhere around?' Joanna took a good long look at WPC Dawn Critchlow's flushed face. 'You mean if she's vanished? Well somebody pulled the trigger. Put it like this. We would be very anxious to talk to her.'

The ground floor of the farmhouse was surprisingly large with numerous small rooms leading off a dark corridor to the left. Maybe once they had been dairies, cooling rooms, stills or pantries. Now they were all storerooms for various bits of equipment. And each time she threw open a door she expected to find the missing girl.

But downstairs there was nothing.

Outside she could hear the men shouting to each other as they systematically searched the outhouses and barns. But the shouts contained no excitement of discovery.

So the work continued.

As she and Mike returned to the main living room the bodies of the two men were being moved into the mortuary van and their shapes outlined in chalk, each pool or splash of blood carefully numbered. The SOCOs in their white suits were still deftly sellotaping samples and transferring them to glass slides. They all knew how meticulous this work must be if they were to secure a conviction through forensic evidence.

One of the SOCOs called her over. 'Take a look at this, Inspector.' He was pointing to the chalked outline where Aaron Summers had lain. 'He was lying on this.'

The rug was faded red and grubby, heavily stained and marked, threadbare and in the centre was a large, circular burn.

'Recent?'

The SOCO shook his head. 'But not that old,' he said. 'At a guess it was probably done about a month ago. In fact,' he said, dropping the rug back and straightening up, 'there are a few burn marks just in this room.'

'Someone careless with a cigarette?'

He shook his head. 'I don't think so. There's no smell of smoke in here and we've found no evidence of either cigarettes or ash in this room. I don't think any of them smoked.'

Joanna looked dubiously at the fire. 'And I suppose it's too far from the fire for it to have been coal or wood falling from the grate?'

'I doubt it. You see the grill at the front serves as an efficient guard. Besides when wood spits from a fire you tend to get numerous small scorch marks. No . . .' He returned to the burn. 'This has the look of a fire started deliberately.'

'Why?'

'I don't know.' The SOCO shook his head. 'I can't imagine why but it does look as though someone deliberately tried to set fire to the rug. And I'd swear there's a faint scent of petrol.'

'We'd better send it off for analysis.'

The SOCO folded it up.

But now there was no excuse for postponing the upstairs search. She eyed the door with distaste. Korpanski pushed it open. Her heart was thumping as she climbed each step, listening to the creak of old wood and knowing only a few hours before Jack Summers had descended these same stairs and reached the bottom.

The warm, stale air hit her as she rounded the bend halfway up and her head drew level with the landing. It was dark as a cupboard, oppressive and claustrophobic and she was glad of Mike Korpanski's heavy presence behind.

The landing was small, dingy and square. And the doors were all ajar. Four of them. There were four rooms to search. In which of them would they find the missing girl?

She chose the nearest door first.

An unmade bed, rumpled sheets and blankets, a heavy, fusty scent. Clothes strewn across the room, yellowed woollen vests, braces. A pair of boots. There was one ornament, a poorly coloured photograph of a long-haired woman, staring into the room. Not smiling. No body.

They moved on.

The second room was an old-fashioned bathroom. Cast-iron bath, standing on splayed toes, permanently stained blue where water had dripped from the taps. Still dripped with a hollow, monotonous plonk. Threadbare face cloths a uniform pale grey colour hanging over the side of the sink. Bald towels and soap that smelt of sheepfat. A steel Gillette razor clogged with iron grey bristles, torn plastic curtains at the window. Mould on the window sill.

No body.

The third door led to another bedroom, surprisingly neat, lacking the stale, musty smell. Instead there was an unexpected scent of the fields reminiscent of flowers and newly mown grass. Sun streamed in through the faded pink curtains and shone bravely through beams of dust. In an attempt to pretty up the room even further *someone* had put wild flowers in a mug and stood it on the chest of drawers. But the water had evaporated and the flowers long since died. There was a picture on the wall, a cheap print of Constable's *The Haywain* in a plastic frame. That and the pink candlewick bedspread darned as carefully as Aaron's sock told her they were in Ruthie's room.

But where was Ruthie?

The third bedroom held the strongest odour of the cowshed and again the fusty smell of an unaired room. No attempt had been made to make this room pretty. Cloth had been nailed across the window and the bedding was heavily stained where someone had lain. Jack Summers?

Joanna let out a relieved sigh. 'She isn't here, Mike. Thank goodness. She isn't here.'

Mike was peering out through the window, watching the men on the ground. 'So where is she, Jo?'

It was a relief to find themselves in the fresh, clean air again and the sunshine seemed to put a brave light on the ugly events of the day. They went around the back of the house to the yard. The dog barked and pulled against his restraint but when Joanna approached it he gave a low, threatening growl before slinking back into his kennel, dragging the chain behind him like Marley's ghost.

She caught up with Mike in front of the barn door, talking to one of the uniformed officers who was staring ruefully down at his shoes. Unmistakable egg yolk, bits of shell and straw were sticking to the black, polished leather.

Mike was laughing. 'McBrine here's had a good look through the henhouse.'

'Plenty of eggs, ma'am. Couple of good layers there.'

She couldn't dissolve her tension quite so easily. 'But no body?'

'No, ma'am. Not even a dead chicken.' He hesitated. 'We've had a thorough search throughout the whole farm. She isn't here. And we could do with some wellington boots.'

She scanned the horizon. 'Then the fields?'

Mike moved towards her. 'Maybe the fields, Joanna. But it might be better if we looked at the facts under our noses. The gun was theirs. Two people were shot. She's missing. I don't have to spell it out, do I? She's either dead or she did it herself and is holed up somewhere. Maybe the question we should be asking ourselves is where would she run to?'

Chapter Four

2.30 p.m.

The contrast between the horrors of the murder scene
and the rural tranquillity of the narrow lane had the
peculiar effect of making both scenes unreal. And
the hot weather simply added to the sense of strangeness. As they walked along the dusty track even Mike
made a grudging comment. 'It's too nice a day for a
murder.'

'Well we've already had two so let's hope Ruthie
Summers is spending the day innocently with her aunt
having spent the night there.'

His answering grunt was doubtful.

They walked steadily for a few hundred yards until
they reached the bend and Hardacre Farm was at last
out of sight. It was just after they had turned the corner
that they spotted the tiny stone cottage almost hidden
behind two tall conifers. Joanna pushed open the
wicket gate neatly inscribed, *Brooms*. The front garden
was a tribute to industry, tidily divided into rows of
sprouting vegetables, tall, caned beans and peas,
carrots, cabbages and lettuces. Again the front door was
contained within a porch but this was not the fancy
glass appendage of Hardacre but a green painted affair
with a shelf cluttered with gardening tools, gloves, a

trowel, a small fork, a wooden trug. And in the corner, cleaned and ready for use, stood a spade and a hoe.

The knocker was huge and old, a fox's head of wrought iron. Mike picked it up and dropped it heavily.

No one came. The cottage was silent and apparently deserted. Joanna felt a horrid, creeping sensation.

Not here too?

Surely there could not be some maniac pacing the moors, blasting away at people who selected such isolation. Never mind the voice of logic which lectured her. Never mind that the gun had been picked up and fired into the sitting room of Hardacre Farm and was almost certainly now being bagged up by the SOCOs.

Had he come here first?

In sudden panic she hammered on the door, louder this time and shouted. 'Hello – Hello.'

Abruptly it was pulled open. Hannah Lockley stood scowling, hands on hips, a strong, dominant woman in her early sixties with a tough, weathered complexion, iron-grey hair mannishly cut by an unpractised hand. The same navy cotton dungarees.

And she looked angry. 'Who are you?' she demanded. 'Bloody ramblers, lost again? I don't know why you always end up here. The path is thatterway.' And she pointed back out through the gate to her right.

Something in Joanna's face must have stopped her.

Mike fished out his card. 'Police,' he said.

Hannah Lockley looked even more hostile. 'So you're the ones with the blasted sirens,' she snapped. 'I've heard them coming and going all morning. What do you mean disturbing the countryside?' Unwittingly she echoed Matthew's views. 'It isn't necessary you know.' Her eyes, cold, pale blue, narrowed with dislike.

They both noted that she displayed no curiosity as to why they were there.

Joanna tried again. 'May we come in?'

Hannah Lockley barred the way. 'Is it poachers again? I've told your lot before. I'm not interested. They can go to blazes for all I care. Let them have the bloody rabbits.'

Joanna frowned. This was a waste of precious time. 'You are Miss Hannah Lockley?' she asked formally.

'Who wants to know?'

'I'm Detective Inspector Joanna Piercy of the Leek Police. Miss Lockley, I'm afraid I have some rather bad news for you. May we come in?'

'No you can't. Whatever you've got to say you can say out here on the step.' She gave a fond glance around the small garden and beyond to the wide panorama of endless green fields and her voice softened. 'There's no one around to hear, at least no one who matters. Just animals, birds and insects, Inspector.'

Mike stepped forward. 'It would be better if we came in, Miss Lockley.'

'And if I don't invite you?'

There was a brief pause, a battle of wills during which Joanna gained the distinct impression that on the old woman's part it was not done without humour. But as for Mike . . .

'Is your niece here, Miss Lockley?'

A veil dropped over the open, country face and the aggression seemed to melt away. 'Ruthie?' she said. 'No. Ruthie isn't here.'

'When did you last see her?'

The hostility was back. 'What's it got to do with you?'

Incredibly still no alarm was registering. 'We've just come from the farm, Miss Lockley. Hardacre Farm. Now please, let us come in. It really would be easier.'

Hannah Lockley shoved her hands into her trouser pockets like a rebellious teenager. 'Easier for you, mebbe.'

'Please.'

Muttering under her breath and without an invitation to follow, Hannah Lockley strode back into the house, throwing behind her a few choice epithets.

They followed her to the kitchen at the back. This too was old fashioned but neat and what had been left unchanged had now returned to vogue. Painted fern green, with a Belfast sink and scrubbed pine cupboards. It was a kitchen to tempt *Homes & Gardens*.

They faced her over a square, stripped pine table.

'Well as you're here,' she said grudgingly, 'you may as well sit down.'

Joanna was struck by sudden curiosity. How would Hannah Lockley take the news? She seemed tough, unemotional. But there had been flashes of sentiment too.

Miss Lockley must have picked up on her thoughts. 'You needn't be careful of me,' she said steadily. 'I'm not afraid.'

Joanna gave Mike one swift, despairing glance before she plunged in. 'This morning, at around ten, a discovery was made, at Hardacre Farm. The milk-tanker driver found two bodies in the sitting room. They'd been shot. I'm sorry.'

The old woman stared straight ahead. But Joanna

knew she had heard by a slight tic at the side of her mouth.

'They were the bodies of two men,' Joanna continued. 'They have been initially identified as Aaron and Jack Summers, who I believe to be your brother-in-law and nephew.'

Hannah's pale eyes flickered. 'So,' she said painfully slowly, 'the idiot son went berserk in the end.'

They had all jumped to the same conclusion.

'There isn't any question that Jack Summers killed his father,' she said. 'They were shot by someone else.'

Miss Lockley's eyes were very shrewd. 'How do you know?'

'A forensic pathologist has examined both bodies and the scene of the crime. I'm sure I don't need to tell you that a shotgun has a very long barrel. It isn't possible that Jack shot his father before turning the gun on himself.'

Hannah Lockley was still incredulous. 'You're sure?'

'Oh yes.'

'And was it their gun that was used?'

'We can't be positive until we've run some ballistics tests on it but at the moment we think so.'

'Then what do you think happened? Who would have . . .?' She ran out of words abruptly.

Mike's dark eyes fixed on the woman's face. 'We wondered if someone had called Aaron back after he'd started bringing the cows in from the field. They were loose,' he added. Hannah gave him a withering look. 'Aaron never would have left the cows wandering. They're valuable animals besides being his livelihood. He wouldn't have done that.'

50

Joanna pursued the point. 'Then can you think of another explanation why the cows were out of the field and loose in the yard?'

'I can't. But there has to be one. You've got your facts mixed up somewhere, young lady.' The look she gave Joanna was reminiscent of her old headmistress. Severe, critical. It put Joanna firmly in the wrong.

Mike pushed on. 'From the scene of the crime it appears as though Jack was upstairs when his father was shot. We think he heard it, came down and . . .'

'He got hit too.' There was something cynical in the woman's face. 'But then Jack always was the fool.'

Again both the detectives knew there was another dimension to the story. 'It appears,' Joanna said cautiously, 'as though the person stood in the doorway and shot both of them from the same spot.'

'And they are both dead?'

'Yes. I'm afraid so.' Joanna had learnt one could not express regret too often in situations like these. 'Tell me, Miss Lockley, the gun . . .'

'I told them it was a bad idea leaving it stood in the porch.' A glimmer of humour softened the hard lines. 'And if your lot had seen it there doubtless you'd have taken his licence off him.'

'We certainly would,' Mike said firmly.

'Was it kept there loaded?'

'Oh I don't know. I don't know about such things. I have no interest in guns.'

The bones of her knuckles were creamy white as she kneaded her hands. Joanna waited for the old woman to mention her niece. Eventually she did. 'And Ruthie?' Again that indulgent, sentimental note.

'We can't find Ruthie. We'd hoped you might know where she is.'

'We've searched the farm,' Mike said.

Hannah's gaze altered. 'But you haven't found her?'

Something brought back to Joanna's mind the girl's bedroom, dead flowers in the vase, water long ago dried up, the flowers themselves desiccated, rattling dry. And the memory set alarm bells jangling in her head. 'Do you have any idea where Ruthie might be?' She might have pointed out the obvious fact that if Ruthie was alive and well she might be able to explain the facts surrounding the deaths in her family, but Hannah Lockley was still looking too bewildered to assault her with this.

'I don't understand,' she said, 'where the girl's got to.'

'We thought you would be able to help us find her.'

Hannah looked blank.

'Could she be staying with friends?' Mike suggested helpfully.

'Or other relatives perhaps?'

'Staying in the town?'

The old lady's eyes were bloodshot. Perhaps the shocking news had finally penetrated. She made a couple of false starts before completing her sentence. 'You don't . . . you don't really see it, do you?' She looked from one to the other searching for some comprehension or empathy. 'None of them. Not Aaron, Jack or Ruthie. They never went anywhere. They never went out except to the market. There is no need for any of us to go out. Except to get our food we stay here.'

'But she isn't here,' Mike pointed out cleverly.

'No she . . .'

'And you haven't seen her for . . .?'

'A while.' She was almost afraid to ask the next question. 'Do you think . . .?' Joanna desperately wanted to deny that Ruthie Summers might be lying somewhere in the fields, shot too, but she wasn't sure the old lady would have believed her.

Hannah's fingers seemed to have formed lives of their own, twisting and knotting. 'Maybe she's on a holiday.'

'But you just said—'

'I know what I said.' There was something wild in her face. 'But I can't think where else . . . Unless.' Her face was unbearably bleak. 'The Landrover,' she said. 'Is it there?'

'Parked outside.'

'So she hasn't gone out in that.'

'No, Miss Lockley.' Joanna felt a surge of sympathy for her. 'At the moment Ruthie Summers is officially classed as a missing person. If you can think of anything – anything that might help us find her, that might help us work out what happened we'd be very grateful.'

She nodded then sat silent for a moment before her pale eyes found Joanna's face. 'Was it that Art Person?' she asked fiercely. 'Was it him?'

'Who do you mean?'

'That Art Person,' she said again. 'We've all noticed how things have been different since he's come. I told Aaron at the time it was a big mistake letting him rent the Owl Hole. I warned him. I told him these city types don't belong here. Money. That's all it was. Just money. He waved a few twenty pound notes in front of Aaron's greedy long nose and that was that. What Aaron

53

couldn't see was that he was mocking us. Mocking us country types, laughing at our ways of doing things. But Aaron always did worry about money.'

Joanna pictured the emaciated body of the farmer and understood what Hannah Lockley meant. Even in death her brother-in-law had looked worried.

And now Hannah had decided to talk it was as though flood gates had burst open and as Joanna listened the picture of the inhabitants of Hardacre Farm grew steadily clearer. 'Aaron was always complaining about the milk cheque and his bull going missing. Said he was having trouble keeping the farm going. Three mouths to feed and the price of hay awful after last year's rain.' Hannah Lockley's mouth twisted in wry humour. 'Trust him to go and die before gathering the best harvest we're likely to have for the rest of the century. That farm would have been fine, properly managed. That was what it needed, to be properly managed. But from the minute that Art Man came he brought nothing but trouble in his wake. Oil and water, I said to Aaron. Oil and water. The day they mix will be the same day those sort of city folk see eye to eye with us. How can they understand us?' She appealed to the two police officers. 'They are so different. We are different. Put them out here and it causes nothing but trouble.'

Mike licked his pencil and repeated Joanna's question. 'Who are you talking about?'

'I can't remember his name,' Hannah said impatiently. 'Some silly art name.'

'And where will we find this person?'

She looked even more irritated. 'I told you. He's at the Owl Hole. It's one of the outlying farm buildings.

Was used as a grain store once. He got hold of it at the end of last year and messed it up but he does pay rent,' she finished grudgingly. 'Though what Ruthie will do with him when she takes over the running of the farm I don't know.'

Joanna was startled to realize that Hannah firmly believed her niece to be still alive, and if alive – innocent. But she let the subject pass unchallenged for now and allowed Hannah to continue. Maybe it was a means of releasing her grief. And maybe she would let something slip that would help them find out who had shot Aaron and Jack Summers.

'Place used to be full of Barn Owls years ago.' She gave a sour grimace. 'At least *they* were some use. Used to keep the mice down. *He*'s done it up like a birthday cake. I don't think he's quite all there.' She gave a scornful laugh. 'He hangs coathangers from the trees.'

Joanna gave Mike a startled glance. 'Who exactly is he?'

'One of these daft, London people,' the spinster said with all the prejudice of country born and bred. 'One of these people who *escapes* to the country bringing their daft London ways with them. Fashion.' She almost spat the word. 'They like to make monkeys out of us. Calls himself a modern sculptor.' Somehow she had managed to modify her Staffordshire burr to a high-pitched, mincing tone with all the affectation of a society ball.

'But you don't know his name?' Mike's pencil was still poised.

'Titus Mothershaw,' Hannah said reluctantly. '*Titus*. What sort of a name is that?'

Joanna smothered a smile and addressed Mike. 'We'd better go and see him.'

'Arrest him, you mean,' the old lady said spitefully. 'It's obvious to me if it isn't to you. Oil and water, you see. And there's your motive.'

Joanna stood up. 'Nothing's so obvious to me, Miss Lockley. And until it is we won't be making any arrests. Now if you do happen to make contact with your niece I would like you to tell her we are *very* anxious to speak to her.'

Mike hesitated before he spoke up. 'As far as you know did Aaron or Jack and this sculptor man have any arguments?'

'Not that I'm aware of,' the old lady said sulkily.

'In fact you said that Aaron was *glad* of the money. And Mr Mothershaw, I suppose, *liked* living in the Owl Hole.'

'Yes, I suppose so.' Said even more grudgingly.

'So there would be no point in him shooting either of the Summers, would there?'

Hard eyes met his. 'They might have argued and I not known. Maybe Aaron had seen sense at long last and had given him notice to quit. He wouldn't have liked *that* after all the work that he's done there.'

'This is pure conjecture,' Joanna said.

'Oh, you think so, do you?' the old lady said. 'Well what would you think of someone who builds obscene sculptures in the garden. He's a monstrous man.'

Joanna couldn't make up her mind to be amused at the old lady's prejudice or to take it seriously. But then this was a murder investigation. Everything must be taken seriously. She tried to uncover the facts. 'You can't think of any specific reason why this "monstrous man" might want to shoot his landlord, can you?'

'No,' Miss Lockley said reluctantly, 'but I can soon find out things.'

'Well if you do perhaps you'll let us know.'

'I certainly will, young man.' Mike's sarcasm was wasted on the old girl.

Joanna tried again. 'Miss Lockley,' she said patiently, 'can you think of anyone who bore the family a grudge?'

The woman's eyes misted over and she looked upset. 'I . . . No I don't think so. Perhaps.' Then she shook her head. 'I can't think anyone would have wanted to kill Aaron. He wasn't a bad man.'

'And Jack?'

'No,' she said. 'No one could have *wanted* to have killed Jack.'

The wording struck Joanna. What could she mean? That Jack might have been killed by accident? A clear vision of the slumped body of the younger farmer, his hands covering the huge wound in his chest, dispelled the idea as quickly as it had formed.

That could not have been her meaning. So she pushed on with her questions. 'How did Ruthie get on with her brother?'

'Very well,' Hannah said wearily. 'I never heard them argue. They were devoted to each other.'

'Really?'

Miss Lockley picked up the note of scepticism in Korpanski's voice. 'That's Gospel,' she said before adding softly, 'I wonder where Ruthie is right now.'

It was a question they would all have liked the answer to.

'And Aaron?' Joanna was still scratching around for some insight. 'How did Ruthie get on with her father?'

Hannah was thoughtful for a moment then she fixed her gaze on Joanna. 'You have to understand Aaron,' she said. 'He was a lonely, gentle man. He didn't say much, especially after his wife died. Ruthie would cook him a meal. Aaron would eat it. He'd dirty his clothes. Ruthie would wash them. I never heard him utter a word of thanks. Every day was the same for them. They ate, they milked, they cleaned out the sheds, they fed the animals, they fed themselves, they slept. They all worked very hard to keep the farm going. They couldn't have managed without her.'

Her voice was soft but the image she was building up was a life of ceaseless toil, day in, day out, year in, year out, of back-breaking work.

'Did Ruthie have a boyfriend?'

The old lady shook her head. 'She never went anywhere to meet anyone,' she said. 'Her life was her father, her brother, the farm, the animals. We were her friends.' Hannah gave a deep sigh then looked straight at them. 'And how's Noah?'

Joanna gave Mike a sharp, panicked glance. Not another one?

'The dog,' Hannah said.

Joanna breathed a sigh of relief. 'We've left him in his kennel. He was chained up.'

Hannah stood up stiffly. 'Then I'd better get over there and bring him back with me. He'll be confused. He isn't used to all these people around. He'll bark himself hoarse. And the milking?'

Nothing could have given them a more vivid picture of the treadmill of a dairy farm than these simple concerns. Two people had been murdered yet the cows must be milked, the dog must not be allowed to bark himself hoarse.

'The farmer from Fallowfield has done the morning milking.'

Hannah snorted. 'Oh he did, did he? Well there's a funny thing, Martin Pinkers getting 'is fingers curled round Aaron's cows' udders.' She gave a harsh cackle then shrugged her shoulders. 'It's been a blighted family, no mistake. But there you are. Spilt milk and no use crying.' Joanna was startled by the old lady's apparent insensitivity. Until she reminded herself that Hannah Lockley firmly believed her niece to be both alive and well – and innocent. 'Though for Aaron the worst part was that business with Jack,' Hannah continued. Her pale eyes fixed at some point across the room. 'You wouldn't understand, being a policewoman. A farmer needs a good, strong son and a wife to keep house. Jack was a bitter blow.'

Joanna was sure she was missing something. 'You were very fond of the family?'

The old woman nodded. 'Especially Ruthie. She is a daughter to me,' she said simply. 'I love that girl.'

'Then where is she now?' Mike was pursuing the point with his usual vigour.

'I don't know,' Hannah said fearlessly. 'All I am certain of is that she is safe. She will come back.'

Considering Hannah's last few sentences the next question might be necessary but it was still cruel. 'You don't think it's possible—' She didn't even manage to finish the sentence.

'That she killed her father and brother? No,' Hannah said vehemently. 'No. It is not possible.'

'Could she shoot?'

'She's a farmer's daughter.' They waited. 'Of course she could shoot.' Hannah gave a peculiar smile. 'Anyone can shoot. You just hold the gun and squeeze the trigger.'

'Was she a good shot?'

'She could hit a rabbit at forty yards and him dodging between tussocks.'

It answered their question.

Joanna stood up. 'And where were you at around six this morning?'

'In my bed,' Hannah said with another flash of humour. 'And there aren't any witnesses to that.'

At the door Joanna paused and Hannah Lockley was sharp enough to read her action.

'I suppose they'll have to be formally identified?'

Joanna nodded.

'And I suppose you'll have to do a post mortem?'

Again Joanna nodded and Hannah Lockley sighed. 'So be it,' she said simply. 'When?'

'Can we pick you up tomorrow morning?'

'All right.'

'At half past eight?'

'Yes.'

'Just one last thing, Miss Lockley. Who stands to inherit the farm?'

The old lady looked affronted. 'Why Ruthie of course. She's a capable girl. She'll farm Hardacre.'

'But if Ruthie is dead?' Mike asked brutally.

Hannah Lockley drew herself up with dignity. 'Ruthie isn't dead,' she said. 'There will be some perfectly rational explanation. I know.'

3.30 p.m.

The heat was still stifling as they returned to Hardacre, stepping carefully through the fresh cow pats, each one with its own cloud of flies. From the milking parlour came the steady hum of the milking machine and the contented lowing of cows gaining relief from the pressure of full udders. Pinkers must be helping out again. The lane was still full of police cars and Joanna could see a line of blue-shirted officers crossing a distant field in a line.

Two uniformed constables were guarding the door.

'You haven't found her then?'

PC David Timmis shook his head. 'She isn't here,' he said. 'Half a dozen officers have been drafted in from the Potteries to help with the search. We've been through most of the farm including the fields. There's no sign of her. Not anywhere. We did find one thing though.' Joanna's interest quickened. 'What?' Experience had told her the smallest detail might be of disproportionate relevance. Therefore no fact was too small. And Timmis was part of the Moorland Patrol. He knew these people and their terrain.

'The hasp on the gate into the field was broken, stuck into rotten wood. It looks as though the cows might have leant a bit too hard on it and it snapped.'

It explained something about the events of the morning. 'So that means neither Aaron nor Jack Summers let the cows out. They never got as far as the field.'

Mike spoke over her shoulder. 'That makes a bit more sense.'

'Martin Pinkers has been quite helpful. He's even mended the gate and done the afternoon milking too.'

She spoke to Mike. 'So we're left with this. The cows let themselves out of the field and Ruth Summers has vanished. I think we should search her room again to see if she's taken any clothes with her.'

'So you think . . .?'

She wheeled around. 'What am I supposed to think, Mike? Her father and brother have been slaughtered. Hannah Lockley wasn't too keen on admitting it but it seems sweet little Ruthie could shoot straight. From a range of less than four feet I don't imagine she'd miss. And while Aaron must have faced his attacker even though she was holding a gun Jack came crashing down the stairs, also unsuspecting. Now what am I supposed to think?'

'All right, Jo,' he said uncomfortably. 'Keep your hair on.'

She sighed. 'I'm sorry. It's been a long day. Matthew seems determined to live somewhere in these wretched moors and I've spent the last six hours expecting to stumble across a third body.' She made a move towards the house. 'Let's get this over with, shall we?'

The sun had moved from the little bedroom with its vain attempt at femininity and now it looked dingy and dark. The scent of flowers was a little less obvious as though Ruthie's presence was itself beginning to fade.

They stood in the doorway for a few minutes, surveying the room until Joanna motioned towards the chest of drawers. 'We'll start there.'

The top drawer was stuck, needing a sharp tug to display white underwear. The second drawer was stuffed full of sweaters neatly folded – and the third and fourth drawer too. From underneath the bed Mike pulled a brown, canvas zip bag. 'I wouldn't have thought she'd have had a selection of suitcases,' he said grimly and slapped it on the bed. 'I bet this is the only one.' He opened the zip and fished around with his hand. It was empty. He slid his fingers through the lining and pulled out a strip of three photographs, head and shoulders, taken in an automatic booth. The bottom one had been snipped off with curving nail scissors. Joanna stared curiously at the faintly anxious face of a woman, probably in her late twenties, her hair pulled away from a thin face that stared – almost pleaded – into the camera. And somehow Joanna felt a faint sense of shock. This dark-eyed, sensitive face looked nothing like the picture she had formed of a healthy, robust farmer's daughter. This young woman was cast from a different mould. Typically Korpanski stared at the picture too but he saw something different. 'How many pictures come on a strip?'

'Four or five. I'm not sure.'

'You need two to send off for a passport,' he said.

Wondering if she had been misled, she stared again at the strip of photographs. Barely visible, on the top edge of the girl's shoulder, she could make out three or four fingertips. As Ruth Summers had sat in the passport photo booth someone had rested their hand on her shoulder. And far from being a work-roughened farmer's hand it looked neat and clean, long, slim fingers with oval, manicured nails, polished, shaped and filed. And it was a small hand. A child's hand? She met Mike's gaze. 'I suppose,' she said reluctantly, 'that if two photos are missing there is a possibility Ruthie's legged it somewhere. But if she did, she didn't take any of her clothes with her.'

'Well I'm not a woman,' Mike said unnecessarily. 'But the stuff in the drawers hardly looked like fancy stuff. I think if my wife was about to hop it she'd leave that scruffy lot behind.'

She was forced to agree with him. 'So where is she?'

Mike sat down heavily on the bed. 'Just a thought,' he said. 'What if this . . .' He was careful not to touch the photograph. 'What if she had a man – a boyfriend – father and brother none too happy about it, losing their housekeeper. They quarrel, she or the boyfriend blasts them both and they leg it, together.'

'Where?'

'To boyfriend.'

'But her aunt says she never met anybody. She was always here.'

'Even here she must have met some men.'

'Who?'

'I don't know, Joanna. Cattle feed salesmen, vets, people at market, other farmers.'

'Yes,' she said slowly, still studying the thin, sensitive face with its haunting dark eyes. 'It could have been like that.' But to herself she acknowledged she was unhappy with the scenario. And yet behind the large eyes was an apology, a sort of veiled guilt. Had she known then what might come some time in the future?

Joanna dropped the strip of photos into the

specimen bag but she couldn't rid herself of the thin, haunting face.

They spent the later part of the sweltering afternoon and the early part of the evening cooking in the Incident Room, co-ordinating the continuing search of the surrounding farmland, filling in forms and swatting the insistent flies. And as the screeches and chirps of a summer night played a high-pitched musical background around them the soft lowing of contented cows provided tenor accompaniment.

They had done three hours of solid work. Gradually the evening stilled. The flies moved out and the midges arrived. Most of the extra officers had gone home. They would return early in the morning. Only a skeleton staff was left as Joanna and Mike planned the following day.

Joanna knew the first obstacle would be the post mortem.

'And then we should interview Martin Pinkers,' she said, clipping together the sheaf of preliminary statements gathered by the uniformed officers. 'Although he doesn't seem to have seen much.'

'Sometimes the lads don't ask the right questions.'

'True. And let's get a print out of telephone calls to and from the farm. If there is a boyfriend it's even conceivable that he has abducted her.'

'You're determined to see her as a victim.'

'Maybe because she looks more like a victim than a killer.'

He gave a snort of doubt. 'And what other leads have we got?'

'If we haven't completely obliterated them I'd like to take a closer look at the tyre marks in the yard and Shackleton's milk tanker.'

'What for?'

'I just want to know whether he really did burn the rubber as much as he says he did. That's all. Just a simple check. You know as well as I do one little lie, another little lie. And why? So we'll check everything he's told us so far.'

The telephone shrilled at her elbow and she picked it up. It was Matthew.

'The PM's fixed for nine thirty in the morning,' he said. 'We'll have them tidily arranged at the morgue ready for formal identification before we start.' He paused. 'Time for a drink tonight, Jo?'

'I'm sorry, Matthew. I've another call to make.'

'Fine.' She could hear the pent up frustration in his voice yet at the same time she knew it would be useless to apologize. It had all happened too many times before.

'So I'll go home to the flat then.'

But he was angrier than usual. And after she had put the phone down she felt uneasy. Part guilt, part her own frustration.

That Mike was watching her with an unfathomable expression in his eyes didn't help at all.

'So where are we going?' he asked.

'Where do you think?'

Chapter Five

Floodlights bathed the front of the farmhouse, picking out the crevices between each stone in sharp, black lines. Even the animals were quiet but it was not the quiet of sleep. She could hear them shift restlessly, a few soft grunts. It was almost as though they were waiting. For what? Maybe it was fanciful but as Joanna picked her way along the lane she could almost convince herself that Aaron's herd of cows were silently waiting to witness justice done, for the police to leave Hardacre Farm in rural peace again.

She would have confided her fancies to Mike but she knew from experience he would not share them, so they walked away from the farmhouse in silence.

Two police had been left to guard the door, WPC Dawn Critchlow and Eddie McBrine, PC of the Moorlands Patrol. Joanna knew from experience that night vigils were usually the worst watch – cold, uneventful, cheerless and boring. But on this rare balmy night the task was almost enviable. Tonight there was a magic around, stars, and indigo sky, a red, setting sun.

Dawn spoke first. 'Off home, are you?'

Mike answered. 'Not yet. We're on a mystery trip.'

'Where's that then?' she asked cheekily.

Joanna answered the question. 'We're going to visit someone who rented a barn from Aaron Summers.'

'A neighbour?'

'Yes.'

'Think he's got anything to do with it?'

Joanna searched around the dim panorama, unable to pick out even that one neighbour's light.

'They've all got something to do with it,' she said, 'until proved otherwise.'

Mike mopped his forehead. 'Why does it seem to get hotter at night?' He slapped his arm. 'And these bloody mosquitoes.'

'Well I'd rather have mosquitoes,' Joanna said, 'than those ghastly, repulsive flies. The way they buzzed around the bodies turned my stomach.'

'Trouble is,' Mike said grumpily, 'we just aren't acclimatized to this sort of heat.'

They left the two officers to their vigil and walked companionably for a few minutes before Joanna ventured to ask, 'You don't mind coming to interview Mr Mothershaw tonight, do you?'

'Well, I wasn't going to go home anyway. Not until later. It's my night at the gym.'

'Bit late for that, isn't it?'

'It shuts late,' he said shortly and she refrained from comment. But she had noticed Mike's increased irritability, put it down to the weather. She had noticed something else too, something that could not be attributed to the hot weather. Detective Sergeant Mike Korpanski had recently been wearing some very flashy ties.

They continued further in silence.

And suddenly the night dropped down from the

sky, like a navy, woollen blanket. The way forward was invisible. 'Now from what Hannah Lockley was saying the Owl Hole is somewhere beyond the milking shed through the trees.' Joanna flashed her torch ahead of them, lighting up a pair of frightened rabbit's eyes and a narrow lane which curved ahead. Either side of the lane tall trees bowed into an archway. All was still. The entire night was holding its breath for the next development. The stillness was oppressive and not for the first time since she had come to Leek Joanna was glad of Mike's bulky presence.

One of the trees was filled with squawking rooks which started quarrelling as the two police officers passed and a few of them were ousted from their perches. They flapped their heavy black wings and croaked their objections before settling back. And all was still again.

Quiet and still.

Mike spoke at her elbow. 'Can't stand the damned rooks. Noisy bloody things, aren't they? No wonder the farmers like aiming pot shots at them. Bloody carrion.'

'Well, it wasn't a rook someone took a pot shot at this morning,' she observed drily, 'but the farmer himself. And it wasn't the rooks that did it. Mike,' she touched his arm, 'do you think that's the place?'

Across the top of the thick trees they could vaguely make out a faint glimmer of light.

'I suppose it has to be. There isn't exactly anywhere else, is there?'

'Nowhere.'

The lane came to an abrupt end in a wooden stile. To the right a narrow path wound through the trees and out of sight.

A round building was vaguely silhouetted through the branches, tall and tapering towards the top.

'It looks a bit like a windmill.'

'A windmill that's lost its sails.'

'What did Miss Lockley say it was? A grain store. Well, let's see what our sculptor has to reveal to us. I don't fancy getting lost in these woods with our killer still on the loose.'

'The daughter.' Mike said the words with difficulty and she knew her apprehension had communicated to him. 'What if it's her. What if she has flipped her lid and she's hanging around here somewhere?'

'As far as we know she'll be unarmed,' Joanna said calmly. 'Barra's taken the gun.' She couldn't resist pulling his leg. 'Not nervous, are you, Mike?'

'Not a hundred per cent happy,' he admitted and she walked the next few yards reflecting on how much their relationship had changed in the five years since she had taken up her post in the quiet, moorland town. Then Mike had been antagonistic, resentful, difficult. And now? Even to herself she was reluctant to admit it. Now she relied on him. They worked well together, her ideas with his practicality, her intuition with his stolid progression, ox like, moving forward. Between them they had gained results. Mike had shed his difficult reputation. But now? She peered at him suspiciously. She wasn't sure. There was something intangibly different about him. He was a bit more edgy, slightly quicker to take offence. It had been there for three, maybe four weeks. And it hadn't made him an easier person to work with.

Her musings were brought abruptly to a halt by

Mike shining a beam to the left of the path. 'What the hell?'

The trees were gnarled and old, bent into curious shapes by neglect and the elements. With very little imagination Joanna could have convinced herself that the wood was peopled with strange beings. She gave a nervous little laugh. Trees. That was all. Misshapen, lumpy trees. The evening was all black now with a seed of red faintly visible on the horizon. They ignored the shapes and carried on along the rough path then stopped.

In front of them stood a sentinel, a man, twelve feet high with arms outstretched as though to grab them. Mike let out a sharp breath.

'What the . . .?'

'Shine the torch on it.'

It was a tree. Again just a tree, initially conveniently human shaped before being formed into a person by someone, presumably the 'Art Person'. Twigs at its head were unruly hair. The trunk formed a body, split at the base into two legs that ended in blackened roots. And the branches that reached down towards the path had been extended with twigs to form skinny fingers.

Joanna shivered. It was monstrously lifelike.

Mike broke the silence. 'The face,' he said. 'Joanna. Look at the face.'

She shone her torch upwards and was both shocked and impressed. With rough carving the sculptor had achieved a reality and expression which altered as she shifted the beam of the torch. And the strange shadows and lighting effects gave the hollow eyes a malevolent gleam. Glass, varnish? Something shone, looking evil, and yet at the same time indifferent; powerful without being conscious of its own power.

She had to admit, the man's work was good. No – not good, brilliant. Brilliant and original and despite the primary reason for interviewing Titus Mothershaw – that he was a murder suspect – she was curious to meet the man behind this creation.

Mike was not so appreciative. 'What does he call this?'

She laughed. Mike could be as bovine as some of Aaron Summers' herd and yet . . . It did her good. 'I believe,' she said, 'that it's a form of art.'

Mike had views of his own. 'Why the hell can't he leave the trees alone?' He touched one. 'It's just silly, this.'

In the darkness Joanna smiled and knew that however fascinating she might find the Tree Man's creator Mike would have nothing in common with him.

'We'd better get a move on.' She teased Mike further. 'Who knows what happens to monsters like these after dark.'

As they wandered along the track they flashed their torches to the left and right, picking out strange carvings in almost all of the trees. The wood carver had been busy. Some were faces so human it would have been no surprise to her to see their lips open, their eyes blink. Some were carvings in stumps, fauns, wood nymphs, grotesque animals and one round stump had been carefully carved to form a pillar box. The whole was like a children's story of some fantastic wood where everything was alive and full of character, and for the time it took them to approach the Owl Hole Joanna *almost* forgot about the deaths. She wondered whether the wood could hold so much atmosphere in the daylight. They were nearly at the strange building when Joanna caught sight of some objects hanging from the trees. Hannah Lockley had been right. Titus Mothershaw did use coat hangers.

A tinkle behind them made Mike swear, turn sharply and flash his torch. Titus Mothershaw had formed wind chimes from small stones, bored with a hole and hung from the branches. Another tree had had its branches bent and lashed together to form an Indian wigwam.

And then, quite suddenly, her torch picked out a finely carved face in the trunk of a tree. She studied it and felt completely attuned to the sculptor's statement. It was something to do with natural beauty *enhanced* by human hand. And it seemed a million miles away from the bodies they had found this morning, people made grotesque, again, by human hand. She moved her torch up and down the bark to study the face better. A knot in the wood formed a nose, a shaped branch, an ear, a gash, the mouth. And now she was doubly anxious to meet this clever emigré from London because the face reminded her, just a little, of Ruthie Summers. 'Bloody crap,' Mike was muttering. 'And I bet he cons people, charges a fortune for these bits of wood. Besides,' he objected, 'it's out of place here. I mean this was a mucky, old-fashioned sort of farm. It just looks stupid, all this art stuff. He should have left the place alone. Belongs in London.'

'Well I like it.' Joanna had an impulse to defend this sculptor's talent. 'But I would love to know what old Aaron Summers must have thought of it. He must have scratched his head. Who knows. Maybe he hated it too.'

But Mike misunderstood her statement. 'Hang on a minute, Jo. I mean I don't like the stuff. But it's hardly a motive for murder, not being appreciated.'

'Oh, Mike,' she said despairingly.

'Well,' he said. 'I bet all this took him hours. And I bet he would be upset if anyone threatened to spoil them. Maybe . . .'

'Come on,' she said. 'Let's hope this sculptor chappie keeps late hours even though he is in the country.'

He must have been watching their approach. Maybe he'd picked out their torchlight.

As they reached the end of the path the door to the Owl Hole was flung open dramatically and a small man in a brilliant, white shirt and yellow bell-bottomed trousers faced them from the centre stage.

'Who are you?'

He had a nice voice, calm and tranquillizing, neither a deep man's voice nor high pitched.

'It's all right, sir. We're the police.'

'The police? Then I assume you're carrying identity cards?'

His accent was cultured. Plummy but educated and not too affected. Eton? Oxford? A public school?

'What exactly are you doing here? It's rather late.' He was frowning.

Joanna took one step forward. 'You've probably heard there's been a shooting up at the farm?'

He smelt nice too. Oranges, spice, soap.

'A uniformed officer came round this afternoon and told me. You can't believe something so horrible would happen out here. And to such simple people. Quite tragic, wasn't it?'

'As you say, sir.' Mike's voice was wooden. Naturally prejudiced against such types he was schooling himself not to display what the contemporary police force called 'negative emotions'.

'Tragic.'

'May we come in?'

The sharp, blue eyes focused on Joanna appraisingly. 'Do. Be my guests. I always have a pot of freshly ground coffee on the hob.' He laughed uneasily and Joanna suddenly realized he was nervous. Of them? For his own safety? He laughed again. 'If you're investigating a murder I daresay you'll be needing lashings of coffee.'

'I don't deny it.'

As they entered the converted barn she took a good look at Titus Mothershaw. He had fine, feminine features with ash blond hair that had a suspicious tinge of pink. It was shaved at the back but the front was long enough to flop across his eyes. He had tanned, smooth skin women would pay for and he was short, about five foot three, a few inches shorter than she. And Mike topped him by a foot. He had neat little child's hands with fingernails carefully shaped into ovals. That guaranteed him a hundred per cent of her attention.

Mothershaw ushered them into a tall, round room, almost the entire ground floor of the Owl Hole. A central staircase wound its way up to the gods and, she supposed, a bedroom and bathroom. The whole was painted stark white, the furniture daffodil-yellow. And from the ceiling was suspended a carving of a Barn Owl in mid-flight. He had done it beautifully, in a pale, sleek wood. But it had been slung too low and Mike bumped his head on it as he crossed the room.

He gave it a baleful look.

Mothershaw ignored the incident except to steady the owl's pendulum swing. Joanna noticed that the spotlight picked out the outline of the owl and threw a huge shadow against the wall. It was as striking as the actual carving. It was a clever idea, this cunning use of light and shade. Mothershaw's home seemed larger on the inside than from the outside, an illusion furthered by the white decor, and white-sprayed branches carelessly stacked in the corner, pricked with fairy lights and satin bows. The effect was almost bridal.

Mothershaw gave a self conscious cough. 'My little grotto,' he said to Joanna. He had clearly already discounted Mike as a philistine.

'It's amazing, Mr Mothershaw,' she said truthfully.

He looked gratified. 'Now tell me,' he said. 'How do you think I can help?'

'How much do you know?'

'Just that there was an accident this morning at the farm and poor old Aaron and Jack were found dead.'

'Nothing more?'

Titus shook his head. 'What more is there to know?'

'They were shot,' Mike said brusquely.

'Oh?'

'Someone shot them.'

Titus gave the same reaction as Hannah Lockley. 'So Jack . . .'

'We didn't say it was Jack. Someone else shot them both.'

The news seemed to shock Mothershaw much more than the original incident. The colour drained from his face. 'Who did it?'

'We don't know – yet.'

Mothershaw's eyes searched their faces. 'Was it their gun that was used?'

'We don't have the official reports yet but we think so.'

He had difficulty speaking his next words. 'And Ruthie?'

Mike's black eyes were fixed on his face. 'Know her well, do you, sir?'

'No. I mean yes.' Mothershaw was still pale. 'I mean. Yes, as a neighbour, you understand?'

Mike nodded. 'We understand all right. See much of her, do you?'

'Just tell me,' he said quietly, clasping his hands together. 'Please. Is Ruthie all right? Where is she?'

Joanna cut in. 'We don't know, I'm afraid. We don't know where she is.'

Mothershaw's eyes were round.

'She's disappeared.'

Mike spoke from the back of the room. 'Attractive girl, wasn't she, sir?'

Mothershaw stared at the shadow of the Barn Owl, still now. 'She was,' he said, 'unusual.'

'In what way?'

'Just not what you'd expect. I don't understand your saying she's disappeared. She's always at the farm. You're sure . . .?'

'We're not sure of anything at the moment except that Aaron and Jack were shot and are both dead.'

'We've searched the farm and surrounding land. We've been doing that all day. There's no sign of her.' Joanna smiled. 'Obviously we're concerned.'

But Titus Mothershaw was too intelligent to fall for that one. 'And I suppose if you don't find her – dead,' he said, 'you'll naturally start putting two and two together.'

Neither Mike nor Joanna felt the need to reply to that.

'You have no idea where she might have gone, a friend, perhaps?'

Mothershaw shook his head. 'I don't think she had any.'

'Boyfriends?' Mike asked.

Again Mothershaw shook his head. 'Not that I know of.'

Joanna glanced once more at his small, neat, child's hands. It could all wait until later.

Instead she asked, 'Have you seen Ruthie lately?'

'No.'

'When did you last see her?'

'Three weeks ago.' There was definitely something wary in his face. 'I called there to pay my rent at the beginning of the month.' He looked from one to the other. 'But she wasn't there.' He thought for a moment. 'She isn't at her aunt's?'

'No. Got any better ideas, sir?'

That made Mothershaw uncomfortable. But then Mike Korpanski had this effect on people. His bulk intimidated them physically but it was his manner that crept under the skin. And Joanna knew sometimes it bore results. He was a valuable friend to the innocent but to the guilty he was a threat. The trouble was Mike made swift judgements. And they were frequently founded on prejudice rather than fact. And although so far she deemed Mothershaw not guilty he was, at the very least, hiding something.

'Is there anything else you can think of about the family that might have relevance to their murders?'

Mike crossed the room, avoiding the Barn Owl this time. 'You see, sir, we're fairly anxious to nail the person who blasted this innocent pair to Kingdom Come.'

Mothershaw almost breathed the next sentence. 'Who says they were so very innocent?'

All Joanna could do was to repeat her last plea. 'If you know anything, Mr Mothershaw, anything at all that might point us towards a motive for the crime it's your duty to tell us.'

But Mothershaw wasn't quite ready to squeal yet. 'I hardly knew them, really,' he said. 'I simply rented this place from them.'

'Come from London, don't you, sir?'

'Yes.' It was almost an admission of a crime.

'So what brought you to this particular part?'

The question relaxed him. He leant back on the sofa, rested his arm along the top of the cushion and crossed his legs. 'You probably won't understand this, Detective Sergeant,' he said comfortably, 'but it was the wood.'

Mike stood rigidly.

'You see I spent months searching for just the right place. Old trees, dead trees, stumps and spare branches. I had to have the right sort of place. When I found here . . .'

'And how did Aaron and Jack react to the carvings?'

Mothershaw drew in a deep, breathy sigh before giving Joanna a sexy grin. 'They thought I was mad,' he said, 'to pay the rent, to transform the Owl Hole, to deface their wood.' He smiled again. 'They as near as suggested I consult a doctor.'

Mike's *'hmm'* summed up his attitude.

Joanna pressed on with the questions. This was always her way. There were certain facts she had to ascertain for the police reports. But the real solution always came like this. Know your victims and know your suspects. Some people, however pleasant and polite they may seem, were capable of murder. And others, apparently truculent, were not.

'Tell me, Mr Mothershaw. Have you ever been inside Hardacre Farm?' Visions of the SOCOs painstakingly lifting prints from the porch, the doors, the corpses crossed her mind.

Maybe Mothershaw shared the same picture. 'To pay the rent.'

Mike leant forward. 'Had you ever noticed a gun standing in the porch?'

Mothershaw nodded. 'Ruthie showed it to me one day. They kept it there to scare the crows off. She told me if the police saw it standing there her father would lose his licence.'

'Too right,' Mike said heartily.

'Was it kept loaded?'

'She told me the bullets were in the drawer of the sideboard.'

'Did you handle it?'

An imperceptible pause before, 'She told me it was heavy. I wondered how heavy.'

'So you picked it up.' Joanna nibbled her thumbnail. This could be the ultimate cleverness, she thought. By this seemingly frank confession Titus Mothershaw had already explained away his fingerprints on the murder weapon.

'Did you get on well with them?' It was too obvious a question.

'Very well the few times I saw them. In fact I'd offered to carve a model of Doric for them.'

'Who is Doric?'

Titus Mothershaw threw back his head and laughed. 'The bull,' he said.

'There's a bull there?' Joanna was concerned for the officers roaming around the farm.

'It was stolen.'

'I don't remember reports of a bull being stolen.'

'They didn't report it to the police. But it was a blow to them. They'd hoped to make quite a lot of money from him.' Mothershaw grinned. 'In various ways. They bought Doric with my first couple of months rent.'

'Mr Mothershaw . . .'

He was instantly on his guard.

'We know you haven't seen Ruthie Summers for a while.'

'That's right.' He was very anxious to confirm.

'So when did you last see Aaron and Jack, alive?'

Titus stared at the ceiling as though giving the question long thought. 'I think it was Sunday afternoon,' he said. 'It was hot. Too hot to work so I thought I'd wander across, go for a walk.' His eyes dropped quickly. 'I just happened to bump into them. They were starting to cut the hay.'

'Enjoy walking do you, sir?'

'Absolutely not!' His grin was disarming. 'I only go for a walk when I'm hunting for materials. Unless I'm bored.'

'Or hot.'

'Yes – or hot.'

'But you didn't see Ruthie last Sunday?'

'No.'

Joanna stood up. 'Thank you very much, Mr Mothershaw. I think that'll do for now. It's late.'

'Is the killer still loose?'

'Yes.'

'So would you advise me to book into a hotel? I mean is it safe round here? It's terribly isolated.'

'Two constables are posted round the farm,' Mike said without sympathy. 'You're probably safer here tonight than you were last night or early this morning.'

Mothershaw shivered. 'At what time,' he asked delicately, 'did it happen?'

'Sometime around six a.m.'

'He won't come back?'

He – so he didn't think it was Ruthie.

'I doubt it.'

'Well, I shall bolt my doors, draw up the bridge and repel all boarders,' Mothershaw said bravely.

'One last thing, Mr Mothershaw. What do you think of Miss Hannah Lockley?'

And here he waxed poetical. 'I think she's wonderful. Such a character, so active. And devoted to Ruthie.'

'Devoted to Ruthie,' Joanna mused, once they were safely outside. 'Why did he just mention Ruthie? Why not Jack – or Aaron?'

*

They walked in silence for a few minutes before Joanna shared her latest thought. 'Some farmers,' she said slowly, 'are old-fashioned. They don't bank money but keep it around the house. What if Mothershaw paid his rent in cash and it was mounting up?'

'And Ruthie?'

'I think we should call the helicopter out to help search for . . .'

'Her body?'

Joanna nodded. 'In this heat,' she said, 'it will be rapidly decomposing.'

Chapter Six

Wednesday, July 8th, 6.58 a.m.

As Joanna cycled along the moorland road she was already aware of the rising heat, the melting tarmac, the mist lifting from the valley and the utter peace. She was alone. No one else was stirring, apart from the birds, singing their dawn chorus.

But because of the heat she had a strange sense of unfamiliarity in these well-known surroundings. The grass was scorched brown, not green and damp. The air was hot, the few leaves were beginning to droop. At first welcome, this desert weather was taking its toll on the moorlands.

She rode along the ridge until she reached the stone walls that skirted Fallowfield and she slowed her pedalling to take a look across the farmyard. She was up before Pinkers. The cows were jostling noisily against the gate, trying to enter the milking parlour. The front door was closed, the bedroom curtains were tightly drawn. The house was still and sleeping. Or was it? She could have sworn she caught sight of a face moving in the downstairs window, which then whisked from view.

She quickened her pace and reached Hardacre moments later.

Here too it was deceptively peaceful, the only visible sign of recent events the police car parked in

84

the yard and the huge caravan of the Mobile Incident Unit.

She dismounted, locked her bike at the back and walked inside the empty room, aware of the stillness of the surroundings, punctuated only by rippling bird-song which seemed to penetrate the Incident Room as though nature itself conspired to cover the whole thing up with birdsong, mooing cows, this deceptive rural peace. It would be tempting to savour the deception, sit still and listen. But Joanna forced herself to change out of her cycling top and lycra shorts into a pale blue cotton dress and loafers – far more suitable for her agenda, accompanying Hannah Lockley in the grue-some task of identifying her dead relatives before attending the dual post mortems. She sat down at the desk, flicked the computer screen on and read through the few facts. They were sparse. Little more than bare details, times, the bodies found and virtually nothing helpful in the statements gathered yesterday, baldly, two men shot, a girl missing. She stood up and crossed the yard to the farm. It was seven fifteen. There was still plenty of time before they had to pick up Hannah Lockley.

Sergeant Barraclough was already hard at work. He was a thorough man, moving around the scene of the crime with meticulous care, collecting and docu-menting every sample. Silently she handed him a photocopy of the strip of photos.

'This is the missing woman,' she said, 'Ruthie. I'd like to know what fingerprints you come up with from the originals.'

He took a good look. 'We've got plenty of prints from her bedroom,' he said. 'We should be able to match them up and see what else they yield. Nice looking thing, isn't she? Sad eyes though.'

'She doesn't look like a killer, does she?' Joanna was aware that she was instinctively defending a suspect – on the strength of a sweet face?

Barraclough had no such scruples. 'They often don't look the part,' he said drily. 'I've met killers who looked more like angels.' He gave a sudden deep, full-bellied laugh. 'And some angels who are unfortunate enough to look like killers too. It could well be her, Joanna.' Still she didn't want to admit it and watched silently as he lifted some clear loops and whorls from the pantry door with deft skill.

'Well?'

'Looks like three distinctly different sets of prints.' He stuck the sellotape to the glass slides before speaking again. 'We need to compare them with the prints from the dead men and the ones lifted from the girl's bedroom. Then maybe we can make some deductions. But it looks as though the only prints in the house belong to one of three people. I wonder what's been picked up from the gun.'

'We'll formally get prints from the corpses at the post mortem.'

Barra looked sympathetic. 'You're going, are you?'

She nodded. 'I should be there.' They both knew she hated it.

Sergeant Barraclough glanced around the room, at the blood spattered walls. 'Well I hope we find someone guilty of this,' he said. 'I wouldn't like to think of the bloke responsible for such butchery roaming free. I mean . . .' For once he seemed at a loss for words. 'I mean there wasn't even anything here to steal.' He

86

glanced around the spartan room, the worn sofa, the threadbare rug, the ancient television. 'So what was the point of it all? What did the murders achieve?'

An embryo of a thought crossed Joanna's mind. 'Unless the Summers hoarded money.'

'In this day and age?'

'Some people still do, especially old-fashioned, isolated, rural farmers. I've seen them pay in cash at the market, pulling out rolls of notes.' For the first time that morning she smiled. 'A month or so ago I saw an old chap try to pay for something with a ten shilling note.'

Barra was incredulous. 'You're kidding.'

'I'm not.'

'Well I suppose the old dear from the cottage would know if anyone did.'

Joanna glanced at her watch. 'I'm picking her up in a little over half an hour. I'll ask her then.'

A second thought flitted unpleasantly through her mind. If they had hoarded cash Ruthie would have known. They had found none. So if there had been money stashed away someone must have taken it. Who better than the missing daughter? Her arguments seesawed from guilt to innocence, from victim to killer.

And despite her instincts Ruthie Summers remained her chief suspect but the only sign she gave to Barra of her turmoil was to mutter, 'If the aunt says they *did* keep quantities of cash around the place we'd better find it.'

Barra gave a loud snort and echoed her doubts. 'If the innocent-looking wench hasn't helped herself.'

'Don't prejudge,' she said. 'She may have an explanation.'

'Well it had better be very convincing. Unless . . .'

His grey eyes were sharply thoughtful. 'I wonder if she saw what happened and fled.'

'Where?'

He shrugged. 'Who knows?'

'I might buy that one,' she said wearily, 'if her aunt hadn't impressed on me what an isolated life she led. But everyone agrees that apart from her father and her brother and the chap from the Milk Marque board there was nobody in their lives. At least nobody who saw them regularly. It was always just the three of them.'

But even as she said it she knew this was not strictly true. There were other people. There was the strange man now living at the Owl Hole. And there were more. There was the aunt. There was the tanker driver. There was Pinkers. There must have been other, neighbouring farmers. And who else? Was there yet another person?

Barra was saying nothing but he watched her carefully and followed her back into the blazing porch, already baking in the morning sun and still full of annoying, buzzing flies.

She swatted one on her arm. 'Where do they all come from?'

He laughed. 'There's always plenty of flies around a farm. I grew up next door to one, in a little cottage on Grindon moor. They don't bother me. You get used to them. I suppose they have plenty of stuff to breed in. Silage, manure, plenty of muck and warmth.'

'Thank you for the graphic comment,' she said drily. 'Especially when I'm just psyching myself up to attend the post mortem.'

*

They were on time to pick Hannah Lockley up from her cottage. And she was waiting for them at the front door, a small, square figure, looking peculiarly old-fashioned in a battered black straw hat and a dark, shapeless dress. She seemed somehow shrunken from yesterday, older and frailer.

'I've had a terrible night,' she said. 'I've hardly slept at all. I can't stop going over and over in my mind what must have happened to Aaron and Jack. How it happened.' She gave them a fierce look. 'Awful. Absolutely awful.'

They watched her lock the door with a huge, old key and tuck it under the coconut mat. Mike opened his mouth to speak but Joanna shook her head. Now was not the time for a lecture on Crime Prevention.

Miss Lockley followed them down the path and into the car before addressing Joanna. 'Who do you think it was, Inspector?'

'It's early days yet.' It was a weak, unhelpful reply.

The old lady's face crumpled as they drove past Hardacre. 'Why do you think they were . . .?' She swallowed.

It was an ideal opportunity. Joanna turned to face her. 'Did they keep cash in the house?'

Hannah gave a deep sigh. 'I can see the way you're thinking, Inspector,' she said wearily, 'but they weren't like that. For all their old-fashioned ways they put their money in the bank. There wouldn't have been more than a few pounds in the house. Nothing worth stealing and definitely not worth killing them for.'

It was a blind alley so Joanna tried another one. 'Have you thought of anywhere your niece could be?'

'No.' The old lady looked thoughtful. 'I've wondered

about that all night and I can't think of anything. But I heard it all on the radio. She must have heard it too. She'll turn up.' She spoke with hearty confidence.

Joanna eyed the old lady curiously. For all the grief she was expressing there was a certain complacency in her manner. Had she worked *nothing* out? Where *could* the girl have gone? More than that *how*? The Landrover was parked outside. They must be four miles from the nearest bus stop. No taxi had reported picking a girl up from anywhere near here. A plea for her to return home had gone out on last night's radio, a hotline set up. No one had rung to say they had seen her and she had not been in contact.

And yet through all this, Hannah Lockley was sure Ruthie would return. Not only that, but she was convinced of the girl's innocence. Joanna wished she could share that same conviction.

She watched Hannah give a self-conscious tug to her hat and listened as she returned to more mundane matters. 'And then when I got up this morning I just didn't know what to wear. I mean – it isn't a funeral, is it? But I felt for their sake I should dress properly. Oh dear,' she said in a sudden flood of emotion. 'This is a dreadful business, isn't it?'

'Yes it is.' Mike spoke woodenly from the driver's seat. 'But all we want to do is our job. We want to get this bloke and shove him behind bars.' He pulled up outside the mortuary before turning around. 'You'll be all right, will you, Miss Lockley?'

Only then did Hannah Lockley's iron self-control break. 'Let's just get on with it,' she snapped.

*

90

Through the open door Joanna could see the mortuary attendants had laid the bodies out side by side, their forms covered with a green cloth. There was a vase of Arum lilies on a small table. They were good at these soft touches conveying their sympathy.

She touched Miss Lockley's arm. 'You needn't actually go into the room if you don't want to. You can look through the window.'

There was something Victorian about the old lady as she drew herself up with dignity. 'I'll do the job properly, thank you very much, Inspector.'

A moment later it was all over, nothing different except Hannah's face was chalk-white.

'I'm sorry,' she said over and over again as they sat her down and offered her a cup of tea. 'I hadn't thought I would be like this.'

'People don't know how they will react,' Joanna said softly. 'But it's always bound to be a painful experience.'

'I hadn't thought they would look so neat,' Hannah said faintly. 'All night I've been lying awake picturing them with holes and blood and something horrible in their faces.' She fished a man's handkerchief out of her pocket. 'But I didn't think they would look so peaceful.' Then her iron resolve broke and she pressed the handkerchief to her face. 'Whatever Paulette would have said I don't know. My poor family. We are cursed. Oh,' she moaned, rocking slightly in her chair, 'if only Ruthie would come home.'

'Perhaps . . .' Joanna said cautiously and could not continue.

It had still not occurred to this elderly aunt that if her niece did turn up alive and well suspicion would *have* to focus on her. But it was not up to Joanna to plant that particular seed in her brain. She took a harder look at the pale eyes and the boney hands and realized. Neither had it occurred to the ageing spinster that her niece might not turn up at all.

Mike took the distressed old lady back to her cottage while Joanna met the two SOCOs at the door and together they waited for Matthew to arrive. The mortician made them a coffee which they drank apprehensively. Traditionally the police hated PM work and the three of them were no exception. The last thing any of them wanted was to throw the coffee up all over the floor. It was with some relief that at twenty past nine they heard Matthew's tuneless whistle as he turned his key in the door. He entered the room looking happy, well rested and animated. He was never more relaxed than when he was about to reveal the secrets of a corpse. Or two. A double treat.

He gave Joanna a warm grin. 'Hi.' And ignoring the others present gave her a hard, happy kiss on the cheek. She met his eyes, recognized the gleam behind them. She never loved him more than when he was in this mood, ready to absorb himself in his work. He ran his fingers through his honey blond hair, always cut a touch too long for real tidiness.

'We'd better get stuck in. No point in hanging around. No time to waste.' He rubbed his hands together and addressed the mortician. 'Wheel them in while I get changed.'

He emerged a moment later in a green cotton gown covered by a huge, blue plastic apron. 'I wonder what little secrets are about to be spilt on to the mortuary floor.' Then he held his hands up. 'Sorry,' he said. 'Sorry.'

He tied her into a cotton attendant's gown and eyed the SOCOs. 'Ready?'

They nodded, pale faced.

An hour later he'd finished and they were sitting together in his office.

'Cause of death,' he said, 'fairly obvious really. Gunshot wounds to the chest. Range of somewhere about four feet for Jack. Much nearer for the old man. Very little scattering of the shot, some scorching and I've fished out quite a lot of wadding from the wound. Interestingly Aaron Summers wasn't going to last much longer anyway. I thought he was emaciated when I first saw him. I'll send a section off to the path lab for confirmation but I'd lay a hefty bet that that ugly lump I pulled out of his stomach was a malignancy. Poor blighter.'

She watched him in surprise. This was a side to Matthew she rarely saw. She had not heard him express pity for a victim before. A pathologist merely reported facts, without emotion. His patients were all dead – beyond suffering – anatomical exercises, text book stuff. But of course Matthew was a doctor too. And what more natural than that he would react to this pathology as would a doctor who would know the suffering and eventual, inevitable outcome of this 'ugly lump' which had eroded Aaron Summers from the inside out.

'How long would he have lived?'

Matthew peeled off his latex gloves. 'We're talking

about weeks,' he said. 'The thing was far gone. I'll ring his GP and find out some more.'

But the real question was, did this discovery have any bearing on Aaron's murder? Surely not. How could it? So she moved to the second figure. 'And Jack?'

'Uum, Jack was in pretty good shape.' He paused. 'Apart from quite a bad old head injury. There was still some depression of the skull and extensive tissue necrosis underneath. It might have been done when he was a child, possibly even when he was a baby. And I think it would almost certainly have resulted in some brain damage.'

She followed him to the sink and watched him sluicing his hands.

He laughed. 'That's the weird thing about this job,' he said. 'Every now and again you get a real surprise. I mean the gunshot wounds were obvious. The rest, well . . .' And at last he was answering Joanna's question. 'But I can't see how either finding affects your case, Jo.'

'Neither can I.'

She watched him filling in the forms in his careful but scrawly writing, something nagging hard at the back of her mind. Something he had said. 'Matthew,' she began slowly. 'What's likely to have caused Jack's skull fracture?'

'I don't know,' he said. 'Maybe he was dropped as a baby, fell downstairs. It could have been anything.' He stopped. 'Has anyone said Jack was retarded?'

'No . . . Yes.'

Hannah Lockley's words when she had learnt about the murders. 'So the idiot son went berserk in the end.' Joanna had heard the words but not followed them up

94

at the time. Only now did they make sense. She nodded and Matthew continued. 'Well, I'd lay a bet he was, at the very least, slow. Now.' He crossed the room towards a blackboard on which was sketched a plan of the murder scene, the sitting room, positions of the bodies, doors and windows. 'As for the major wounds. The shot Jack received was just a little off centre and angled while Aaron's was full blast central chest.' With his finger he traced a line from the front door to the spot which marked the point where Jack's body had been found. He spoke to one of the SOCOs. 'Can you remember the exact measurement?'

'Just under four feet.'

Matthew nodded. 'The assailant took one or two steps inside the room. Jo, he was no nearer. The shot in the bodies isn't very scattered and even on Aaron there's practically no scorching. Besides, shotgun wounds much over four feet are rarely fatal and that couldn't have suited our killer. I suppose . . .' He paused for a moment. 'I suppose that you've already worked it out that Aaron might have been the designated victim while Jack's happening on the scene was a bit of bad luck.'

'I had considered that possibility,' she said cautiously.

'And Aaron has to have been shot first otherwise he would have been near enough to have grabbed the gun from the killer. Understand what I'm saying, Jo. There was blood on the floor. The killer took two steps forward, stepped in it.'

But Joanna shook her head. 'We've found no bloody footprints, Matthew.'

'Not enough for prints but particles, invisible to the

naked eye. Put it like this,' he said. 'I'd like to see some shoes.'

'Or wellies?'

He nodded. 'And I'm sure some would have splashed on the top too.'

This was what had always impressed her about Matthew. Not just the work he did on the slab but the piecing together of the facts.

She watched the mortician wheel the two bodies out of the room before turning her attention back to him. 'How long would Jack have taken to die?'

'A minute or two. No longer. And by the way, in case you want to know, neither had fired a gun in the last couple of days. And now it's time I wrote my reports.' He gave a last glance at the two officers, busy bagging up the samples for the forensic lab. 'Have you got all you want?'

'Yes, thanks, Doctor.'

'Including their fingerprints?'

'Yes.'

'Then I'll ring the coroner and we'll pop them back in the fridge to await further instruction but you can tell the relatives we should be happy to release the bodies for burial quite soon. It's a straightforward case and I don't think there's anything more to find. Not from these two anyway.' He grinned at her. 'Time for a coffee?'

They were settled in his small office before he broached the subject of Ruthie. 'Found the missing girl yet?'

'Nope,' she said. 'No sign.' She reached across the desk to touch his hand. 'How you do love your work, Matthew.'

His green eyes gleamed. 'And how you love yours.'

For a long moment they held each other's gaze and Joanna was conscious that their early moments had been just like this – light-hearted bantering that had suddenly got out of hand.

And then she had found out that Matthew was married. She closed her eyes to blot out the memory.

'Of course,' she smiled, 'stating the obvious. If we *had* found Ruthie Summers dead what we would now be investigating would be a very ugly triple murder. It's even possible that it was done on the spur of the moment as the gun was habitually kept in the front porch. It might even have been loaded. Damn.' She clenched her fist. 'If we'd known how casual they were about their firearms we'd never have stamped his gun licence.' She returned to her original train of thought. 'But if we had found Ruthie's body I suppose it would have made things easier because we could be certain that this was the work of an outsider. As it is . . .' Even now she hated to say it. 'She's the chief suspect.'

Matthew was silent for a moment. 'I suppose,' he said, 'that you have considered the possibility that she might have wanted to spare her father the agony of dying and shot him to prevent further suffering.'

'A euthanasiac killing? And Jack?'

'Maybe he got upset and she . . .' Even Matthew found it difficult to say.

But the memory of the heart-shaped face, the pensive dark eyes and the slightly nervous twist to the girl's face made her shake her head. 'I don't think so,' she said. 'Whatever the explanation I don't believe that's it.'

'So what is?'

Joanna shook her head. 'I simply don't know.'

'So where do you start?'

'With her photographs, then to the bank. No one can live on nothing. If she withdrew money that'll give us a sign of premeditation. Plus an indication of guilt. And, I suppose, if there has been no withdrawal it sort of tips the scales in her favour.'

'And towards her death,' Matthew observed.

'One step at a time, Mat,' she said. 'At the moment when I say it tips the scales in her favour I simply mean being innocent of the crime. I don't like jumping to conclusions. We'll put some pictures of her on the national TV and keep our fingers crossed she turns up. I really do hope we'll find her.'

Matthew grinned at her. 'Proper little terrier, aren't you?'

'Woof, woof.' She stood up then. 'I'd better get back to the Incident Room,' she said. 'Mike will be wondering what's happened to me. Time's leaping forward. We should start interviewing potential witnesses.'

'Anyone special?'

'A particularly unsavoury specimen called Pinkers,' she said. 'He runs a neighbouring farm and he's milking poor old Aaron Summers' cows at the moment.' She gave Matthew a mischievous smile. 'Much as I'd love to burst in Rambo style with the heavies, I think in reality Mike and I will go prodding round his cowsheds and see what we can come up with.'

'Well don't forget your wellies.'

'I won't.'

'No other suspects in your sights?'

She gave a deep sigh. 'It's usual form to interview the person who found the body at some length. Statistically speaking the last person to have seen the victim alive is also the first person to find them dead – if you see what I mean.'

'Of course. I think I've watched you deal with enough homicide cases to have gleaned the way you work.' He leant across the desk impulsively. 'Let's have dinner tonight.'

'Oh, Matthew. You know what the hours are like during a major investigation. It's impossible.' But he carried on looking at her, his eyes bright, happy and pleading and she gave in. 'Oh go on then,' she said. 'I'll come late to the Mermaid. And you'd better tell them to keep my dinner hot.'

12.30 p.m.

'Surprise surprise,' she said to Mike, finding him sitting in her office. 'Gunshot wound to the chest.' And quickly she filled him in on the other, unexpected findings of the post mortem.

She had the pleasure of watching Korpanski turn green as she told him about Aaron's stomach cancer. 'I'm glad I wasn't there,' he said. 'The way Matthew chops up those bodies with such relish turns *my* stomach.'

She felt a compulsion to defend him. 'Well, just think of the number of times he's helped us convict the guilty. Or release the innocent,' she added.

She leant on her elbows across the desk. 'No one's *said* anything about Jack being strange, have they?'

'Well I got the feeling there was something there. You know, people made suggestions, didn't they?'

She thought for a moment . . . and remembered Shackleton's comment on the day of the killings.

At the time she had not picked up on the remark. Only now was she wondering about the significance of the question. '*Did Jack finally flip?*' And later on that day Hannah Lockley's, '*So the idiot son finally went berserk?*'

She crossed to the window of the caravan, feeling tired in the unaccustomed heat. 'They did tell us, didn't they, Mike? They were all feeding us clues. It's simply that we didn't really understand what they were saying.'

Mike broke into her thoughts. 'I know everyone claims that brother and sister were devoted,' he said slowly, 'but I can't help wondering if . . .'

He had her full attention. 'What?'

'What if Jack became violent for some reason and went for her?'

She shook her head. 'There's no sign of a struggle.'

'She could have tidied up afterwards. What if *he* picked up the gun and pointed it at her. There was a struggle. It went off, killing him and then she turned the gun on her father.'

'No. Everything's wrong with that theory. The range, the sequence of events. However it happened it was not like that.'

But his thoughts had put another picture in her mind. She had said this before at the previous investigation of another shooting, accidental that time. Whoever picks up a loaded gun should remember. In unpractised hands it can go off, possibly accidentally. It might kill someone.

'More likely is that Aaron was about to go for the cows. One boot on, one boot off. Our killer comes to the door, picks up the gun. Aaron backs off, the killer fires. The sound brings Jack down. He gets it too.' She gave Mike a swift glance. 'Aaron must have been near the gun when our killer arrived but he felt no need to protect himself. The person who picked up the gun aroused no suspicion in Aaron. So I think that points to someone he knew well. And that as we know, is a narrow field. There are not too many people in their circle of familiars. And if the gun was wiped clean afterwards I suppose it reduces suspicion on Ruthie. Her prints would have *belonged* there.'

'And the sculptor bloke who spent a few minutes explaining why his dabs would be found on the gun.'

'Hmm.' Joanna was unconvinced.

Mike tried again. 'Perhaps one of them, maybe Aaron, picked up the gun. Ruthie tries to take it from him. It goes off, killing her father.'

'So what about Jack?'

Mike frowned. 'Well.'

She fixed him with a frank stare. 'When we get the right answer, Mike, you know as well as I do that the whole thing will fit quite perfectly into place. Until we do every other theory will leave discrepancies and unexplained events. So let's just plod our way through a normal investigation beginning with this afternoon.' She smiled and touched his shoulder. 'What time have we fixed the briefing for?'

Mike wiped some sweat away from his brow. 'Two thirty.'

'In that case we've got time to visit Mr Pinkers first.'

*

Martin Pinkers' farm was a neglected old house, stone built, like his neighbour's and surrounded by dry-stone walls. There was an extensive range of farm buildings which again looked less dilapidated than the outbuildings at Hardacre. The surrounding fields were dotted with plump Friesian cows with bulging udders and Joanna noted a second field full of healthy, energetic young heifers who butted the hedge as they passed. Two more fields held the oblong hay-bales and in the yard stood a full range of farm machinery, JCBs and plenty of trailers, rakers and muck spreaders as well as a new looking combine harvester. Obviously business was good for Martin Pinkers. Underneath the dilapidation there was undoubted prosperity. Unlike his neighbour's farm. *So what was the difference between the two farmers?*

They made their way round to the side door, accompanied by a cacophony of noise, dogs, hens, cockerels and a few anguished groans from some cows in a shed.

Pinkers himself opened the door, still dressed in the navy dungarees, tied around the middle with a belt of string. And his thin, weasel face was even less attractive the second time around.

He gave a toothy leer. 'I thought I'd be seein' you sooner or later.'

'Have you got time to answer a few questions?' Mike asked casually.

Pinkers gave the burly policeman a searching glance. 'Oh, yeah,' he said, 'I got time all right.' He gave the yard a fond glance. 'Farm's quiet now,' he said, 'and it's too hot to get the 'ay in until the sun goes down a bit. The lads can turn it. Come in, won't you. It's cool in the 'ouse.'

He led them into a small, smelly room dominated by a huge television set and settled back into a wide armchair covered in stretch nylon covers, filthy cream with pink roses. Cats had caught their claws in the threads and pulled them down in long trails. Even now they were prowling around the base. One leapt up and Joanna put it firmly back on the floor. Since James had deserted her almost three years ago she had felt no affection for cats.

Pinkers was watching her.

'You should just throw it,' he said. 'It won't hurt them. The cheeky animals. They got nine lives anyway.'

Joanna couldn't resist it. 'Unlike your neighbour, Mr Pinkers,' she said drily, 'who did not have nine lives.'

'More's the pity,' Pinkers growled. 'He would have been able to tell us then who shot 'im and saved you a lot of time with innocent people who got nothin' to tell.'

'Quite.'

Pinkers' eyes flicked across to the other side of the room towards Mike, and Joanna knew he was pondering the question. Who was the greater threat, she or Korpanski?

She settled back on the sofa, smiled and crossed her legs. 'Now tell me, Mr Pinkers,' she said briskly. 'What really happened yesterday?'

'Nothin',' he said.

'We don't mean about the murder,' Joanna said easily. 'Just tell us your movements yesterday. What did you do?'

Pinkers scratched his sparsely covered scalp. 'Woke

103

around five. I always do. You'll find most farmin' folk wakes early.'

'I'm sure.'

'And your neighbours at Hardacre?' She was having to drag the statement from him.

'I suppose so,' he said grudgingly. 'As I said. Most farmin' folk do waken early.'

Joanna shifted on the sofa. 'And then what?'

'I has a cup of tea.'

'Right. Live here alone, do you, Mr Pinkers?'

'I got a wife and I got two sons but I does most of the work here.'

'Do your sons actually live here?'

Pinkers nodded.

'And their names?'

'Emery and Fraser. But they was asleep in bed I can promise you.'

'How old are they?'

'Seventeen and fourteen,' Pinkers said reluctantly. 'They're just boys. They got nothin' to do with this.'

'And you're sure they were asleep?'

Pinkers glared at Korpanski. 'Yes I am. My wife and I can give testimony to that.'

'OK,' Joanna said. 'If we need to interview them at some later date we'll let you know. So let's get back to yesterday morning, shall we?'

'Suits me.' A note of surliness had crept into Martin Pinkers' voice. 'I gets the milkers in nice and early. And there was a couple of calves I wanted to take to market. Not that you get much for them these days. Hardly worth it, price has gone down so much. And they always takes some separatin' from the mother.' He thought for a brief moment. 'I wouldn't be surprised if it wasn't nearly seven when I started the milkin'. Ask anyone. Anyone. They'll have heard the machines.'

It was a neat trick. But they could not ask anyone anything. There was no one around to ask. Except his family and the animals.

'So did you take the calves to market?'

He hadn't been expecting that. His big hands fumbled. 'I didn't quite manage it yesterday. Like I say. They takes a lot of separatin' from their mothers.'

There was something here but Joanna did not know what.

'What time do you normally leave for the market?' She was edging closer, but blindly.

Pinkers' sunburnt face looked suddenly bleached. 'Not so early as you'd think.'

The three of them all knew this would be an easy statement to check.

'But not so late either, Mr Pinkers. It was after ten when Shackleton called. Surely that would be a little too late?'

The question shook him. His thin mouth worked painfully.

Joanna's eyes were fixed on him. 'It's a fine farm you have here, Mr Pinkers.'

Something furtive moved across his face which made him look even more weasel like. 'I been lucky,' he said. 'That and hard work.'

Mike spoke up. 'And how did you get on with your neighbours, Mr Pinkers?'

The farmer looked from the burly detective back to Joanna and they both knew instinctively that the farmer was trying to gauge how much they already knew.

'We had our disagreements,' he said finally.

'About anything in particular?'

Pinkers cleared his throat noisily. 'He blamed me for everything that went wrong.'

'What sort of things?'

'Oh some cows went missing one day. He got the idea set in his head that it was me what took them.'

'How unfortunate.'

Pinkers wasn't fooled by the mock sympathy.

'So who did *you* think had stolen the cows from Hardacre?'

'Oh rustlers,' he said, 'people from the city.'

'And what would city people do with a couple of cows, Mr Pinkers?'

He looked surprised at the question. 'Why – sell them, of course.'

'Where?'

'There's abattoirs that won't ask questions.'

Joanna gave Mike a swift glance. Cattle rustling? This all sounded more like the Saturday Western than rural Staffordshire. Mike smiled and hunched his big shoulders.

Joanna moved on. 'When did you last see the Summers, Mr Pinkers?'

He thought for a moment. 'Well, I haven't seen Ruthie for a while. Not for a month or more. But Aaron – why I saw him only last week. He was at the market, selling a couple of barren cows he had no more use for.' He scratched his wispy grey hair. 'Fetched a good price they did too.'

'And Jack was with him?'

'No. Jack must have been back at the farm, minding things.'

'I would have thought Ruthie would have done that.'

'Oh, Ruthie, she liked comin' to the market. Enjoyed it she did, more than usual she'd have a couple of dozen eggs she could sell. Bit of pin money.'

'But she wasn't there last week?'

Again Pinkers thought back for a moment. 'No,' he said slowly, 'she weren't there.' Then his face took on an enlightened look. 'Mebbe,' he said, 'there was no eggs.'

But there had been. Joanna recalled the young constable, his face rueful, staring down at his shoes, covered in egg yolk and broken shell. So whatever the reason that Ruthie had not been at the market it had not been because she had no eggs to sell.

Joanna gave Mike a swift glance.

'Do you mind if we take a quick look around the farm?'

Pinkers shrugged his shoulders. 'Why should I? I got nothin' to hide.'

The barns were cool but clean, recently hosed down. There was a vague smell of disinfectant, a much stronger scent of fresh cow dung but it was not unpleasant. It reminded Joanna of childhood days, spent hanging round a local farm, feeding lambs from babies' bottles.

She and Mike tramped through each barn with their huge, high roofs, the breeze whistling through the eaves. They were home to darting swallows, feeding their young from fragments of insects in their beaks. Bales of straw were stacked in the corner, giving out a sweet, strong scent of the field. Again Joanna breathed

in and was reminded of her childhood. Until the
shadows of herself and Sergeant Mike Korpanski, huge
against the barn wall, jerked her back to the present.
Then their shadows were joined by a third shadow with
a dog stuck to his heels as though by a short string. A
couple of times Pinkers' dog turned to look at Mike and
gave a low, warning growl. Mike shook his foot at him.
He had a healthy dislike for dogs having fed one or two
with his ankles as a junior policeman. They walked to
the end of the final barn which had been partitioned
off. It was from here that the bellow was coming from
an anguished animal. Joanna peeped over the bales
and came face to face with a dribbling cow, the whites
of its eyes rolling. It gave a painful grunt and Joanna
looked enquiringly at Pinkers. 'Her first calf,' Pinkers
said without sympathy. 'They always have a difficult
first birth. That's why we pair them with a Hereford.
After that . . .'

Joanna glanced back at the wild, unhappy animal.

Motherhood in its least glamorous pose. Surely
nothing at all to do with the double murders? And yet.
She glanced again at the wretched animal.

But there was nothing else to see so they left the
barn and returned to the yard, passing the bright, new
combine harvester.

Mike put his hand on it. 'Cost a lot of money, did it,
Mr Pinkers?'

'I bought it secondhand.'

'Still expensive though.'

The farmer nodded. 'But worth it,' he said
grudgingly.

'How much?'

'A lot.' His horny hand caressed the shiny red paint.

Joanna watched him carefully. There was real avarice in the gesture. 'Tell me, Mr Pinkers,' she said suddenly, 'do you have a gun?'

'Course I do. Most farmers do. I got a licence for it. But I thought . . .'

'What did you think?'

The farmer's face froze.

'You thought that they were shot with their own gun? We haven't had the forensic report yet, Mr Pinkers.'

Pinkers recovered himself. 'Shackleton told me,' he said sullenly. 'He said it was their gun was on the floor.'

Joanna gave him a sunny smile. 'Of course,' she said. 'Shackleton told you. Dear me. My colleague, Detective Sergeant Korpanski and I were beginning to get horribly suspicious of you.'

The farmer gave them both a dark scowl and mumbled something unintelligible.

It was Mike's cue. 'Do a lot of shooting, Mr Pinkers?'

The farmer nodded reluctantly.

'And what do you shoot?'

Pinkers gave them both another hard stare. 'Crows,' he said.

There was little to report at the briefing. House to house interviews had merely reinforced the picture of a family who had guarded their privacy and discouraged friends or visitors. Most local people seemed to feel that the shootings were somehow connected with the fact that Jack was 'strange'. No one had ventured how.

Joanna frowned. 'What did they mean – strange?'

Police Constable David Timmis read from his note-book. 'A Mrs Rowan from a neighbouring farm said that most of the time he'd be fine but he had an unpredict-able streak in his character. Her dog had bitten him one day. Accidentally, she said, when they had been playing. Jack had pretended to take the dog's slipper and had been teasing him with it. When the dog bit him Jack kicked it so hard he broke a couple of ribs. And it had to be put down. She said it was as though Jack didn't know his own strength.' Timmis faced Joanna squarely. 'I got the impression she was really fond of this dog. It seemed she hated Jack for what he'd done.'

'Really?'

'Yes.'

'Did she say anything else?'

Timmis glanced back at his notebook. 'She said he had a fascination with fire. Aaron and Ruthie had to watch him all the time. They were afraid one day he would set the barns alight. And with all that hay . . .' They could all fill in the details. Blazing ricks, a year's abundant harvest, the result of hours of work, months of the right weather conditions, years of managing the land, all destroyed in minutes.

'Apparently they found him one day lighting sticks and paper in the middle of the floor. He said he was cold and needed to get warm. He'd burnt the rug.'

So that explained the scorched mark that had com-manded Barraclough's attention.

'Go on,' she prompted Timmis.

'Because of his unpredictability with fire Jack wasn't allowed to smoke, according to Mrs Rowan.' Timmis smiled. 'When he went to market he'd try to cadge cigarettes off the other farmers. But if Aaron or

Ruthie saw him smoking they'd take it off him and the person who'd given it to him would be ticked off "good and proper". But Mrs Rowan said she'd noticed something. Jack wouldn't smoke his cigarette, not properly. He'd puff away at it until the end glowed red and then he'd simply stare as though he was in a trance. And poor old Aaron and Ruthie were frightened to let him out of their sight for what he might do. Mrs Rowan said that all that watching took its toll on Ruthie.'

'She seemed to know the family very well,' Joanna observed.

'Apparently Ruthie used to clean there a couple of times a week.'

'She did?'

'Mrs Rowan's got a thriving business going with barn conversions and holiday lets. Ruthie used to clean up after the visitors had left.'

So. Not such an isolated family. Ruthie went elsewhere twice a week.

Joanna turned to Mike. 'I think we'd better see this Mrs Rowan ourselves. She obviously knew our missing person very well.' She spoke again to PC Timmis. 'Did you have a good look around?'

'I did.'

'And?'

'There was no sign of Ruthie and Mrs Rowan said she hadn't seen her for nearly a month.' Joanna drew in a deep breath. There was something in Timmis' statement that disturbed her. She smiled at him. 'Well done, Timmis. Now tell me. What did Mrs Rowan think of Ruth Summers?'

'She seemed fond of her. She just said what a nice, quiet person she was, reliable, kept house for her father and brother. She did say Aaron and Jack couldn't have managed without her.'

Joanna felt she must check on the most significant fact. 'But she hadn't seen her for about a month?'

'No.'

'And the last time she actually did see her?'

'She'd popped up to Hardacre to give Ruthie her week's wages, said she'd been short of change. She said Ruthie seemed perfectly normal, herding the cows in and singing.' Timmis gave a sheepish grin. 'Mrs Rowan said Ruthie had a "sweet" voice. She said she was always singing.'

Again the words conjured up a pretty, idealized, almost Victorian picture, a milkmaid, collecting eggs in a basket, herding cows, singing. Guarding her brother, protecting her dying father, singing. Aiming a shotgun at them, squeezing the trigger. Still singing? That thin, sensitive face, the deep, dark eyes that had stared out of the photograph. Life had been a struggle for Ruthie Summers. How old had she been? Judging from the photograph late twenties. Had she known her father was dying? Yes, Joanna thought so. She would have seen that he was slowly starving to death as the cancer stole his nutrients. Joanna struggled to shake herself free of the conviction. This girl was not a singing killer. Whoever had called at the front door that morning, stood in the bright, hot porch and raised that heavy gun to their shoulder to murder first the old man then the younger, it had not been Ruthie. It had not been she who had watched Jack collapse against the wall, watch him slowly bleed to death before calmly putting the gun down and walking away from Hardacre, leaving the Landrover still standing in the drive.

Or had she?

Timmis continued. 'She hadn't come to work since then. She'd rung in sick. At least, her father rang.' Timmis hesitated before saying the next sentence. 'I got the impression Mrs Rowan was none too pleased at Ruthie's bunking off.' He grinned self-consciously. 'It's the height of the season.'

'Yes,' Joanna said. But her mind was speeding through the facts. Guilty or innocent where the hell was Ruthie? And tagged on to the tails was a more personal question. Why was she more intrigued over the fate of the farmer's daughter than finding the real killer?

The answer came back clearly, shining bright. Because to solve one part of the puzzle would lead to the solution of the other. And . . .

'Mike,' she said, 'do you realize no one's actually seen Ruthie Summers for about a month?'

Mike thought for a moment. 'It could be chance.'

'It *could* be,' she said slowly.

'We've searched the house and grounds thoroughly.'

'We should search again.'

'What do you think you're going to find?'

'Something,' she said confidently. 'Something.'

She glanced around the room at the tense faces. They needed a breakthrough, something to pull them along and convince them they would succeed in finding the killer. She addressed them. 'Did anyone you interviewed seem to hold a grudge against the family?'

A sea of blank faces. No one had.

She tried another avenue. 'Did anyone mention a place where Ruth Summers might have gone?'

Again nothing.

'Have any other farmers had animals go missing?'

Blank faces and shaking heads.

'So, we're left with this.' She held up the posters she had had printed. 'We must find this girl. We need to find out *exactly* when she went missing. Date and, if possible, time. We'll keep interviewing neighbours but I want you to focus your questioning on Ruthie Summers' disappearance.'

She caught sight of a familiar shock of brown hair. 'McBrine, cleaned your shoes yet?' He grinned. 'I have but there's still a damned awful stink. Rotten eggs,' he said. 'I can still smell them.'

'That's not the eggs,' one of his mates quipped and she could sense the briefing was in danger of descending into gutter humour. But the mention of eggs made her thoughtful.

'We've been promised the final report on the gun tomorrow. That might give us something. Kitty . . .' she addressed a leggy young blonde police cadet, 'did you get anything from the bank?'

'Negative, I'm afraid.' She gave a rueful grin. 'Nothing's been taken out of their account for ten days.'

'And then how much?'

'Just twenty pounds.'

'And before that?'

'Two weeks. Another twenty pounds.'

'And the balance?'

'Two hundred.'

'Any savings?'

'The bank manager didn't think so.'

She turned slowly to face Mike. 'Now I'm even more convinced. Ruthie Summers is dead.'

Chapter Seven

By the time she and Mike had logged all the information on the computer and run through the collected statements the rest of the day was gone. She borrowed one of the squad cars to drive out to the Mermaid but was still late reaching the pub and Matthew had already finished his meal. The barmaid brought out a plate of dried up minted lamb casserole and new potatoes and she wolfed it down hungrily.

He was watching her eat with amusement, saying little until she finally cleared the plate.

'How goes it?'

'It's early days yet.' She felt unaccountably defensive. And yet it was barely thirty-six hours since the murders. Not even the brightest optimist would expect a twenty-four hour arrest where there was no obvious suspect. But underneath she knew what was needling her.

'I think apart from Ruthie being missing,' she said, 'the biggest puzzle is the motive. I just can't think of one. I mean *why* would someone murder a couple of farmers who by all accounts kept themselves to themselves, never harmed anyone and never went anywhere except to the market once a week to swap country tales, buy and sell a couple of cows and flog hens' eggs?'

Matthew swallowed a smile. 'No leads?'

'Nothing much. Nothing of significance anyway. The girl was just a farmer's daughter. She worked around the farm and kept house for her father and brother.' Then she remembered Ruthie Summers' part time job. 'Though she did clean for a neighbour's holiday lets a couple of times a week. Maybe there's something there.' But even to her it sounded unconvincing.

'So the missing daughter?'

'Hasn't turned up. I don't have a clue where she is.'

Matthew said nothing and this irritated her further. 'It doesn't mean to say . . .'

He covered her hand with his own. 'I wasn't saying anything, Jo. This is a police case. Nothing personal.'

She laughed. 'I know. I'm sorry. And I'm talking about work again.'

'Yes you are.' But he spoke with humour and she could tell something had pleased him today.

'Matthew?'

He sat back, smiling, his green eyes bright and merry before tossing the details of a house across the table. 'I've been thinking,' he began, 'about our dilemma as far as buying a house is concerned.'

'And?'

'Maybe you're right. Maybe isolation isn't such a good idea. With these murders and things.'

He took a long swig of beer. 'Do you know the village of Waterfall?'

She did. A beautiful, unspoilt village with straggling stone cottages sitting around a triangular village green

116

and an excellent pub. It was quiet and popular, lived in by farmers and farm workers and a couple of commuters from the Potteries. Interested, she picked up the details and scanned them.

A stone residence, needing renovation, room for improvement, subject to planning conditions. Three bedrooms, bathroom, two receps., a kitchen. And the photograph on the front pleased her, showing a neat, symmetrical house with original stone mullions and a small, manageable front garden. Behind it she could just pick out the spire of Waterfall church. She turned the details over. No price. 'How much?'

'£98,000.'

Matthew pulled an envelope from his pocket. The back was smothered with calculations. But the bottom line was clear. If she could sell her cottage in Cheddleton they could afford to buy it with enough money left over for the renovations.

Matthew could barely contain his excitement. 'I know you're busy, Jo, but please take a look at it. I think you'll like it. And I would like to be settled in a house together before the autumn. I hate the long nights.' He hesitated. 'Alone.'

She watched him over the rim of his wine glass. His eyes were still on her, warm, but faintly questioning. 'I'll try to go some time tomorrow,' she promised. 'But it might be late.' She pocketed the details and picked up his glass. 'Another drink?'

'No – I'll have a coffee.'

Standing at the bar she glanced back at him, sitting down, his honey blond hair dropping over his face as he sat, studying the calculations on the back of the envelope. She felt a pang of affection for him, longed to put her arms around him, bury her head against his chest.

She brought two cups of coffee back to the table and sat down opposite him, reaching across the table for his hand.

'Stay with me tonight, Matthew,' she said.

He took a deep breath and she knew he had something else he wanted to say.

She waited.

He took another gulp of air.

'Spill the beans,' she said. 'What else is there?'

It came out in a rush then. 'Jane's going to stay with an old friend for a couple of weeks.'

Her heart sank.

Matthew gave a brave smile. 'Sort of a holiday.' She could guess the rest. 'She doesn't want to take Eloise.' His smile was a painful twist. 'Cramp her style.' And then the words came tumbling out. 'I mean the weather's good and Eloise has got lots of friends round here at the riding school. I've already rung them up and she can go up there most days and help with the horses. I can take a bit of time off, be with her a bit.'

She was trying to tell herself it was silly to be jealous of a twelve-year-old child, of his daughter. But it didn't work. Joanna sat, still and awkward and said the wrong thing. 'It isn't fair of Jane to dump her on you.'

'It isn't like that.' He was angry. 'I'm glad to have her. She's my daughter, the only child I have – so far.'

The last two words were spoken with a harsh tone and she knew these issues would always come between them, Eloise, Matthew's love of children, his desire to have more – and her determination *never* to be a mother.

'Jane has her for most of the time,' Matthew said reasonably. 'I do very little for her.'

'You pay her keep and school fees.'

'Naturally.' The harshness had turned to frank hostility. Superstitiously she fingered the house details in her pocket.

'Please, Joanna. Please try and get on with her.'

'It's a two way thing,' she said petulantly.

Matthew's hand shook slightly as he rested the coffee cup back on the saucer. 'She's twelve years old, Joanna,' he said reasonably. 'You're years older than she is. And she is my own flesh and blood. I love her and she's gone through a lot.'

'Because of me.'

Matthew sighed. 'Don't – be – difficult,' he said. 'Please.'

So now she had her answer. Eloise would always be present.

'If we had kids of our own . . .'

She banged her coffee cup back down on the saucer. 'Not that again. How many times do I have to tell you? I – don't – want – children. I have no intention of giving up a promising career just to be stuck with some squalling little brats. I like my work. I like my life. And my job isn't nine to five. It simply doesn't leave time for bathing babies, changing nappies and shoving bottles down their throats in the middle of the night.'

'But it isn't always like that.'

She was angry now. 'Matthew – you left your wife because you wanted to. Because, you said, you loved me. I never ever put any pressure on you. I never rang you or contacted you. This has been largely what *you* wanted. I was content. And I've made it quite clear, from the start, that whatever my commitment to you I don't want children. If what you wanted was an earth mother who could present you with a quiverful of sprogs you will have to form a relationship with someone else – or go back to Jane.' The words almost stuck in her throat. And suddenly Matthew looked older, much older. A thirty-something man with a wife and child already. Less boyish and more responsible. He passed his hand across his forehead and she had an ugly feeling in the pit of her stomach. She had gone too far this time. He was regretting leaving Jane.

She stood up. 'I'm going home.'

Politely he stood up too.

'Alone,' she said and left the pub.

Chapter Eight

Thursday, July 9th, 8 a.m.

She didn't know what made her drive straight past Hardacre towards the wood where Owl Hole stood. It was an instinct that drove her to see Titus Mothershaw again – alone – that morning. She had left a message for Mike to say she would see him at nine, in the Incident Room. She had an hour.

Titus opened the door wearing a grey towelling wrap-over that stopped just short of his boney knees. His hair was tousled and he looked sleepy, but his grin was welcoming.

'Well this is a surprise, Inspector. Nice and early for a social visit.' He gave a huge yawn and looked past her, along the winding path through the woods. 'No sidekick today?'

She shook her head.

'Then coffee, I think, to celebrate.'

But his easy manner, far from making her relaxed, made her all the more nervous so she began with an apology. 'I'm sorry to call so early but we've got a double murder case on and we have to work long hours.'

His eyes were warm. 'Well I hope you get the time back.'

'That or get paid overtime.'

She followed him into the strange, unreal room. How would she describe it? Clinical? Futuristic? Unique? Interesting.

Mothershaw stood in the centre of the room. 'So what brings you here – again?'

She decided to be as frank as she dared, in the hope that it might draw out an answer. 'I'm desperate to find Ruthie.'

He was adjusting the silvered branch in the corner of the room, his back to her but she clearly saw his shoulders stiffen. And his answering voice was low and strained.

'What makes you think I can help you find her?'

She watched the small, child's hands adjusting the branch and decided not to mention the passport booth photograph. She must keep a card up her sleeve, retain the ability to surprise him.

'She was an attractive young woman.'

Mothershaw said nothing. Not an agreement then, but no disagreement either.

'And she did live only a couple of hundred yards along the lane.' She tried a long shot. 'Did you buy your eggs from her?'

He turned around, laughing. Showing white teeth, a look of genuine merriment. 'Now what sort of a question is that?'

His reaction put her at a disadvantage and he knew it. He grinned again, confidently glanced down at his bare legs. 'I think I'd better go and put some proper clothes on.'

She deliberately didn't watch as he ran lightly up the winding steps and disappeared into one of the upstairs rooms. There was the sound of running water, the toilet being flushed, footsteps overhead and he reappeared in pale blue cotton trousers, loose fitting, pulled in at the waist with a thick, ethnic leather belt and a lemon silk shirt, short-sleeved, showing slim arms touched with the palest of tans. His feet were bare. She had to remind herself that this man was a suspect in a double murder investigation. He was not a social acquaintance.

She settled back on the white leather sofa, cool against her legs, even in this heat. Mothershaw disappeared into the kitchen and returned balancing two mugs of steaming coffee on a tray. He fished out a pink cork mat from a tiny drawer in the glass coffee table and set her mug down on the polished surface. All his movements were elegant, neat, controlled and graceful. He could have been a classical ballet dancer or an actor.

Joanna took a great gulp of the coffee. The flavour was just right. Strong but not bitter, milky but not creamy. She watched him over the rim of the mug and made a bet to herself that Mothershaw was a decent cook too.

'Tell me a bit about your work, Mr Mothershaw,' she began.

He raised his eyebrows. Whatever he had expected from her line of questioning it had not been this.

'No one calls me Mr Mothershaw,' he said. 'My name is Titus.' He chuckled. 'Like it or hate it it *is* my name.'

To point out the incongruity of a senior investigating detective putting herself in this position, firstly to visit a suspect alone and secondly to use his

Christian name on friendly terms, would have seemed unnecessarily stiff and awkward. Joanna said nothing.

It was left to Mothershaw to break the silence. 'Why do you want to know about my work? I would have thought it would have born no relevance whatsoever to your investigation.'

Joanna watched him steadily. 'We never know what's relevant until the case is wound up.'

Mothershaw blinked. 'You can't mean you suspect me of . . .?'

'We suspect everybody.' Joanna managed to turn the statement into a joke. 'Even the cows.'

Mothershaw laughed guardedly.

'What brought you to Staffordshire?'

His blue eyes looked wary. 'You've seen my work.'

Joanna nodded. 'It's very good.' She took another gulp of coffee. 'Especially the Tree Man.'

Mothershaw looked pleased. 'Personally I think he's a masterpiece.' His accompanying laugh was attractively self-deprecating. 'But then I would say that, wouldn't I? However, in my defence, I must say that everyone who sees him does make some comment.' His face changed. 'Everyone, that is, except Mr Summers.'

'Aaron Summers?'

'Oh no. He thought it was a rather intricate scarecrow. I mean Jack. He had . . . a bit of a thing about it.' He paused. 'I don't know whether you know much about Jack but . . .'

'I know he was strange.'

Mothershaw shook his head. 'That,' he said, 'is a polite understatement.'

'Just remember I didn't actually *know* him,' Joanna

reminded the sculptor. 'I only saw him after he was dead.'

Mothershaw's eyes flickered. 'Well he *was* strange,' he said. 'And he had a fixation for setting fire to things.'

Joanna began to understand. The scorched feet of the Tree Man. 'Are you trying to tell me . . .?'

'I caught him one night trying to burn it.' Mothershaw's chest was heaving with anger. 'A *masterpiece* like that.' He leant forward in his chair, his eyes blazing. 'I can never repeat a work, Inspector. Once the inspiration has gone I move on. I could never make another Tree Man. It simply wouldn't be possible. If that crazy lout had destroyed it Tree Man would no longer exist. Do you understand?'

Joanna nodded. There was around Titus Mothershaw the aura of a fanatic as well as a genius. 'Is Tree Man for sale?'

Mothershaw drew in a sharp breath and relaxed back in his seat, shaking his head. 'You don't understand the way I work,' he said. 'Like all my pieces he is for sale and he isn't. The fact is I would never let anything I had created go to a home where it wasn't *fully* appreciated. Price is immaterial.'

'What do you live on?'

Mothershaw gave her one of his crooked smiles. 'I'm not short of money,' he said, giving an elegant waft with his hand. It was a self-indulgent, artistic gesture.

'But why here?' Joanna pursued the point. 'Why did you come here? It isn't a well-known area – there isn't an artists' colony here. How did you find this place? And how did you know the Summers had somewhere to rent?'

Mothershaw looked pleased with himself. 'Have

you any idea how difficult it is to find a wood both suitable and available for my sort of work? So many trees have protection orders slapped on them. I scoured the country for this place. But it was worth it.' He gave another wide smile. And this time there was frankness and honesty behind his eyes. It was an attractive and tantalizing expression. Again Joanna reminded herself that this man was a murder suspect.

But, like Ruthie's face, as hard as she looked, she could see nothing of a cold-blooded killer in Mothershaw's bright eyes. However, as Sergeant Barraclough had reminded her, appearances can be deceptive.

Mothershaw stood up and held out his hand for her mug. 'Another coffee, Inspector?'

'Thanks.'

He disappeared into the kitchen, returning two minutes later. 'I know people think my work's all twaddle and hype,' he said with disarming frankness. 'But there is real depth.'

'I know. I could see that.'

Mothershaw stared at her. 'I knew you did,' he said. 'I knew you appreciated my talent. You see. I simply couldn't find that depth in London. Besides that. No raw materials. No wood, sticks, leaves. Nothing. London is a barren desert. No inspiration. And all that traffic. Dreadful for the lungs. Whereas here I find magic everywhere. In the trees and the sky, the birds and the animals. Even the people . . .'

'The people, Mr Mothershaw?' Joanna felt the pricklings of unease. Mothershaw looked less comfortable. 'The farmer and his son?' The feeling of disquiet was growing. 'Was Jack Summers the inspiration for the Tree Man?'

Mothershaw glanced away.

'Did he recognize himself in the statue?'

Again Mothershaw said nothing.

'Was that why he tried to burn it?'

There was vague hostility in Mothershaw's eyes now. 'I didn't expect the police to be so perceptive.'

'It strikes me that you didn't expect Jack Summers to be so perceptive – or his family. They were smart, Mr Mothershaw. Did Ruthie and Aaron take exception to the mockery of Jack?'

Mothershaw frowned. 'No,' he said. 'No.'

'Not even Ruthie who was so fond of her younger brother?'

Mothershaw gave a little cough. 'Far from being critical, a Philistine, or disapproving, Ruthie,' he said quietly and with undoubted sincerity, 'was my greatest fan.'

Again Joanna was reminded of the picture she had formed of the farmer's daughter, herding the cows, singing as she moved. A quick glance at Mothershaw told her he was having a very similar vision. There was a faraway dreaminess in his eyes.

She felt a sudden flash of unease in this sterile, futuristic house. 'Take me for a walk back through the wood,' she said suddenly. 'I'd like you to point out some of your work.'

So together they left the Owl Hole and walked through the overgrown wood with its watching faces and strange imagery carved in the bark until they stood in front of the statue. Mothershaw stared up at the face. 'It's funny,' he said. 'I created this monstrosity using Jack as a model. But he changes as the light hits him at a different angle. At the time I saw Jack as stupid but

not malevolent. Definitely not malevolent. Yet sometimes when I look at the face although I can see Jack
his features are superseded by someone else, some
other personality trying to gain attention. Someone
evil and clever – not like Jack at all. Perhaps it's the
way the light catches him. Shadows have funny, unpredictable effects. They create expression.' He stopped.
'They absorb it too. Oh . . .' he turned away from the
statue. 'Maybe old Aaron was nearest the truth when
he said, "The owd buggar is useful for scaring crows.
Nowt else." '

But Joanna was still studying the sculpture. Had
the face Titus Mothershaw been portraying been
superseded by another face, that of his original model's
sister? 'Did Ruthie Summers look like her brother?'

Mothershaw thought for a long moment. 'I wouldn't
have thought there was any resemblance,' he said
slowly. 'In fact I would have sworn there was no resemblance at all. But . . . There was something, something
quite subtle that told you they were brother and sister. I
suppose it was a family resemblance.'

Unaccountably Joanna felt she had moved a step
closer to understanding the dual murders. Yet Mothershaw had said nothing, had he? And looking around the
wood she could see no face that looked even remotely
like the picture taken in the photo booth. Last night's
dark had deceived her. By daylight the face carved so
skilfully into the trunk of the tree looked nothing like
the passport photograph of the missing farmer's
daughter.

The child-sized fingers touched a blackened area at
the base of the figure. 'Look at his poor, scorched little
toes,' he said. 'If Lewis Stone hadn't shouted to say

128

there was a fire in the wood I might not have come out in time.' He looked around and shivered. 'Who knows? The entire lot might have gone up in flames and I might have gone up too.'

He looked to her for sympathy. But she was pre-occupied. It had been dark. How had he known it was Jack who was torching the Tree Man?

They continued their walk along the path, Titus Mothershaw still musing to himself. 'I was surprised Jack recognized himself in the statue,' he said.

'And how did he react?'

Mothershaw smothered a smile. 'To say he was angry would be an understatement.'

'And Ruth? Was she furious too?'

Mothershaw's mouth opened, fish-like, as he fumbled for words. 'She couldn't very well say any-thing.'

And Joanna was left to wonder. Why not? There would be time to ask all these questions – and more – later.

Her eyes were drawn to the edge of the wood and beyond, to the rolling hills neatly divided by dry-stone walls. She listened to the cawing of rooks and the twit-tering swallows. All so innocent, so traditional, so very deceitful.

They had reached the wicket gate that marked the end of Mothershaw's strange gallery and she had played for long enough. It was time to glean some facts. 'How often did you actually go to the farm?'

Mothershaw realized the politenesses were over. His answer was equally curt. 'Once a week, just to pay my rent.'

He was staring over her shoulder, back into the

wood. And Joanna knew his gaze was fixed on the Tree Man.

'What was the relationship between you and Ruth Summers?'

Mothershaw gave a vague shake of his head.

'What did you think of Ruthie?'

Mothershaw's answer was as strange as his carvings. 'She was a dryad,' he said dreamily. 'Insubstantial. A wood nymph, a girl who belonged here.'

'And where do you think she is now?'

His thoughts must have been miles away, if on this planet at all.

'Returned to the woods,' he said, 'from whence she came.'

9 a.m.

'Bloody crap.' Mike was scornful when she related the conversation to him. 'And I don't know what possessed you to go there on your own. It wasn't sensible. In fact it was positively dangerous.'

She felt the need to defend herself. 'I thought he might open up a bit more to me – alone. I want to find Ruthie.'

But Mike was glaring at her. 'And he says she's turned into a fairy or something.'

Joanna was silent as Mike continued. 'If what he means by that is that he's raped her, strangled her and buried her in that mutilated wood of his he should say so.'

'I don't think that was what he meant at all.'

But Korpanski faced her squarely. 'So what did he mean then?'

'Maybe,' she tried. 'Maybe he meant she was eth-ereal, without substance and that's why he isn't too worried by her disappearance.'

'Utter crap,' Mike repeated his earlier sentiments. 'She's flesh and blood and perfectly capable of pulling that trigger. So calling her a . . . What did he call her?'

'A dryad.'

'Yeah. Well. Calling her a dryad isn't going to get her off the hook. And what's more, it's a safe bet that it's his fingerprints that are on that picture from the photo booth.'

'Agreed.'

'And I've got another suggestion. I bet you any money that he's used her too as a model for his sculptures.'

'That's where you're wrong,' she said, frowning. 'I thought he would have done. I mean – if he used Jack – she would have seemed an obvious model. Attractive, with a certain aura around her. Maybe it's hidden,' she said thoughtfully. 'Maybe somewhere in the trees there is a wood nymph with Ruthie's face.'

'And if Jack recognized himself as Tree Man,' Mike said in a flash of inspiration, 'I wonder what Ruthie would have thought of a model of herself as a wood nymph?'

She stood up. 'After we've seen Hannah Lockley,' she said, 'I am going to buy you your lunch. Because you've earned it, Mike. You are beginning to under-stand the complexities of modern art.'

'Heaven forbid,' he said fervently.

*

She got off on the wrong foot with Hannah Lockley – a mere slip of the tongue but the old lady was razor sharp.

They had been shown into the stuffy parlour, three-piece suite draped with fussy antimacassars, a teak coffee table in the centre, a print of a vase of flowers over the tiled fireplace. 'Mrs Lockley . . .'

The old lady's face became fierce. 'I'll have you know I'm a Miss. I am not married. I never have been married. I owe no man anything.'

Joanna quickly apologized and tried to smooth over the awkwardness by asking her how long she had lived in Brooms. The old lady shot her a suspicious look.

'This cottage was always in the family. I was brought up here. My father was farmhand at Hardacre, my mother helped in the dairy.'

'You must have known Aaron Summers quite well?'

The old lady nodded.

'And your sister?'

Miss Lockley gave a proud nod. 'Ah – Paulette.' There was a note of adoration in her voice.

'Your sister was younger than you?'

'There was ten years between us – and a great deal else. I took after father, large, strong, robust. Paulette was my mother, right down to the fine bones, the unhealthy constitution. My mother was what farmers would call a poor breeder.' Hannah Lockley gave a tough smile. 'She would have fetched no money at market. Two children in twenty year o' marriage?'

Joanna smiled. But the words were forcing her to realize things, to look at the past as well as the present. Maybe somewhere back there was some clue to the events of two days ago. So she began to probe blindly. 'You must have grown up with Aaron.'

'Yes.'

And he must have been nearer you in age than your sister.'

'That's right.'

'Were you fond of him?'

Hannah Lockley shrugged her shoulders. 'So, so.'

'But he married your little sister instead of you.'

Hannah Lockley gave a harsh cackle. 'She were prettier.'

'But you remained close neighbours.'

'My father stayed on as farmhand.'

'Even though his daughter had married, "the boss's son." '

It was a feeble joke and Hannah Lockley ignored it. 'My sister was very fond of Aaron,' she said. 'They were very happy. The tragedy began with her dying so young, leaving the two children. And then there was the accident.'

Joanna watched the old lady carefully. 'What exactly was "the accident"?'

'Has no one told you?' There was mild surprise in the old lady's face. 'Everyone knows the facts. We never tried to hide them. But it has nothing to do with the shootings.'

'Can you be sure of that?'

Hannah Lockley pressed her lips together.

'Was the accident how Jack fractured his skull?'

The old lady nodded. 'As you know my sister died when poor old Jack was no more than a baby and Ruthie was six. She had to be a little mother to him as well as keeping house for Aaron. Well Aaron had the farm to run, didn't he, otherwise we'd all have been left to starve. He might even have lost the children too. So he had no choice. And it isn't exactly a generous living neither. Anyway Ruthie took little Jack out in the yard one day, in his pushchair. It's cobbled, you know, and she must have been going a little fast. She tipped the child out and he must have landed on his head. She did tell her dad but Aaron was so worried Ruthie would get into trouble he did nothing, you see. After Paulette died he had an aversion to all things medical. Stupidly he blamed the hospital for Paulette's suffering. But in this case he did wrong. It seems Jack's brain swelled and the damage was done. Maybe if he *had* been taken to hospital sooner it mightn't have been so bad. But . . .' She sighed. 'That family has not been blessed with luck.'

'And now they've been wiped out,' Joanna finished.

'Yes. Except Ruthie.'

'You still think she'll turn up?' Mike was incredulous.

The old lady gave him a confident look. 'Yes,' she said simply. And then something of their suspicions must have filtered through to her. 'And it's no use your thinking she had something to do with the shootings. She and Jack were inseparable. She looked after him when he came out of hospital. Hardly let him out of her sight. She loved him like he was her own child, stopped him from coming to any harm. And Jack was still strong. He did the work of two men at Hardacre.' Something sentimental flashed over the leathered face. 'He'd follow her around like a great, shambling dog but he'd work like a strong, steady horse. Working, eating, sleeping, steady as the day.'

She sat still for a while, absorbed in the memory as though Jack, Aaron and Ruthie were all still working at Hardacre. 'Ruthie was so like her mother, small and slim, none too strong, with those big, dark eyes. Clever too. If Paulette had been educated she would have been a lady. But she married Aaron straight from school. She wanted a home of her own and Aaron promised her I could live here, in the cottage, for my entire life.' Hannah Lockley gave Joanna a twisted smile. 'That's the trouble with we country girls, Inspector. We might have the same talents and clevernesses as the town and city girls but we don't always know how to put them to our advantage. And Ruthie was the same. You see our families don't want us too educated. They want to see us in our own homes, sitting in front of our own hearths. It's what all the folk round here want for their daughters and it's what I want for Ruthie. It's better than education.' Her eyes met Joanna's with a touch of defiance. 'Jack never would have married. We all knew that so when Aaron died Hardacre would go to Ruthie. Hardacre, the Owl Hole, the cottage. The lot. Lock, stock and barrel. She'll manage the farm and Jack too for all she's slight and small.'

Had she still forgotten that Jack was dead and Ruthie missing? Something else struck Joanna. Had Hannah Lockley known her brother-in-law was terminally ill? And if she had known what bearing, if any, could it possibly have on the murders?

Joanna eyed Mike with desperation. He gave a small nod and an almost imperceptible grin. 'Miss Lockley,' she began tentatively. 'Did you know Aaron was ill?'

The old lady's shoulders twitched. 'It was obvious,'

she answered in a low voice. 'Anyone could see he wasn't right. But he had an unholy terror of doctors.' The tears were rolling now. 'I told him to go and see someone, that maybe they could cure him. He just told me to mind my own business. He said it was acid in his stomach. Even when he was bringing up blood.' Mike was standing in the doorway, thick legs slightly apart, his face as inscrutable as a sphinx. And Joanna noticed he didn't take his eyes off Hannah Lockley but stared, unblinking, as he spoke.

'Where is Ruthie?'

But if Joanna had hoped that abrupt tactics might shock the old lady into a confession she was disappointed. Hannah Lockley too could be as inscrutable as a sphinx.

'I don't know,' she said simply. 'So it's no use your keep asking me. I have no idea where she is. And I have no idea why she's staying away. It's a mystery.'

Mike stepped forward. 'You must have *some* idea.'

She looked startled, intimidated by Korpanski's bulk. 'I don't,' she said. 'I don't. Please, don't try and bully me.' She looked from one to the other like a nervous rabbit, eyes flicking jerkily. 'I'm every bit as confused as you are.'

'So you don't think she's running away from a double murder?'

The old lady looked shocked. 'Most certainly not,' she said. 'If you *knew* Ruthie you'd understand.'

Round and round, Joanna thought irritably. Round and round. And they were getting nowhere.

She must try another tactic.

'You didn't tell us *everything* about Jack, did you?'

The old lady looked affronted. 'I did . . .'

Mike picked up on Joanna's tack. 'You didn't tell us that Jack enjoyed setting fire to things.' The old lady's manner changed to one of furtiveness. Her eyes slid away from both the detectives.

'Who told you?' she said at last.

'One of your neighbours.'

Her lip curled. 'I bet it was that . . .'

'Your bloody brother-in-law and nephew are shot,' Mike spoke furiously. 'Your niece has disappeared. Don't you understand? We have to know . . .'

Hannah Lockley drew herself up to her full height. 'It has nothing to do with it.'

'Let us decide. Miss Lockley, we don't know what's important in this case and until we do even if you go to the toilet in the middle of the night we need to know.'

'There's no need to be crude, young man.' Hannah Lockley stared him out.

Joanna smiled. Somehow, this old lady had got the better of Mike, though he was twice her size and had the authority of the Staffordshire Police department behind him. She was reminded of the scorched rug Barraclough had rolled up on his first day's investigations. 'Did Jack ever attempt to burn down the farm?'

Hannah Lockley was suddenly subdued. 'He had to be watched,' she admitted.

'When we first came,' Joanna said, 'you mentioned ramblers. Are there many ramblers in this area?'

The old lady looked at her with something approaching respect. 'You've got quite a memory, young lady,' she said grudgingly. 'I did mention ramblers and there are too many. Especially in this sort of weather. Crowded as a street in the middle of London, it is sometimes. There is a public footpath crosses the boundary between Hardacre and Fallowfield. But they don't stick to it. They wander through the farms, into people's gardens. Cause no end of trouble. They leave the gates open, let their dogs chase sheep. And apologize? No they don't.'

Mike's dark eyes were sharply intelligent. 'Would their path take them anywhere near the farmhouse door?'

She could read his mind. The previous weekend and the days following had been the hottest recorded temperatures in Staffordshire for twenty years. Half of the population of Leek might well have been wandering the footpath. The local residents took full advantage of the surrounding countryside. Not a quiet, rural area then, but busy and full of trippers. The old lady brightened. 'The footpath crosses the boundary on the Top Field.'

Joanna never could get used to the different names for various fields. They all looked the same to her. 'Which do you call the Top Field?'

'Right by the door of the farm, across from the lane. But surely . . . ramblers . . . What for? Why would they want to shoot a couple of farmers?'

'I don't know.'

But now Joanna had pursued one seemingly insignificant fact she was remembering another.

'Tell me about the cattle that went missing.'

Again the old lady looked cross. 'Can't we keep anything from you? That has no bearing on the shootings. I'm sure. And I don't know how you came to know about it anyway.'

'Just tell us,' Mike said.

Hannah Lockley looked at him with dislike. 'It

started at the very end of last summer,' the old lady began reluctantly. 'Just as the leaves were turning. A few good cows went missing. We all thought it was Pinkers.' She looked from one to the other with a face taut with concern. 'You have to understand. We *never* had any proof. Four of Pinkers' best milkers had gone dry. Dave . . .'

'Shackleton?' Mike interrupted.

'Yes. Dave Shackleton. He told us Pinkers' milk production was down, that he was having real problems. If you lose production, let Milk Marque down, they cut your cheque. And then your quota. And you never get the quota back. So Pinkers really did have a problem. One day Aaron went to fetch in the cows. Early one morning it was, ready for milking. He came in and said that a couple had gone missing. Hell to play there was. It's a big farm but our cows are tagged, in the ear. If they had gone on to the road someone would have spotted them and fetched them back. We took a look around. There was no gaps in the hedge and the gate was fastened. So someone must have taken them out of the field. Naturally we thought of Pinkers. So we went down there and took Noah with us. He always had a good nose did Noah. Could sniff a Hardacre cow out like it was smothered in peppermint oil. Anyway, he went wild outside one of Pinkers' cowsheds. We tried the door but it was locked. Next thing we know is Pinkers is standing there, his shotgun pointing right at us. "One bloody step", he says, "and the dog gets it. One more step after that and you does too". Miss Lockley gave Joanna a bold stare. 'Have you ever had a gun pointin' right at you, Missus?'

It gave Joanna the perfect chance to redress the

score. 'I'm not a missus,' she said, with dignity. 'I'm a Miss, like you. I have no husband to thank for my position either, Miss Lockley.' The old lady flushed.

'But to answer your question no. I have not had a gun pointed at me and I hope I never shall.'

But it was a vain hope. Villains were getting ever more violent. And guns were readily available, without licences or with them. Joanna shivered. It was only a matter of time before she too stared down the barrel of a gun, as had Aaron and Jack Summers.

She gave Mike a weak smile. 'So did you get the cows back?'

Hannah Lockley shook her head. 'We didn't,' she said. 'But Dave Shackleton told us about the miracle that had happened in the meantime. Surprise surprise,' she said sourly, 'Pinkers' milk production was back up to quota.'

'And the tags?'

'You can easily take the tags out and the pretend barren cows have miraculously turned productive.'

'And the accreditation papers?'

Hannah Lockley looked scornful. 'Barren cows can go in the freezer. Stolen cattle can easily take up their identity.' She chuckled. 'Not the best of steaks but the cheapest.' She gave Joanna a hard stare. 'Do you believe in virgin births?'

'Uumm . . .'

'I don't suppose I need to tell a clever young lady like you that calves come from bulls and cows,' the old lady persisted. 'The vet does the insemination if you pay him. Otherwise you need a bull. And cows what don't have calves don't produce milk neither. Do you get me? So when old Doric, Aaron's bull goes missing and Pinkers' cows start getting fatter with calves and no vet has been in attendance or semen bought we know who the daddy is. Now do you understand?'

They both nodded.

'But there was no proof, was there?' Joanna asked.

'Not a shred,' the old lady said comfortably. 'Not a single shred of evidence. But then who needs evidence? Not that the courts would be interested in a couple of farmers squabbling over some animals. Now what else do you want to know?'

'I want to know what Ruthie's relationship was like with her father.'

The question earned Joanna a hostile stare. 'Perfectly normal. However deep you dig you won't find anything there, I promise you.'

'And when did you last see Ruthie?'

'About a month ago,' she admitted. 'But I don't see her every day.'

'Wasn't it unusual not to see her for such a long period?'

The old lady shrugged. 'It happens,' she said, 'sometimes.'

'Perhaps she's with a boyfriend.'

Miss Lockley's face softened. 'I have wondered,' she said. 'She is such a pretty girl. And I know Dave Shackleton's quite fond of her. He gets on well with Jack too. And a young family will be so good for Hardacre.'

'How did Ruthie feel about Shackleton?'

'I'm not too sure about that,' she said. 'Personally I think she's too good for him. But who else is there?' Her accompanying smile was anything but comfortable.

'Miss Lockley . . .' Joanna stood up. She was more

141

than ready for her lunch. 'We may ask you to come back to the farm with us at some point, just to see if you can spot anything different.'

'What do you mean?'

'I don't know,' Joanna confessed. 'Anything that may help us to discover who murdered two members of your family. Maybe tomorrow? Perhaps in the afternoon?'

The old lady gave a determined nod of her head. 'I'll come,' she said, 'provided it's all been cleared up.'

As they closed the small gate behind them Joanna felt a sudden wave of confusion. 'We've been there for more than an hour,' she said. 'And yet we've found out nothing.'

Mike was ahead of her. 'You call that nothing? The fact that Pinkers threatened them with a shotgun after they'd found out about his petty pilfering? I don't call that nothing, Jo.'

'I suppose it makes him worth a second visit but this business with the cows . . .' Mike was striding ahead of her. 'It's hardly a motive for murder, is it?'

Mike turned then, shielded his eyes from the glare of the sun. 'Maybe not to you and maybe not to me. But to these farming sorts. They have different priorities.'

'Oh come on, Mike.' The heat was making her irritable, the swarms of buzzing flies doubly so. 'You can't seriously think Pinkers blasted the pair of them into Kingdom Come over a couple of cows.'

'I think it's possible,' he said stubbornly.

'Then what about Ruthie?' She turned to face him. 'Where does she fit in to all this?'

142

But Mike had no answer to that one.

They drove back towards the town to find a pub with a garden that served meals and pulled up outside the Three Horseshoes, famous both for its truly delicious home cooking as well as the stupendous views towards the Roaches, a rocky outcrop overlooking the moorland. They settled at one of the tables, Joanna baring her legs to the sunshine.

The action reminded her of something. She took her sunglasses off, folded them carefully and faced Mike across the table.

'What about this rambler thing, Mike? Worth pursuing, do you think?'

He gave her a withering glance. 'Rambling – at seven in the morning, Joanna?'

She sighed. 'So you don't think it's worth an appeal?'

He put his pint glass down firmly on the table. 'Now I didn't say that.'

2.30 p.m.

The team were assembled back at the Incident caravan and there was a pile of faxes. Mike picked up the top one. 'Preliminary reports on the shotgun,' he said. 'Linked with the murders, injuries, etc. Wadding taken from Aaron Summers' chest matches the stuff from inside the barrel of the gun.' He gave Joanna one of his rare, broad grins. 'That should be enough evidence to please the courts.'

There was a stirring around the room. No one needed to point out that for the gathered evidence to even *reach* the courts they would have to produce a viable suspect.

Mike glanced through the second sheet. 'Blurred prints of all the family. Suggest miscreant was wearing gloves.'

There was a titter from the back of the room.

Joanna sighed. 'Anything of real value?'

'Prints on the photographs, Jack Summers.'

'Jack Summers? But the hands are . . .'

'They might be Mothershaw's,' Mike said grimly. 'But the prints are those of her brother, the deceased.'

The sentence conjured up the dreadful picture of the surprised face, glancing down, the meaty fists trying to stem the flow of blood from the gaping wound in his chest. Joanna shivered.

'She must have showed the picture to her brother.'

And now there was something else bothering her. Why had Ruthie not been seen for a month? Where had she been?

Because the picture didn't fit in with her being the killer. She couldn't have vanished for a month only to appear in the doorway, the shotgun in her hand. Or could she?

What sort of a woman was Ruthie Summers?

Chapter Nine

'So where now?'

The Incident Room was stifling. There seemed more flies than ever, great, black clouds of the things. And she could have sworn they were bigger, noisier and more inclined to settle on her bare legs and arms. Even on her hair. She shook her head, annoyed.

They drank luke-warm coke and she made a decision.

'Let's take the car up to the Rowans' farm,' she said suddenly. 'Ruthie worked there. It's just possible she could be hiding up there.'

Mike looked dubious. 'With all the publicity?'

'Well let's go anyway,' she said irritably as a blue-bottle with a buzz like a Spitfire landed on her arm. 'I can't stay here, Mike.'

So they drove along the bumpy lane passing Fallow-field, sleepy, with no sign of human activity, before turning out on to the main road and travelling the half mile to the track that led to the Rowans' farm. The Rowans went in for tourist accommodation. Three gold coronets sat beneath the name on a swinging green sign. They rattled across the cattle grid before climbing the slight incline towards the prosperous-looking farm nestling into the side of the hill. The drive was smooth and without ruts, carefully tarmacked, the verges neat and well tended, an electric fence keeping the cattle from straying. The stone house at the top looked in good condition with original stone mullions. All looked neat, organized and in good order. Joanna pulled the car into the yard and switched the engine off. Ahead was a tall Dutch barn neatly stacked with hay-bales. To the left was a long row of barn conversions, each one with the twee name of a bird painted around a picture on an oval metal plaque. There was a Robin Cottage, a Magpie Cottage, a Thrush and a Blackbird Cottage. Above the name each had a hanging basket filled with red and blue flowers, salvias and lobelias. There was a pale green Mercedes parked outside Blackbird Cottage and the door was standing open. A child ran out, stared at the two police officers and ran straight back in again. They crunched across the gravel to the front door of the farmhouse.

Again there were signs of zealous work. The path was swept, the flowerbeds tended. No weeds. Someone worked very hard to keep this place attractive. Through the front door wafted a pleasing scent of polish and cooking, cakes and a casserole. The entire atmosphere was one of well controlled domesticity and when Mrs Rowan came out to meet them the illusion was furthered.

A size ten, neatly dressed in a short-sleeved check shirt, tied at the waist and skin tight jeans, chin length blonde hair pleasantly ruffled by the wind. She looked about thirty. And her husband who arrived a second later to take up his arm-squeezing position behind her was also dressed smartly, slim and dark with the attractive air of a reprobate. He too was impeccably dressed in cavalry twills and a white, polo necked shirt.

Though the day was broiling neither was sweating and it struck Joanna that they seemed poles apart from the two moorland farmers whose murder she was investigating.

She made brief introductions and noted that Mrs Rowan's manners were as impeccable as her appearance. 'Do come in,' she said pleasantly. 'Would you like a coffee?' She gave Mike a conspiratorial smile. 'Or a beer, Sergeant?'

Mike replied stiffly. 'Not on duty, thanks, Mrs Rowan.'

'Oh – Arabella, please. And this is Neil, my husband. Shall we go into the kitchen?'

It was a lovely room completely fitted with oak units, the ceiling criss-crossed with low beams festooned with sprigs of drying herbs and flowers. And at the far end was a dark green Aga. Joanna's eyes wandered around the room approvingly. She would love this kitchen, with its scent of wood smoke, welcome even on such a hot day.

Mrs Rowan slipped on an oven glove and fished a baking tray of a dozen or more scones out of the oven. All were perfectly symmetrical, wonderfully risen and uniformly browned. Joanna watched Mrs Rowan's precise actions. This was how Matthew would like her to be. Domestic, neat, ordered – and home-bound.

What had seemed at first pleasantly organized was now stifling. She shifted in her seat.

Mrs Rowan stopped looking at Mike and focused her attention on Joanna. 'I do holiday lets,' she explained. 'Barn conversions, home cooking, on the farm. People love it,' she said, 'especially the city dwellers. Especially families. They arrive in their green wellies and play farms for a week or two. They even begin to talk quite knowledgeably about Friesians and Herefords and Pot Bellied Pigs. They pay generously for this pleasure. And then they're quite happy to return to their stuffy cities and money-spinning jobs.'

Joanna was surprised at the note of mockery and cynicism in the woman's voice. Why did Arabella Rowan dislike her clients so much? This was a well organized business, one which obviously earned her a good living. There was an air of prosperity at the Rowans' farm which had been lacking from either Fallowfield or Hardacre. So why despise the people who paid for the privilege of spending their holidays in the country? Why bite the hand that feeds you, Mrs Rowan?

She looked sharply at the woman and formed an opinion. She was clever, hard working and perceptive. She was also a perfectionist, obsessional and ambitious. She would not take kindly to anything that threatened her ordered existence. There was also a ruthless side to this woman and it was less attractive than the superficial version, the size ten, blonde, amenable, feminine woman.

And Mr Rowan?

Joanna turned her attention to the man instead. He was slim and dark-haired, handsome in an ordinary way. His was not an interesting face but rather a neat, orderly collection of inoffensive features. It was a negative brand of good looks rather than any one, positively attractive feature. She noticed that he was saying nothing but stood directly behind his wife with a slightly foolish grin fixed on his face. He was clearly not as intelligent as his wife and he was probably a philanderer. Even as the thought formed she wondered how she had reached that conclusion. Yet any woman would have picked up the calculating question in his eyes, the sliding glance across her breasts, her hips, her legs. And there was a boldness around his eyes, a restlessness about his broad fingers. She glanced again at Arabella Rowan's firm chin.

But he was afraid of his wife.

And his wife knew it and used it to her advantage.

And Ruthie? Had she been forced to repel Neil Rowan's unwelcome advances? Or to the sheltered farmer's daughter had he seemed romantic, a godsend, a hero, a Siegfried? How would Arabella Rowan have reacted to advances made by her husband to her chambermaid?

Arabella Rowan spoke. 'I suppose you're here about Ruthie.'

It was shrewd of her to guess that. Most people would have referred firstly to the double shootings of their neighbours. But Arabella, with her clever brain, had realized that it was their contact with the missing girl that had warranted a visit from the two senior officers on the third day of their investigation.

Her blue eyes opened wide as she spoke again. 'What a dreadful thing to happen to the poor girl's family. Hardly bears thinking about.'

'No.'

'And have you any idea where she is?'

Joanna could have sworn Neil Rowan's eyes flickered. Certainly he started breathing quicker and a touch more noisily. His wife must have noticed too and gave him a sharp, admonishing glance.

'No. That is the reason why we've come,' Joanna admitted. 'I don't suppose you've any idea where . . .'

'Well she isn't here.' At last Neil Rowan had spoken. They all turned to look at him.

'When did you last see her?'

It was Arabella who answered Mike's question, turning her blue eyes full on him. 'Quite a while ago,' she said crisply. 'And I wasn't too pleased at her simply not turning up without a word of explanation. This is the busiest time of year. I needed her.'

'So when *did* you last see her?'

'About a month ago. Early in June. I can't give you the exact date. She simply didn't turn up one morning. There was no explanation.'

'Did you ring Hardacre Farm?'

'I certainly did.'

'Who did you speak to?'

'Oh I don't know. The brother and her father sounded the same to me.'

'And?'

'They said she wasn't well and that she wouldn't be in for a while.' Arabella Rowan looked slightly ashamed of herself. 'To be honest I told them she could stick it and that I'd get someone in from the town. I was very angry.'

'And did you?'

Mrs Rowan frowned. 'Did I what?'

'Get someone in from the town?'

'Yes I did – as a matter of fact.'

Mr Rowan reinforced his wife's statement with a nod and a widening of the fatuous grin. Arabella was taking no notice of him, probably a normal attitude for her.

'How well did you know the Summers family?'

'Not well. Not really well at all. We didn't *know* them. We were simply *acquainted* with them. They were neighbours and Ruthie was a perfectly sweet girl. She was quite clean too and reliable.' Arabella swivelled her head around to give her husband a swift glance. Of warning?

'So do you have any idea who might have wanted to shoot her father and her brother?'

'Most definitely not *anybody* from around here,' Mrs Rowan snapped. 'The entire idea is quite appalling. It must have been someone from outside.'

Joanna reflected how much more comfortable these crimes were when committed by 'someone from outside'. It was too convenient. She must destroy that illusion. 'We don't think so, Mrs Rowan.'

Arabella Rowan gave a little jerk. 'Why ever not?'

'Because someone not only knew the gun was there but had the opportunity to check it was loaded.'

Both the Rowans stared uneasily at her.

'And how did you get on with them as neighbours?'

The answer was predictable. 'Very well. Very well indeed.'

'You saw them often?'

She might have known Neil Rowan would be the type to bluster. 'Hardly ever. Not socially at all. But when we did, at the cattle market and such like, we were perfectly amicable neighbours.'

'Nice,' Mike said mockingly.

The Rowans gave him a suspicious stare but Mike's square face was innocence itself.

Joanna cleared her throat. 'Was it at the market that Jack Summers kicked your dog?' Neil Rowan looked annoyed. 'Yes it was, as a matter of fact. Though what it's got to do with the murders . . .'

'Probably nothing,' Joanna put in soothingly.

'And why he took it into his foolish head to . . .'

'I understood the dog bit him, Mr Rowan.'

Neil looked uncomfortable. 'Well yes. But . . . He's a farmer. He should have had more patience with a dog. Animals are unpredictable things.'

'Like humans,' Mike said.

The farmer looked at him with hostility. '*Some* humans,' he said carefully. 'Only *some*.'

'And as a result of Jack's violence your dog had to be put down.'

'Hardly a motive for murder,' Arabella said acidly. 'Though the dog did suffer. And we were angry – at the time. His rib was broken and it stuck in his lung. Poor thing.'

'You were fond of the dog?'

'Yes we were, actually. Very fond.'

'So you were none too pleased with Jack Summers.'

'As I have already said.' Arabella's voice was even more concentratedly acid. 'Hardly a motive for murder.'

'I'm not suggesting it is,' Joanna said calmly. 'But someone – and we feel it was probably someone local – pulled the trigger on two defenceless farmers. Used their own gun. We don't know why. And so we can't guarantee the same thing won't happen again. In this area of the country most rural households possess a shotgun. Some of those gun licence holders are lax in

152

keeping their weapons locked away. There is a real danger.'

'Surely not,' Arabella said faintly.

'We believe there is.'

Mike was surveying both the Rowans from beneath his lowered eyelids. Joanna could read his mind. If they felt there was no danger why not?

Joanna spoke. 'You own a gun, Mrs Rowan?'

'Of course we do.'

'Double barrelled?'

Neil Rowan scowled. 'What's that got to do with it? They were shot with their own gun, weren't they?'

'I just wondered if you were familiar with the handling of a gun.'

Neil Rowan thrust his face forward. 'I am,' he said, 'as are most of the farmers around here.' It was left to Mrs Rowan to apologize. 'I'm sorry, Inspector,' she said contritely. 'This business. It's shaken us up terribly. We were fond of Ruthie. And for this to happen to her father and brother – neighbours of ours. It's terribly upsetting.' She smiled. 'You do understand, don't you? We really are worried about Ruthie. Where do you think she can be?'

Joanna studied her. Arabella Rowan seemed genuinely upset. Far from her assumption that Arabella might have resented the attentions of her husband towards the girl had it created a common bond?

'We wish we knew,' Mike said grimly. 'I don't suppose she ever mentioned any friends of hers, maybe even from outside the area?'

'No.'

'She was a very – sweet – girl.' Neil Rowan somehow managed to look ashamed.

And it struck Joanna. 'Was she a happy girl?'

The question seemed to agitate Neil Rowan. He moved across the room abruptly to stare out of the window. 'Happy?' He passed his hand across his face. 'Happy?'

His wife's voice cut in. 'Of course she was a happy girl.'

Her husband turned around. 'Except I thought . . . I thought she always carried a sort of sadness with her.' He gave an apologetic smile. 'Like a grey cloak.'

His wife's eyes opened wide. She was dreading what he might say. He seemed not to notice. 'I always wondered whether Ruthie's air of grief was something to do with her brother's accident. She felt responsible, you know.'

'Neil.' His wife's expletive shaped a warning.

It was Neil Rowan who had all Joanna's attention now. 'Do you think there was anything else at home that was upsetting her?'

But his brief moment of freedom was over. He shuffled his feet, returned to the table and flopped into the seat. 'I don't think so,' he said. 'Hardly knew the girl – really.'

His wife's glance was sugar-coated poison. 'But she was nice, wasn't she, dear, in her own way.'

'Quite.' He nodded obediently.

Joanna addressed her next question to them both. 'Did she have a boyfriend that you knew of?'

Both the Rowans looked blank.

'Maybe Dave Shackleton?' Joanna prompted.

'The tanker driver?' Arabella Rowan looked genuinely startled. 'Oh, I wouldn't have thought so.

There was something a bit . . . a bit . . . nicer about Ruthie.'

'But she was a farmer's daughter.'

Arabella Rowan gave a stiff smile. 'You shouldn't be so anxious to typecast people, Inspector.'

Neil Rowan put his cup down firmly on the saucer. 'Ruthie was a bright girl,' he said. 'Way above Shackleton. For goodness sake, he was a bloody tanker driver. She was . . !'

What was she? Titus Mothershaw had described her as a dryad, a wood nymph. How had Neil Rowan seen her? Joanna waited.

'She was a perfect flower in bud.'

It was an odd expression.

Arabella Rowan stood up. 'I'm awfully sorry,' she said, returning to the gracious hostess role. 'But I think you've had a wasted journey. We really can't help you. We can shed no light on this utterly distressing business. And neither of us knows what's happened to poor little Ruthie. I'm so sorry.'

The last three words were spoken with true, unaffected depth of feeling. Joanna looked at Arabella Rowan closely. She was pressing her hands together hard. 'I'm sorry,' she muttered again. 'But we can't help you.' Then she added. 'Do you need to search our farm now?' Joanna shook her head. She had to get back to the Incident Room for the briefing.

'Fine,' Neil Rowan said heartily. 'Well – any time. Any time at all. We'll do anything we can.'

'Good.' Mike gave Rowan one of his friendly grimaces and they left the kitchen.

But they were still in the hall when the storm broke.

It was Arabella Rowan's voice. And she was furious. 'Bloody philanderer. Now see where it's got us.'

They headed back to the car. Joanna made a face. 'Interesting,' she said. 'Most interesting.' And she started up the engine.

'Seems obvious to me,' Mike observed. 'Rowan tried to get inside little Ruthie's knickers.'

'And his wife knew all about it. So where does that leave us, Mike?'

His face was serious. 'We should take a better look around their farm.'

They were back outside the Incident Room within five minutes. The officers were assembled in the courtyard, most with open necked shirts, loosened ties, rolled up sleeves. But before Joanna climbed out of the car she wanted to say something else to Mike. 'If Neil Rowan had made advances towards Ruthie it would mean somebody else had intruded on that tightly knit little family group.'

'Yes?'

'And Mrs Rowan is patently fond of her little storybook lifestyle. I'm certain she would do anything to preserve it.'

'Yeah. So she wouldn't have appreciated her husband fumbling in the cleaner's petticoats.'

'No.'

Mike summed up. 'Well it might be a sort of motive for getting rid of Ruthie Summers. But I don't see what Aaron or Jack would have to do with it.'

She sighed. 'Neither do I.'

She stared out across the green fields spattered with

black and white cows, contentedly munching the grass. Her eyes moved past the dry-stone walls to the yellowing hay fields, their harvest almost collected in. There was no sign of the weather breaking. Not yet. When she turned back Mike was watching her. 'Where's that optimism you're usually so full of, Jo?'

'Temporarily abandoned,' she said with a laugh.

'Why? We've had worse cases than this one.'

'I think it's Ruthie,' she said. 'This image people had of her is so at variance with the image of a killer that it seems reasonable to suppose that she is either dead or has been abducted.'

'So?'

'*So why can't we find her?*'

'Because,' Mike suggested, with a wave of his hand across the wide expanse of fields, 'there's so many places her body could have been hidden. Haystacks and river beds, barns, badger holes, fox earths. Besides there's miles of countryside.'

She opened the car door. 'Then let's mobilize troops to search every inch because I am convinced that it will be only through finding Ruthie – dead or alive – that we will know who shot her father and brother . . .'

She had expected little from the briefing, nothing more than a general sharing of facts. She was anxious that the officers were all aware that the Rowans could be implicated in Ruthie Summers' disappearance. But Sergeant Barraclough had something up his sleeve. He called her across and handed her a leaflet, blue-grey, printed on coarse paper. She looked at it without comprehension.

'BPAS?' She looked to Barra for explanation.

'It's just a thought, Joanna. We decided to comb through the entire house, every drawer and cupboard and one of the junior officers came up with this. The British Pregnancy Advisory Service,' he explained. 'We wondered what it was doing in her room, hidden at the back of a drawer, in her underwear.'

'You mean . . . you thought she might be pregnant?'

'What if she's having an abortion – now. What if that's where she is?'

Joanna took the leaflet with her and left Mike to finish the briefing. She disappeared inside the Incident caravan, picked up the phone and dialled the 0800 number.

A soft voice answered. 'Hello. This is the British Pregnancy Advisory Service. How may I help you?'

Wincing at the Americanism Joanna gave the details out curtly. She was a police officer. *Not* a fallen woman. 'All I need to know is have you taken a call from a girl in this area, recently, in the last few days.'

'I'm not able to tell you that,' the woman said regretfully. 'Confidentiality.' She began the usual fender of . . . 'You'd want the same level of confidentiality if it were you.'

'But this is a murder investigation. I'm a police officer.'

The woman's voice was soothing. 'If you want to call round to our offices – with a warrant – we might be able to help you. Otherwise . . .'

Joanna felt confounded. 'Then at least tell me where you would send such a girl. Which hospital do you use?'

'A private one in Macclesfield,' the woman said reluctantly.

Joanna took the number and redialled.

The answering voice was brisk. 'We have no one of that name here. I'm sorry. And quite honestly if such a girl had had an abortion here she would be home by now. We only keep them in for one night.'

Joanna went outside the caravan to find Mike discussing the Rowans' land with the assembled officers.

'Start with the barns,' he was saying, 'before moving on to the fields. You know the drill. Freshly turned earth. And take sniffer dogs. The helicopter will be working through the afternoon with heat seekers.'

A few of them nodded. Mike noticed Joanna and raised his eyebrows. 'Success?'

'A blind alley, I'm afraid. The BPAS use a private place near Macclesfield and they only keep the girls in for one night. Ruthie's been missing since early Tuesday morning at the very least. Even if she had been having an abortion she would have been home by yesterday.'

'Unless there were complications.'

She nodded.

'So where now?'

'We'll send a couple of uniforms around the local hospitals, not only Macclesfield but the North Staffs, and Buxton too. See if that bears any fruit.'

9.30 p.m.

The sun was just setting as she descended the hill towards the tiny, pretty village of Waterfall, a cluster of stone cottages and a pub scattered around a triangular village green complete with a spreading chestnut and a bench seat. It was powerfully silent as though the entire village slept through the dying embers of another summer's day. Unlike the town there was no distant hum of traffic, no sound of lawn mowers or the thump of music. The church clock struck once as Joanna wheeled her bike towards the square stone house, the estate agent's details in her hand.

It wasn't big, according to the details. The rooms were modestly sized. But it had three bedrooms and two reception rooms and a small, Victorian conservatory at the back. Joanna walked around to the rear and peeped over the wall.

It transported her to her childhood. A rusting swing in the long, orchard garden which backed on to the church. For a moment she rested her elbows on the wall and closed her eyes, waiting for her father's voice to call her in for tea.

There was nothing. Nothing but peace, stillness, memories.

So she returned to the front garden, tidy but unimaginative with rows of thirsty looking wall flowers. As she pushed the wicket gate open to take a closer look Matthew's BMW drew up on the verge. It was perfect timing.

He jumped out of the car, grinning at her. 'So you made it.'

'I couldn't resist it. It's such a lovely evening and I've worked hard enough for one day.'

'Are you getting anywhere with the case?'

'A few blind alleys. None of them have led anywhere – so far.' She glanced around at the village. 'It's a peaceful place, isn't it? Seems a hundred miles from the death and destruction of Hardacre. And yet it's less than five, as the crow flies. Matthew,' she said impulsively. 'Why don't we take a quick look around the house, get a takeaway and eat it in my garden with a bottle of chilled wine I just happen to have in my fridge?'

He looked uncomfortably back towards his car. And that was when she noticed Eloise, slumped in the front seat, her blonde hair catching the last of the fading light.

She looked to Matthew for an explanation.

He threw his hands up in the air. 'A phone call,' he said, 'from Jane, early this morning. She got the chance of an early flight.' He looked sheepish. 'I mean – what could I do? She just stuck Eloise on the train and I had to pick her up. I'm sorry, Jo.'

He moved back towards the car, his face mirroring his emotions. Pride in his daughter, a fierce love, but there was embarrassment and guilt too.

Joanna stood glued to the spot because she had her own feelings about Matthew's daughter. Sure, Eloise had intelligence and resilience, strength of character and stamina. But it was tempered with a vicious, feminine spite which she had inherited from her mother. And Joanna knew that the emotion Eloise felt for the woman who had finally parted her parents was pure, undisguised hatred. Against it she felt powerless. There was *nothing* she could do to deflect it. She looked again, longingly, at the cold, stone peace of the house. When she and Matthew were living together there would be many such visits from Eloise. The question was, was their combined love strong enough to withstand such a destructive force?

She doubted it.

Watching the girl flick her long, pale hair out of her eyes, she caught Eloise watching her in the wing mirror. The girl smiled.

She watched Matthew urge his daughter to get out of the car and take a look inside the cottage.

She heard him try to persuade her to join them in the pub. She did not, however add her encouragement to his but stood still and watched.

Matthew returned with a sigh. 'Says she's knackered after the train journey.'

'Well we've got the key,' she said steadily. 'We may as well take a look and then you can take Eloise home.'

Inside all the promises of the brochure were fulfilled. There were minor, cosmetic blemishes, plaster peeling, flushed formica doors, damp patches and leaking taps. But the proportions of the rooms were perfect. The high ceilings and long, Georgian sash windows were original. And the kitchen overlooked the garden as well as the field at the back and Waterfall church. Even better there was a small Victorian conservatory at the back which overlooked the orchard with tufts of grass and apple trees. It was long, green, shady and very pretty.

Upstairs there was a decent sized bathroom, a master bedroom with an attached room easily big enough for a shower, sink and toilet, two more reasonably sized bedrooms and a dry loft. Joanna felt her excitement grow and refused to be discouraged by the stone sink and array of spider-filled cupboards which served as a kitchen. She and Matthew pushed open the French windows to the conservatory and then walked outside to look at the outbuildings, a coal house, a shed and a small garage, probably too tight a fit for his BMW. But it would take Joanna's Peugot 205 without any problem. And more importantly, her bike.

Matthew nosed around the shed before giving her a straight look. 'How would you feel about keeping Sparky here?'

'I'm not mucking out a horse every day.'

'We could pay a schoolgirl in return for allowing her to ride him when Eloise is with her mother. And when she's here . . .'

Joanna shuddered. 'Are you suggesting Eloise would spend most of her school holidays here – with us?'

He took her hand. 'For part of the time. In the holidays. Jane's flat is too small. There's nothing for Eloise to do there.' Then the common refrain. 'She *is* my daughter.'

'But she isn't mine. And I won't suffer her malice to expiate your guilt for leaving Jane. That was your decision, Matthew, not mine. She can come here – as agreed – every other weekend, for part of the school holidays. Not all the time.'

'But Jane doesn't mind.'

'I do,' she said.

'Please, Joanna, be fair,' he begged and she hated herself for letting him even catch a glimpse of her childish jealousy.

At the same time a cold feeling gnawed at her

stomach. She simply couldn't supply what he wanted, an open-ended welcome to his daughter.

'I'd better go,' she said quickly. 'How long will Eloise be with you?'

'For a while,' Matthew said shortly.

Joanna held out her hand. 'Then goodbye,' she said, 'for a while.'

Chapter Ten

Friday, July 10th, 6.45 a.m.

After a sleepless night she rode her bike the few miles to Hardacre before seven in the morning, stopping in the herd of cows being driven along the lane by a yawning Pinkers. He was working hard these days, running the two farms. He greeted her pleasantly. 'Good morning, Inspector. Lovely day for a ride. Keepin' fit, are you?'

She let her gaze wander deliberately through the herd before riding up on the verge to avoid being trampled. 'You have a fine herd of cows, Mr Pinkers.'

'Oh they are that.' He grinned.

'Good milkers?' she asked carelessly.

He shot her a sharp glance. 'They 'ave a fair yield.'

But her dislike for the farmer was steadily mounting. Hannah's story had been a dirty one. Moorland farming was a scratch at a living. To rob your own neighbour of his most valuable beast might well be to destroy his livelihood and Hannah's story, told simply, with little emotion, had the ring of truth behind it. And she was convinced, as the Summers family had been, that Pinkers had stolen the cows as well as the bull. She frowned at something pricking her memory. The bull's name. Doric. Wasn't it something to do with Greek architecture? Doric columns, firm, plain, strong? Who, in this environment, had named a bull with such classical insight? Titus Mothershaw?

Ruthie?

She watched Pinkers drive the cows into the field where they immediately bent their heads and started grazing. Pinkers stood back and watched her as she cycled on.

Apart from the tape across the door there was no sign of the recent activities but she was anxious to go back in. She was no believer in ghosts but there had to be something here, some motive, some mark, a sign.

She looked up at the grey, stone facade, unmistakably neglected and old, with the bright glass porch the only visible attempt at prettiness. She pulled the tape back and PC Timmis seemed to appear from nowhere. 'You're bright and early, ma'am.'

'It's the only way I can get to use my bike these days. What with the heat and the extra hours.'

He grinned. 'Hard done by, are you?'

She smiled abstractedly. 'Get the kettle on will you, Timmis. And stop cracking jokes at my expense.'

He vanished back into the house.

She mounted the three stone steps but instead of stepping straight into the house she turned and stood still for a while, listening to the birdsong, the cows mooing and the soft peace. She stared across the wide green valley and wondered which field or tree root, hedgerow or barn held Ruthie Summers' decaying body now. In such weather putrefaction would be swift. Then she passed through the jewelled lights of the glass porch. But today they did not evoke stained-glass windows or the distant sound of psalm singing. Only apprehension. She dropped her gaze. Glass only formed the roof and the top half of the porch. Below were wooden panels stained green. And here was a jumble of old wellingtons, worn shoes, a blackthorn walking stick and a tall, metal umbrella stand. This must have been where the gun had stood. She looked upwards, to the Victorian lantern, dusty and clogged with spiders' webs. Then she reached out to touch the wooden door of the farmhouse, fingering a huge, rusting key which stuck out of a wide keyhole. The door must *never* have been locked. It was stiff and warped, swollen by damp. It would have been almost impossible either to close it or to lock it. One of the floor tiles was loose and rocked underfoot. A huge, black fly buzzed into her face and she panicked, swept it away with a brusque movement of her hands. She felt it brush against her fingers and shuddered. Then she jerked back and conjured up the vision of how it had happened. Here the assailant must have stood. The farmer must have backed into the sitting room, one wellington on, the other still in the porch. The assailant had picked up the gun, aimed and fired. And then Jack had come running down the stairs . . .

She had gone over this sequence of events so often in her mind that she could picture it clearly. Only one part of the picture was missing, the face of the assailant. She dropped her eyes to the floor. There was no sign. Nothing here. No footprints. One could almost believe that *no one* had stood here to do those awful things. No one had pulled the trigger.

No one? Or a dryad, a wood nymph?

Shaking away the vision she stepped inside.

The room looked different today, a typical scene of the crime a couple of days after the SOCOs had gleaned every bit of evidence from it. Marked with tape, heavily chalked where the bodies had lain. Most of the blood had been cleaned up. But there were still signs, easy to interpret for the practised eye, dark stains, and paler ones where evidence had been removed.

Joanna crossed the room towards the kitchen and met Timmis, holding out a mug of tea.

'I was just coming to find you.'

She took the tea and passed through into the kitchen to peer out of the glass panel in the back door which overlooked the courtyard – and the henhouse.

She frowned. What was it about this damned henhouse? Why did it still bother her, this wooden shack, full of eggs for police constables to smash underfoot when they searched it?

Drawn towards it she rested her tea on the work surface and opened the back door. Outside the courtyard was noisy with the clucking of hens and the squawking of the cockerel who strutted outside the low door of the henhouse. She pushed it open. Inside was dark, the ceiling low. And there was a pungent scent. Rotten eggs and manure. Joanna looked at the floor. Broken eggshells. And now it was *her* shoes which were plastered in egg, yolk and shell.

She stood still, closed her eyes and began to think . . .

Superintendent Colclough was lying in wait for her at the door to the Incident caravan. The warm weather was not suiting him either. His face was purple and sweating. She heard his wheezy comments to the two

PCs as she approached, wishing the lads a good morning, and cursing as he skated across a cow pat.

'Morning, Piercy.' He gave a pointed glance at his shoe and she smothered a smile and avoided dropping her eyes to hers, similarly covered in farmyard debris.

Colclough gave her a wide, chinny grin. Considering how little progress had been made in the first few days of the murder he seemed in remarkably good humour. After all, they had not discovered a motive, the missing girl, or the killer. And Colclough was a man who loved twenty-four-hour arrests. They made him puff out his chest and polish his medals. But then, politically speaking, this murder was hardly of significance. It wasn't even earning headlines – any more. The local papers had moved away from the tale of rural crime and back to another story of arson in a terraced house in Meir. A woman and her two children had been burnt alive. And the tale was one of marital infidelity, romance and a large helping of illicit sex. The fact that the man in the case was married and a prominent professional had led to moralizing, prudery and allegations of hypocrisy. But it was the two dead children's screams which had wrung the city's hearts and grasped the headlines.

Sentimental stuff compared with the shooting of a couple of lonely farmers. She could almost see Colclough dismiss it as an *insignificant* crime.

Not to her.

She wished him a good morning and followed him inside, Colclough settling down comfortably behind *her* desk as though he had the idea of spending the entire morning watching her work.

'Things going all right are they, Piercy?'

'Slowly,' she replied guardedly.

'Good.' He rasped his hands together. 'Well this is the place to be,' he said, looking around the Incident caravan. 'Nice rural setting. Solving country crime. Hot day.' His tone was jocular.

She couldn't resist a dig. 'Flies, mosquitoes and the stink of cow dung,' she said lightly. 'Not to mention . . .' And she glanced at both their shoes.

'Be poetic, Piercy,' he said, frowning. 'This ugly cynicism doesn't suit you.'

'No, sir.' And she sighed and dropped into Mike's chair.

Already it was hot. The flies were buzzing up the windows.

Colclough leant across the desk, his blue eyes sharp. 'So what's the story so far? No sign of the girl?'

'Not hide nor hair.'

Colclough winced. 'Nasty way with words you have, Piercy.'

'Sorry, sir.'

It was still early and she was sick of apologizing.

'So where are you up to? What's on the agenda?'

He must have had a better night's sleep than she with her constant thoughts about Eloise . . .

Colclough was watching her. 'So?'

She forced herself to concentrate on the present. 'Mike and I thought we'd haul Shackleton in for questioning.'

'Shackleton?'

'The tanker driver, sir.'

'So what's the lead?'

'Not much,' she admitted. 'He discovered the bodies. There's been some question whether he had a

170

relationship with the missing girl.' And she added the bit about the BPAS leaflet.

Colclough made a face. 'Nothing more definite than that?'

'He was fond of her. He seemed genuinely upset by her disappearance.'

'Hmm.' Colclough's eyes bored into hers. 'But no sightings?'

'No, sir.'

'Passport?'

'She'd never been issued with one.'

The question showed how little Colclough under-stood. Ruthie Summers had probably never been out of Staffordshire, let alone to a foreign country. And alone?

'Bank account?'

She shook her head. 'The bank account is negative. She didn't take any money with her. There had been nothing more than small, regular withdrawals, barely enough to cover their food.'

'And response to your leaflets?'

'Nothing.'

He drummed his fingers along the desk. 'Any other leads?'

'No, sir. Not unless you want to consider the cattle rustling.'

Colclough gave a hoot of laughter, setting his jowls wobbling like poorly set jellies. 'Cattle rustling? Think this is the Wild West, Piercy?' He stopped laughing abruptly. 'Keep a grip on reality.' He stood up. 'It seems to me that you really haven't got very far at all. Now what's all this about cattle rustling?'

She could hardly expect him to understand unless he too had immersed himself in these people's lives.

'Three good milkers and a valuable bull were stolen from Hardacre last autumn. At the same time the Summers' neighbour, a Martin Pinkers, acquired some new milk producers and a couple of his cows became pregnant without visible signs of a live bull or the vet's artificial insemination.'

'And what's this got to do with the murders?' he asked irritably.

'There was bad blood between the two farms.' She paused before producing her trump card.

'When Aaron and Jack Summers challenged Pinkers with the theft of the animals he levelled a shotgun at them. They were frightened enough to back off.'

Colclough was impressed. 'I see,' he said thoughtfully. 'So are you hauling him in this afternoon?'

'No evidence, sir, yet. We've asked Miss Hannah Lockley to return to Hardacre with us.'

'To what end?'

'I simply want her to take a really good look around. I have the feeling we're missing something *inside* the farmhouse, sir.'

Colclough had cheered up. He liked action. Plans.

'Sounds sensible to me, Piercy.' He beamed.

'And everything else so far has turned out negative,' she said. 'There's no sign of Ruthie Summers. The prints on the gun are all smeared but they're family all right and the photographs we've found of Ruthie bear her prints and her brother's only. No one else's.'

But one photograph was still missing. And was it Titus Mothershaw's fingers which rested on the missing girl's shoulder?

'There's something else I've heard,' Colclough said slowly. 'I keep hearing talk about Jack Summers. Not

right in the head, could fly off the handle. Unpredictable. Is it true?'

'Jack Summers had an accident as a baby,' Joanna
said reluctantly. 'At post mortem Matthew could see
the damage quite clearly. He fell from a pushchair . . .'

Unbidden the phrase wandered into her mind. Did
he fall or was he pushed? Had Ruthie's sweet angel face
concealed a devious and malicious character?

' . . . Jack Summers *was* strange and unpredictable.
That's true. He needed direction but he worked hard
enough on the farm.'

'Was he violent?'

'No recorded assaults on other *people*,' Joanna said
cautiously, 'but he kicked a neighbouring farmer's dog
so hard the animal had to be put down. And he set fire
to things.'

Even as she spoke she felt disloyal. Jack Summers
was not under investigation. He had been murdered.
He was a victim. So why did she keep picturing the
Tree Man's face when the light caught it from the left to
show a determined viciousness?

'Forensics found a rug which had been drenched in
accelerants and lit,' she said reluctantly.

'And was that the rug Aaron Summers' body was
found lying across?'

Colclough did this, pretended to be ignorant of the
facts. And then when you felt you had to spell out
everything . . . everything . . . he would trot out some
seemingly insignificant detail that proved he knew the
case. Knew it back to front, forwards and backwards.
He could trip the unwary up.

'Yes, sir.'

'And what about this artist fellow?'

'Sir?'

'The sculptor who lived in that derelict windmill sort of place in the wood. What sort of contact did he have with the family?'

'Not much . . .'

'I suppose he was friendly with the farmer's daughter too.'

'He *knew* her,' she said. 'He's admitted to nothing more.'

Mentally she was still cursing Colclough's thirst for detailed knowledge so early on in the case. And it proved to her how little she knew about *anybody*.

They both glanced across at the board. The photos of Ruthie had been blown up. Her face stared out at them dumbly. Mothershaw's hand was clearly visible, resting on her shoulder. Colclough's eyes seemed to stick on the hand.

He knew.

'I'd be very suspicious of this sculptor fellow, Piercy. Artists, crimes of passion. Strangers in their midst. You know what havoc townies can cause in these rural communities.'

She almost laughed. 'I can't see him pulling the trigger, sir.'

Colclough's eyes bored holes into her. 'Like him, do you, Piercy?'

She shifted uncomfortably. 'I don't think he's guilty although I agree with you that he probably is not unconnected.'

'What the hell do you mean, not unconnected?'

'I don't know, sir. I simply feel that his presence could have been the catalyst for subsequent events.'

But she did know. She had put her finger on the

throbbing pulse of the case. Colclough was right. Strangers could cause havoc in isolated rural communities, like this.

Colclough was still studying her. 'And relationships within the family?'

'Good – by all accounts. Brother and sister were devoted.'

'And father and daughter?'

'I've heard no one say anything to the contrary. They seem to have been a close-knit family. There has been no suggestion that there was anything *within* the family that led to the shootings.'

'So what did?'

Joanna had no answer.

Quite abruptly Colclough looked bored, hot, ready to leave.

'Check the whole thing out, Piercy. That's my advice. Check everything. And don't trust people.'

She thanked him for the advice.

'Oh – and all leave is cancelled until further notice.'

'Yes, sir.'

Mentally her heart gave a little skip. She had the perfect excuse for seeing nothing of Miss Eloise. The child could have her father all to herself until the case was solved or scaled down. But the nasty, nagging little voice refused to remain silent. 'You won't be able to avoid Eloise when you and Matthew are living together. She will be there when you wake up in the morning, when you return home from work at night. She will be there if you have to visit the bathroom in the middle of the night. And if she can't sleep one night Matthew will leave your bed and go to his daughter.'

It was a future she was reluctant to face.

8.30 a.m.

She watched Mike's car turn around in the yard before approaching him and sticking her head in through the window. 'Congratulations,' she said. 'You've just managed to miss Colclough.'

He climbed out and locked the door. 'And what did he think?'

'Not very impressed so far. I think he thinks we're being a bit slow.'

Never at his best first thing in the morning Mike grunted.

Inside the Incident Room the telephone was ringing. Joanna picked it up. 'Are we ready to tackle Shackleton?' she asked. 'Because he wants to make a statement.'

Mike's eyes gleamed. 'Where is he?'

'At the station.'

'Tell them to give us twenty minutes to get down there,' he said, 'and a long, blank tape.'

They found Shackleton in the waiting room. He stood up nervously as they entered. He had lost weight since they had last seen him. And he looked as though he hadn't slept much either.

'Have you found out anything yet?'

Joanna felt some sympathy for the man. He had known the family well. She had not. Hers was not an emotional involvement in the case but a professional one. She had often considered the painful role for relatives and friends in murder cases. And judging by the raw grief in Dave Shackleton's face he was still suffering.

They led him into an interview room and switched on the tape.

He began talking straight away. 'Have you not found Ruthie?'

She studied his open, sunburnt face and answered evasively. 'Nothing definite. But our investigations have turned up various relevant facts.' It was time to play rough. 'Facts we're certain will have a bearing on the case. For instance, Mr Shackleton, why didn't you tell us you were having a relationship with Ruthie?'

He flushed a deep, embarrassed red. 'I weren't,' he said. 'I mean – I was fond of her. Really fond of her. I'm not denying that. I did like her a lot. But she weren't interested in me.'

'Not ever?'

Shackleton looked even more uncomfortable.

Joanna picked up the thread. 'So she *was* interested in you – until someone else came along.'

'No, no,' he protested. 'It weren't like that. There was no one else.' There was a short pause while he thought. 'I'm sure. I'm sure. It were Jack.'

Korpanski pounced on his words like a cat on a mouse. 'Are you suggesting she was having an incestuous relationship with her own brother?'

'N-No . . !' Shackleton stammered. 'It-it-I-I didn't mean that.'

'So what did you mean?'

He turned to Joanna gratefully. 'Having to watch him all the time. He was getting worse, you see. More violent. More difficult for Ruthie to manage. She weren't free.'

'To marry you? Are you suggesting that Jack Summers was a bar to you marrying his sister?' The cobra in Mike's voice would have paralysed a harder, tougher man than Shackleton.

'No – No.'

'You would have liked to have married Ruthie, wouldn't you, Shackleton? Nice farm, Hardacre. Worth a bit. And she was a pretty girl.'

'I had no designs.'

'So was it *your* baby she was carrying?'

Shackleton looked astounded. 'Ruthie . . .? Ruthie . . .? A baby?' He dropped his face into his hands. 'I never knew,' he said, hugging his arms. 'I never knew. I – loved Ruthie. We all did. She was light as thistledown, graceful as a flower. You don't understand, you police. She was lovely, beautiful. Good. And gentle. If you had seen her tending those animals you would know.'

Again that image, a girl, herding cows, singing . . . singing. Shooting . . . Shooting?

'And she had the most terrible conscience about Jack. Knew it was her fault he was like he was. Blamed herself. Never stopped blaming herself.'

And Shackleton *still* didn't realize it. He had had the perfect motive for wanting to wipe Jack Summers off the face of the earth and thus free Rapunzel from her castle.

The two police officers exchanged glances.

'You'd better tell us everything, Shackleton,' Joanna said. 'Everything you know.'

And the questions became even more direct.

'When did you last see Ruth Summers?'

Shackleton licked dry lips. 'I don't know. About a month.'

Mike towered over him. 'Think.'

'Middle of June.'

'Didn't you think it strange that the girl had vanished?'

Again Shackleton's eyes held that haunted, hunted look. 'Yes,' he said finally. 'I did. I thought it was very peculiar. Because Ruthie was always there.'

'Did you ask her father and brother what had happened to her?'

Shackleton nodded and Joanna had to ask him to speak into the tape recorder, which elicited a soft 'yes'.

'And what did they say?'

'Silly things. They'd say she was out the back when I knew she weren't. Or they'd say she'd gone shopping when the Landrover was parked up. They were lying.'

Joanna gave Mike another swift glance. So Aaron and Jack had tried to cover up Ruthie's absence. Why? And where had she been? Missing for weeks *before* the murders.

There had to be a connection.

They pressed Shackleton for more.

'I been visiting that farm for fifteen years,' Shackleton said. 'And there *was* something unusual going on. But I didn't know what. How could I? They didn't confide in me. They shut me out.'

'Did you ever attend the local cattle market?'

'Sometimes. Occasionally. If my round was finished early I'd go along, out of interest, see what the animals was fetching.'

Mike bent over him. 'It must have been quite a pipe dream for you,' he said, 'thinking that one day, if you played your cards right, you might even own your own farm, buy and sell your own animals.'

Shackleton shifted uncomfortably on the hard chair.

'When did you last go to market?'

'Middle of June.'

'Do you mean June 10th or June 17th?'

'I can't be sure. One or the other.'

'And did you see Ruthie then?'

Shackleton thought for a moment. 'No,' he said. 'No. She weren't there.'

'And the week before that?'

Shackleton smiled. The memory must have been conjured up. 'I remember now,' he said. 'I saw her June 10th. Because she were teasing me about it being my birthday a couple of days later. Said she'd keep me some eggs.'

Joanna nibbled her thumbnail. Those bloody eggs again.

'And the following week?'

Again Shackleton needed to think about it. 'No,' he said. 'She weren't there.'

'Thank you. Now tell me about Martin Pinkers and the missing cows.'

Shackleton flushed. 'We had no proof,' he said. 'I can't point the finger when I don't know.'

'But Aaron Summers thought Pinkers had taken the bull. He went there.'

Shackleton ran his fingers through his springy dark hair. 'And that was a disaster,' he said.

'Why?' Mike was playing the innocent.

Shackleton looked from one to the other uneasily.

Joanna smiled. 'Because Pinkers threatened them with a gun, didn't he?'

Shackleton looked relieved. 'Yes,' he said.

'And then a few months later both Aaron and Jack are found shot.'

Shackleton said nothing.

'Do you think Pinkers carried out his threat?'

Dave Shackleton looked confused. 'I did wonder,' he began. 'But I *went* there, didn't I? I went there to tell him about the shootings and to use his phone. I *can't* have thought he did it, can I? Or I wouldn't have gone.' He was looking to Joanna for reassurance. But she couldn't give it to him. Instead she let the silence grow. Sometimes silence elicited more facts than questions. Silence was uncomfortable. People would speak to break it.

So she let the silence hover for a couple of minutes while both she and Mike stared at Shackleton. Then suddenly she put her arms on the desk and leant forward. 'Now tell me about Tuesday morning,' she said quietly.

Shackleton swallowed. 'I was doing my round,' he said slowly, 'as I do every morning. I collect the milk from four farms. Hardacre was the third. I always leave Fallowfield until last.' He grimaced. 'Pinkers can be awful late with the milking. I often have to wait for him to finish.'

'Tell us about the four farms.'

'Firstly I call at Wheatsheaf,' Shackleton said. 'That's farther out on the Buxton road. Then secondly I go to the Rowans' place.'

Joanna interrupted. 'Did you see Mr Rowan that morning?'

'Not him.' Shackleton gave a shrug. 'He has all sorts of people to do his work for him. Doesn't like getting his hands dirty. Or his poncie shirts.'

'Bit of a ladies' man?' Mike put in.

The comment seemed to put Shackleton at his ease. 'That's right,' he said. 'He does fancy himself something rotten.'

Joanna waited patiently before continuing. 'So to get to Hardacre from the Rowans' you must have passed Fallowfield.'

Shackleton nodded.

'Did you see Martin Pinkers there?'

'I heard the milking machine. I didn't actually see him. He must have been in the sheds.' Shackleton was fidgeting with his hands, pressing his fingers together, bleaching them white, displaying his tension. Joanna listened intently.

'Anyway – I drove past Fallowfield into the Hard-acre drive but the lane was blocked with cows. I couldn't understand what was happening. They hadn't been milked. Their udders were full. Some of them were dribbling. And the machine was quiet.' He shivered. 'Like a ghost town the place was,' he said. 'No sound at all. No tractors busy around the field, no machinery, nothing but the blasted cows runnin' riot.' He frowned. 'I knew something was wrong when nobody came out to meet me. Before I went inside the farmhouse I knew something terrible must have happened.'

'What was your guess?' Joanna asked curiously.

Shackleton sucked in a long, deep breath. 'I tried to make myself believe they'd overslept.'

He was evading the question but they let him carry

on. He would answer *all* before he left. There was something open and honest about the ruddy face. Shackleton would not be good at concealing either facts or emotions. Or so Joanna thought.

'Carry on, Mr Shackleton,' she prompted.

'I parked the tanker up by the milking sheds, where I normally go. I still hoped that either Aaron or Jack would be in the milking sheds. Perhaps the machinery was broken down.'

But Joanna was convinced Shackleton had not thought this at all. She caught his eye and straightaway Shackleton flushed a deep, tomato red. He'd been found out.

'Then I went to the farmhouse.'

'I suppose you hoped you'd see Ruthie there?'

After a pause Shackleton nodded – briefly.

'The door to the porch was standing open.' He started gulping again as though short of air.

'Was the door wide open or ajar?'

'Wide open. The weather was hot. They were glad of any breeze. It was always standing open – except when they were out. Then they closed it.'

This, Joanna knew, was true.

'So the gun would have been clearly visible to whoever came to the front door?'

'To get some air through.' Shackleton flushed. 'You don't understand. They didn't think about the gun. To you police it's really important.'

'It turned out to be of significance to them,' Joanna commented drily.

'They just forgot about it. It meant nothing to them.'

'Until somebody came to pay them a call, picked it up and blasted the pair of them through the chest.'

Shackleton worked his chin.

'Go on,' she said.

'I saw Aaron first. At least I saw his feet. Sticking up. One boot on. Then I saw Jack sitting against the wall with that . . . that' Shackleton's eyes were filled with pity, with pain and with disgust. 'With that big hole in him. There was blood everywhere. And such a smell. A sick, sweet scent. And flies. They were everywhere. Like an old-fashioned butcher's shop before they had those funny blue lights in them.'

And Joanna was vividly reminded of the swarming bluebottles in the pretty, jewelled lights of the Victorian porch, so deceitfully like the stained-glass windows of an ancient church, the sunshine streaming in over the muddy wellington boots, the umbrella stand.

'Did you see anyone else around?'

Shackleton's head jerked up, his face guarded. 'Who do you mean? I would have told you if I *had* seen anyone.'

'Would you?' Joanna murmured. 'Would you have mentioned if you had seen someone simply near the farm, perhaps on the footpath?'

'I didn't notice,' Shackleton said quickly.

'Just think, Mr Shackleton. Think. Anyone? Anyone at all?'

Shackleton's eyes were wide open. 'I didn't see any *one*,' he said slowly.

'So what did you see?'

'A dog,' Shackleton said, bemused. 'I saw a dog.'

'Do you mean one of the farm dogs?'

Shackleton shook his head slowly. 'No,' he said. 'That's the point. It *wasn't* one of the farm dogs. It

184

wasn't Noah and it wasn't Pinkers' mangy old hound.'
Dave Shackleton was getting excited now. 'It was an
Alsatian,' he said. 'Loose, sniffing along the lane.'

'Was it with anyone?'

'It didn't have to be,' Shackleton said excitedly. 'I
know whose dog it is. And it never goes out alone.'

'So whose dog is it?'

'I don't know his name but I've often seen him on
that walk.'

'What does he look like?'

'He's a big man. Tall, big stomach. He always wears
those long shorts, down to the knees.'

Joanna smothered a smile. 'Bermudas?'

'That's right. And they're always really brightly coloured. And he wears a T-shirt, usually white with some
writing on it.'

'And you saw the dog when you drove into Hardacre Farm that morning?' Joanna gave Mike a swift,
excited glance. It was the first *real* break.

Shackleton leant across the desk. 'I did,' he said,
'and I'm perfectly sure. I *know* it was that very morning
because I can remember fretting the dog'd chase some
of the cows.'

'Do you know where the man lives?'

'No – somewhere in the town.' Shackleton paused to
think. 'I've a fancy I've seen the dog somewhere near
the supermarket.'

Joanna turned aside to Mike. 'Get that description
out,' she said sharply. 'No one fitting that description
has come forward to say they were in the vicinity of
Hardacre that morning.'

Mike nodded and allowed himself a broad grin.
This was the point in any murder investigation when

the pulses quickened and the nose began to twitch. They were starting to discover things.

Joanna sat back, surveyed the tanker driver and decided to play the game a little dirty. 'Mr Shackleton,' she said, her face a blank mask, 'I have to ask you this, you understand.' Shackleton nodded – apprehensively.

'Did you touch the gun?'

He looked affronted. 'No. I did not. I know enough about police work not to touch the murder weapon.'

'So if your fingerprints had been found on it you would be very surprised?' she asked innocently.

Shackleton studied her face carefully. 'You're bluffing,' he said. 'But if my fingerprints were to be found on the gun I can tell you. I have handled it more than once. Me and Ruthie would go and shoot crows sometimes.'

The image was wrong. The dairy maid, singing as she herded the cows. Shooting crows? Joanna sat up.

'Shooting crows, Mr Shackleton?'

Shackleton was unperturbed. 'It's just a way of letting off steam.'

But the mention of Ruthie Summers brought the subject of the questioning round neatly.

'Do you have *any* idea where Ruthie might be?'

'I wish I did,' Shackleton said hoarsely. 'I really wish I did. I'd give anything to see her again.' And he stumbled to his feet, knocking his chair over, spending ages attempting to right it.

Anything so the two police officers could not see his tears.

But they could.

Chapter Eleven

9.45 a.m.

Joanna watched him shuffle out before turning to Mike. 'So what do you think?'

'He could have shot them both *before* starting his milk round, murdered or abducted Ruthie Summers.'

'But why, for goodness sake?'

Mike shrugged. 'Hostile family, reluctant girl-friend? I mean Ruthie was *never* going to leave Jack behind, was she?'

Joanna glanced down at the photograph in her hand. 'I can't believe that she would have condoned her lover slaughtering her father and brother before setting off into the sunset with him.'

'No?' He watched her with rising impatience. 'You're judging her whole personality on the strength of a *picture*. What if she wasn't sensitive or caring? What if she was a nasty piece of work who argued with her father and brother one morning and blasted the pair of them with an available shotgun? After all *she* would have been the one who would have known it was there, whether it was loaded or not. And plenty of people have seen her fire it.'

Joanna still felt compelled to fight Ruthie's corner. 'But everyone says Ruthie was gentle, pleasant, good natured. She cared for Jack for years, didn't she? No one has said anything about her being irritated by looking after him, just guilty.'

'Well guilt can mount up, Joanna. She *did* cause his injuries in the first place. Maybe she just got pissed off with looking after him one day. She might even have got frightened. He *did* have some nasty habits with boxes of matches. After all. It was all her fault.'

'It was an accident,' Joanna protested.

'How do we know? No one *saw* what happened all those years ago. And Jack was too young to tell. What if she lost her temper with him and went for him. Plenty of reason for guilt in that case.'

'She was a child of six.'

Mike watched her steadily. 'Funnier things have happened,' he said. 'Children can do peculiar things, in temper. And don't you psychologists have a special name for it?'

'Sibling rivalry.'

'Yeah well. The point I'm trying to make is that we don't really *know* anything about Ruthie Summers. We've never met her. Everything we know about her is seen through someone else's eyes.'

'I suppose so.' She hesitated before bringing up the next point. 'Why do you think Aaron and Jack covered for Ruthie's absence?'

Mike shrugged. 'Who knows? It's anybody's guess. Maybe it's simply coincidence that no one saw her.'

And again she conceded the point.

'OK,' Mike said. 'So let's move on and start looking at someone else apart from the wretched girl. What about the man walking his dog?'

'I'd be more interested,' Joanna said slowly, 'if it wasn't for the time difference. Aaron and Jack

Summers were shot early in the morning, round about six a.m. He was presumably around at ten, four hours later.'

'So if he's completely innocent why hasn't he come forward?'

Joanna tapped her pencil on the side of the desk. 'I don't know,' she said. 'Unless . . .'

'He doesn't read newspapers or watch television? Pull the other one,' Mike said scornfully. '*Everyone* must know all about the shootings. There have been notices up everywhere, headlines in the local papers, local radio every hour and pieces on the TV. He *must* know all about it.'

Joanna met Mike's dark eyes. 'Are you suggesting there's a reason why he hasn't come forward?'

He nodded.

'Then let's find out what that reason is.' She picked up the phone and linked up with the police press officer, shot a few facts down the line and smiled at Mike. 'Now we sit down and wait,' she said.

They heard the announcement on the ten o'clock bulletin. This time complete with description. '*Police are searching for a man said to be walking an Alsatian dog in the vicinity of Hardacre Farm, where the double murders took place some time early on Tuesday morning. He is said to be a large man who frequents the area, often wearing a T-shirt and Bermuda shorts. They are appealing to this man to come forward as they are anxious to speak to him.*'

Joanna sat back, satisfied. 'So let's see what this brings in.' She watched Korpanski with a trace of amusement. He hated inactivity. And his predilection for fancy ties had persisted even through the scorching weather. Today it was smothered in liquorice allsorts. Yesterday it had been Blue Whales. She stretched her arms over her head, yawned and grabbed hold of the bottom of his tie. 'So what's with the ties, Korpanski?' she demanded. 'You must be roasting hot. Everyone else is working in open necks. Even the uniformed officers.' She gave him a sideways smile. 'So who are you trying to impress?' Korpanski flushed a dull, plum red and wriggled uncomfortably.

'Well let me guess. It won't be WPC Dawn Critchlow who has legs like milk bottles.' She decided to tease him further. 'I simply can't imagine you with anyone who has legs like milk bottles, Mike.'

Korpanski cleared his throat and stopped looking at her.

'And Detective Sergeant Hannah Beardmore has been lurking around the Leek police force for at least seven years. I don't think she's suddenly decided to awaken your male libido.'

'Shut it, Jo.'

'On the other hand Police Cadet Kitty Sandworth is not much more than seventeen years old. Round about half your age. Mike.' She paused. This was dangerous territory. 'And you're a married man.'

Korpanski stood up. 'For goodness sake, Joanna.'

So she had scored. 'Quite,' she said softly. 'So let's leave it, shall we?'

Korpanski inhaled deeply as though he was dragging on a cigarette and Joanna watched him with a little private niggle. She and Korpanski had worked together for almost five years now. Their names had been linked, despite her *amour* with Matthew. Besides,

Kitty Sandworth seemed to her a mere child. A nymphet. So why should she feel a prickle of jealousy? Was it because Korpanski had never worn fancy ties for her? She watched him through new eyes and the silence thickened in the stuffy little caravan until Mike cut through it. 'So what are we going to do for the rest of the day then? Just sit here and talk about ties?' There was more than a hint of defiance in his voice.

'Oh – I don't think so.' Joanna fumbled along her desk top and found the BPAS leaflet. It was a forlorn hope and yet, stubbornly, she clung to it, this blind optimism, that somewhere, somehow, they would find Ruthie Summers both alive and innocent.

'Let's tour some of the local nursing homes and hospitals.'

As usual Korpanski could read her mind. 'You still think . . .?'

And to him she could admit it. 'I want to – very much.'

12.00 p.m.

Before they spent the afternoon trawling round the local nursing homes it seemed worth a visit to Ruthie Summers' doctor. He proved a friendly Chinese man with a wide smile, crooked teeth and amazingly accentless English. His name was Peter Foo.

The receptionist ushered them into his surgery and he beamed a welcome. Joanna thought what a reassuring doctor he seemed. Surely Aaron, Jack and Ruth would all have confided in him.

It seemed not. 'I've got all their notes out,' Doctor Foo said with one of his broad grins. 'But I don't seem to have met them too often. I hadn't seen Jack for more than four years. And that was for something quite routine that can have had no bearing on the case at all.'

'And Aaron?' Joanna asked cautiously.

'I was in a difficult position here,' Doctor Foo glanced at his computer screen. 'You see according to my records, I received a telephone call from Mr Aaron Summers' sister-in-law to say he was unwell. She wanted him to consult me.'

'And?'

'I did telephone Mr Summers,' the doctor said, 'but regretfully he was not willing to come to the surgery.' He smiled. 'He had a very fatalistic view of life, death and disease. Common amongst farmers and country folk but hopelessly out of step with modern, interventionist medicine. In fact it seems unfortunate but I never did see him.'

'You saw the results of the post mortem?'

The doctor nodded. 'I did and I was not surprised. From what Miss Lockley had told me I guessed he had a malignancy somewhere. And to be honest, Inspector Piercy, I'm not so sure that his tumour would have been operable anyway. From the size of it he'd had it for quite a while, probably years. He may have taken the wisest decision. For all the wrong reasons, of course.'

Joanna moved to more sensitive ground. 'And Ruth Summers?'

Immediately the doctor's manner changed. 'I'm sorry,' he said awkwardly, 'but I have spoken to the Medical Defence Union. While both Aaron and Jack Summers are dead and therefore *anything* I know *might* have a bearing on their murders, Ruth Summers is, as far as we know, still alive. I can't reveal any medical detail.'

'She is a potential witness in a murder inquiry,' Joanna said sharply, 'as well as being our prime suspect. She has not been seen *since* the murders. In fact up to now, no one we have questioned seems to have seen her in the last month. We're *very* anxious to find her. So anything, anything at all that might help us would be vital to the investigation.' She decided to cast the dice. 'Doctor Foo,' she said earnestly, 'I'm not interested in knowing *all* her medical details. I simply want to know one thing. Was she pregnant?'

The doctor's eyes flickered.

Joanna tried again. 'Look,' she said, 'if it'll help you I'll explain. If Ruth Summers was pregnant and she *was* seeking an abortion you just might hold the answer to her whereabouts. She *might* have seen something on Tuesday morning.'

The doctor sat still for a moment before picking up the telephone. 'Let me just speak to the MDU again.' He covered the mouthpiece. 'I'm sorry,' he said with a disarming smile, 'I'm really *not* trying to obstruct you in your enquiries. I want to know who murdered two of my patients probably as much as you do. But this confidentiality thing – it's a minefield. I promise you.'

'It's OK,' Joanna said.

The doctor spoke quickly into the telephone, explaining the circumstances concisely. Two minutes later he replaced the receiver. And his manner now was open and relaxed. 'She never *actually* consulted me,' the doctor said. 'That was part of the trouble. However I do have something logged here . . .' He flicked the screen to another patient. This time Ruthie

Summers, aged twenty-seven, address, Hardacre Farm. 'Patients can drop urine samples off at the surgery for testing,' he said. 'We send them to the path. lab. On June 16th Ruth Summers did in fact leave an early morning specimen of urine at the surgery, giving the date of her last period as May the first.'

'And?'

'It tested positive,' the doctor said reluctantly.

Joanna leant back in her chair. So her hunch had been right. Ruthie Summers *had* been pregnant. This opened up an array of possibilities. Suicide, an abortion, an escape from the claustrophobia of the farm. And it didn't need an 'A' level in Biology to point out that for Ruthie Summers to be expecting a baby there had to have been a love affair. So not quite the chaste dairy maid.

She addressed the doctor. 'Then what happened?'

'We informed her of the test result by telephone and made her an appointment for the ante-natal clinic the following week.'

'And?'

'She didn't turn up.'

'So then what did you do?'

The doctor sighed. 'I rang the farm,' he said, 'but I only ever spoke to either Aaron or Jack. They always said Ruthie was out. And . . .'

'Because of confidentiality you couldn't tell them what you were ringing about.'

The doctor shrugged. 'That's right.'

'But what did you think happened to her?'

The doctor gave a rueful smile. 'I didn't think,' he said. 'That's the trouble. I have four thousand patients on my list with only one part-timer to help me. I daresay the midwives will have chased her up. They would normally even call at her home but I really didn't have time to do anything more. I'm sorry.'

There was something defensive in his manner. The pleasant Doctor Foo was worrying about his neck on the line. Litigation, a neglected pregnancy. Joanna leant forward. 'Tell me, Doctor,' she said and placed the leaflet on the desk, 'if Ruth Summers had decided to opt for a termination by the BPAS what would happen?'

'The patient has the absolute right to privacy.'

'Even from her own GP?'

The doctor nodded.

They called in at a pub for lunch, sitting outside on wooden benches.

Joanna waited until they were settled with a drink and a plate of sandwiches. 'I think we've found her,' she said.

'Don't be too confident.'

'No, I really think she's in one of the nursing homes run by the BPAS. In fact we'll check the first one this afternoon and get some of the uniformed lads to ring the local hospitals, just in case something happened and she was admitted.'

'But they've already put out a missing persons quest.'

'She could have used a different name.'

Their first port of call was to a converted Victorian house, pronouncing 'The Elms Private Nursing Home' picked out in black lettering on a white painted board.

They took the car up a drive that was darkened by bending pine trees, and welcomingly cool in the shade. The house was large, bay-windowed and somehow quite forbidding. Joanna sat, mesmerized, in the driving seat, full of hidden fears and old memories. Once, only once, she had thought she must come to a place just like this, to rid herself of what she had *imagined* she carried, something she had thought of as a hostile, unwelcome foreign body. The prospect of a child had been awful, frightening. For a few days she had worried. And yet it had been nothing. Nothing but worry and guilt, a temporary upset, the doctor had called it. It was only now that she realized the baby she had *thought* she carried would have been Matthew's much longed for child. A consolation for the intermittent loss of Eloise. Eloise ... Suddenly weary and depressed she wondered how he was getting on with her.

Had Ruthie Summers faced such a prospect too? Had she come here, with her suitcase, to dispose of just such a problem?

The answer hit her like a thunderbolt. Surely not. If Ruthie Summers had been pregnant by Shackleton there would have been no need for an abortion. He was a free man, wasn't he? He loved her? So he would have married her. But if it had been Mothershaw's child she had carried?

She rang the bell and spoke to a neatly uniformed matron who also produced the confidentiality plea. Joanna pointed out that there was a possibility that Ruthie Summers was a vital witness to a double murder. And confidentiality melted, like chocolate on a hot day.

Nevertheless The Elms drew a blank as did all of the five other nursing homes used by the BPAS so the journey back to the farm was subdued. Joanna *knew* there was a significance about Ruthie Summers' pregnancy but for the life of her she didn't know what it was. It infuriated her and at the same time frustrated her. Mercifully Mike was silent until they reached the outskirts of the town.

'Mike,' she said suddenly. 'Look. We can't find Ruthie. But we could have a go at speaking to the father of her child.'

He glanced across at her. 'So who are we talking about?' he demanded. 'Neil Rowan, Shackleton, or . . .' she knew he was watching her out of the corner of his eye, 'are we talking about that sculptor fellow, the one you're so fond of visiting on your own early in the morning when I daresay he's still in his pyjamas.'

Joanna burst out laughing. This was the old Mike. The jealous Mike, the Mike whose loyalty guarded her like the Dogs of Fo outside Chinese Temples. This Mike she knew. Well.

'Actually,' she said, still giggling, 'he wears a rather fetching grey towelling dressing-gown.'

Mike growled.

'Anyway, I didn't mean Mothershaw. I was thinking of Shackleton. I think we should call round and speak to him. Who knows,' she said, 'we might get lucky. There's just a chance he's been hiding Ruthie Summers there all along.'

Mike grunted but turned the car around and they headed towards the Southern end of town, to the rows of terraced mill workers' cottages and Victory Street.

It was a diminutive place, barely bigger than a dolls'

house, one of a row of five. Shackleton's was the centre one, the height of the bedroom window scarcely six inches above Korpanski's head.

They banged on the door and Shackleton himself pulled it open, staring confusedly at the two police officers. 'I only spoke to you this morning,' he said. 'Has something happened? Have you found Ruthie?'

'We'd like to have a look round your house.'

Shackleton grasped the point quickly. 'You mean you think Ruthie's here? You've got to be joking. She wouldn't have come here.'

Joanna eyed him steadily.

Shackleton ran his fingers through his hair distract-edly. 'If she was here I'd have told you. There's nothing I'd like more than to see her. But there's no one here but myself and my mother. We live alone.' He looked sharply at Joanna then Mike. 'Why here?'

'Because there are so few places she *could* be. She hardly knew anyone. And we know you were fond of her.'

'I *am* fond of her,' Shackleton said with simplicity. 'But if she had done that to her father and her brother I wouldn't have hidden her because she wouldn't be the Ruthie I knew.'

And the honesty in his eyes forced Joanna to acknowledge that he was telling the truth.

Mike was shuffling impatiently. She could read his thoughts. Why weren't they getting on with it?

But Shackleton stood his ground. 'Have you got a warrant?'

'We can easily get one,' Joanna said wearily. Confi-dentiality, warrants. She was sick of red tape.

Shackleton eventually gave a brief nod. 'All right,'

he said. 'But don't say too much to my mother.' He jerked his head backwards, into the house. 'She's old. She isn't very well and I haven't said too much to her about . . .' A spasm temporarily twisted his features. 'She was fond of Ruthie.'

'We'll be as delicate as a pair of courting butterflies.' Joanna gave Mike a sharp glance, but his face was impassive.

Shackleton shrank back against the wall and Mike strode past.

It was a tiny house with no room to swing a cat. A diminutive living room cramped by a bulky three-piece suite and a table folded against the wall. Kitchen through a glass door, bathroom added on beyond that, a lean-to with a flat roof and mint green bathroom suite.

There was no place downstairs they could have hidden Ruthie Summers.

Narrow stairs, dark. At the top two doors. One stood open – Shackleton's room. Bed covers thrown back. Hot, stuffy. Overalls on the bed, small wardrobe, chest of drawers. Nothing underneath except a pair of boots and a thick layer of dust.

The other room.

The door was shut. Joanna knocked, opened it slowly.

Dim inside. A hump on top of the bed. She must be lying down in the afternoon heat. She caught her breath. *Ruthie?*

No. Strands of white hair across the pillow.

'Mrs Shackleton?'

The old lady sat up slowly. An ancient woman with a creased face who eyed Mike with malevolence. 'Who are you?' Then she called out. 'David . . . David.'

She pulled a cardigan tightly around her shoulders as Shackleton entered the room. 'It's all right, Mother.' He sat down on the bed and soothed her. 'It's all right. They're friends of mine.'

The old lady was staring trustingly up at his face as Shackleton gently explained.

'You remember I said Ruthie was missing and there had been an accident up at Hardacre?'

Joanna winced. *An accident?*

The old lady nodded dumbly, tears rolling down her cheeks.

Shackleton continued his explanation. 'These are police officers. They're trying to find her. That's all.'

'So what are they doing *here*?' They had been deceived. The old lady's voice was surprisingly sharp. 'They won't find Ruth Summers here.'

Joanna searched the old woman's face. There was a note of hostility that was mirrored in the lined eyes. Shackleton's mother had not liked or loved Ruthie Summers but had resented her. For having the potential to rob her of her son?

But Shackleton seemed oblivious to her emotions as he dropped his arm around his mother's shoulders. 'Don't worry,' he said. 'They'll find her.'

The old lady gave a brave smile and touched her son's face. 'She thinks she's too good for you,' she said. 'But really you're too good for her. She'd be lucky to have you.'

'I know,' Shackleton soothed. 'I know.'

Joanna moved back towards the door. This bedroom was even tinier than the other, filled by the double bed. There was no question that Ruthie Summers was here. She would have left but Mike was peering out of the window, bypassing the yellowed nets gathered in his meaty fist.

'Come and have a look here, Jo.'

She saw instantly what he meant. A tiny garden, narrow but long. And at the end was what *might* be termed a potting shed.

It was clear that Ruthie Summers was not and never had been in the house. But in the shed? It was worth looking.

'Thank you,' she said to both of them. 'We'll leave you now – after we've taken a look around the garden.'

Instantly the alarm was there. Shackleton stopped tucking the cardigan around his mother's shoulders and stared at Mike, open mouthed.

It made them doubly curious to look inside.

They galloped down the stairs, passed through the kitchen and out of the back door. Neat rows of cabbages and carrots, beans and peas were laced up bamboo canes. At the back was a display of flowering sweet peas bright enough to match the deceitful picture on the front of a seed packet. They approached the potting shed.

It was a neat affair, timber clad, not much bigger than a chicken coop but just about big enough to house Ruthie Summers. Reluctantly Shackleton handed them the key.

'You're wasting your time, Inspector.'

The hostility in his voice made him seem a bigger man somehow than the curly-headed, pleasant-mannered tanker driver.

Joanna tugged the door open. Inside was dark. A rag had been nailed across the one, small window. Joanna tore it off to let in light.

Lawn-mower, gardening implements, rows of fertilizer and weed killers, slug pellets. A bench across the back. Ruthie Summers was not here either. Joanna took one frustrated glance around before finding the object of Shackleton's frozen stare. Beneath the bench. Magazines. She could almost guess what they were. More as a matter of form than curiosity she pulled one out.

Shackleton's mother would never have allowed him to read such magazines inside the house. It was the potting shed or nowhere. But it was nothing worse than very soft porn. At a guess most schoolboys would read nothing less polluting. Grinning blondes with huge breasts and scanty knickers. Plenty of proffered bottoms.

Hidden fantasies. And they had intruded on them.

She replaced the journal and gave Shackleton a sympathetic smile. 'It's all right,' she said. 'I'm sorry.' His face, first pale, was now crimson. She tried to explain further. 'We had to.'

They emerged into the sunlight, she still trying to allay his embarrassment. 'That's the trouble with murder cases. You *have* to invade, everywhere. Nowhere is sacred. I'm sorry,' she said again. 'This need go no further. We had to *know*.'

She waited until they were back in the car before she exploded. 'Dirty magazines. For goodness sake. Are we no nearer finding out *anything* about this case than a pile of dirty magazines? Are we to spend all our time discovering *nothing*?'

Mike let her rant continue as she did a five-point turn in the narrow road. 'Just for once I wish someone would tell us something of real significance. Anything that might have some bearing on this wretched case.' She accelerated along the road then stopped. 'And for my money I'll back Hannah Lockley.' She took her eyes off the road for just a moment. 'Mike, let's take her back to Hardacre. Now.'

'What for?'

'I'm convinced that there is *something* back there.'

'When Barra's been over it with a toothcomb?'

'Got any better ideas?'

'No, but . . .' His two-way radio bleeped and he listened intently.

Joanna changed gear. 'We *must* have missed something.'

But Mike held up his handset. 'Well whatever it is we won't get there this afternoon, Joanna,' he said. 'The man who was walking his dog has turned up. His name's Lewis Stone and he lives at the back of the supermarket in town.'

One of the great advantages of being in the police, Joanna decided as she parked at the base of the jumble of flats that seemed to project higgledy-piggledy right into the car-park, was that she could leave the car anywhere without attracting the attentions of the over-zealous traffic wardens. Neither was it likely to be invaded by the group of youths sitting on the wall, watching them.

'So which one . . .?'

But she and Mike could have picked out Stone's flat by the deep barking that came from behind a tall door blocking off a concrete yard.

She banged hard. 'Hello.'

The only answer was some more, frenzied barking.

Then a man's gruff voice spoke. 'Who is it?'

'Mr Stone?'

'Who wants to know?'

'The police.'

'Shut up, Nathan.' The door was tugged open.

He had the Alsatian throttled by the choke chain. That was her first impression. Her second was how accurate Shackleton's description had been. A big man with a swollen beer belly, a white T-shirt inscribed with a four XXXXs, bright cotton shorts to the knee. Shaven head, blond stubble, an earring, very dark eyes.

'Mr Stone?' Joanna asked.

'Yeah.'

Joanna glanced nervously at the dog's slobbering jaws. 'Would you mind putting your dog out of the way so we can have a civilized conversation?'

Stone eyed Korpanski warily. 'You police too?'

Mike's answering stare was wooden. 'Detective Sergeant Korpanski, Leek Police.'

'That's all right then.' Stone wiped his finger across his nose. 'Can't be too careful, can yer?'

They followed Lewis Stone across the yard, up the metal staircase and he pushed open the door at the top. Inside was a tiny flat, relatively clean and organized. Joanna was pleasantly surprised. Stone led them through a lime-green painted kitchen and into a sitting room, well decorated, again in beige and lime green. She settled on a flowered sofa expectantly. The dog was quiet now.

Joanna opened the questioning. 'We believe you

were walking near Hardacre Farm on the morning of July 7th.'

'That's right. I go there to walk my dog. Big dog like Nathan needs a lot of exercise.'

'I'm sure.'

Stone grinned in Joanna's direction.

'Why didn't you come forward, Mr Stone, and tell us you'd been near Hardacre Farm on the morning of the murders?'

'I didn't put two and two together,' he said. 'I heard there'd been a shooting. I didn't know it was *that* farm.'

'But the date?'

Stone leant back and rested his arm on the ridge of the sofa. 'Look, love. Every day's the same to me. I get weekends as well week days off, you see. Every day.'

'But you *were* there on Tuesday morning.'

'Yeah I was.'

'At what time?'

Stone thought for a minute. 'About seven, half past.'

Joanna stiffened and shot a swift glance at Korpanski. Shackleton had claimed to have seen the dog at ten. Not seven.

She eyed Stone curiously and gave him the chance to retract. 'You're sure it was at seven a.m.?'

Stone nodded. 'I heard the farmer whistle the cows in,' he said, grinning.

Joanna stiffened. 'You heard what?'

Stone pursed his lips up and gave a couple of toots. 'Like that,' he said. 'And the cows, they just come jostling through the gate.'

'You're absolutely certain? At seven o'clock?'

'Of course I am. The minute I heard old Summers whistling I put Nathan back on his lead.' He leered at

Joanna. 'Can't take no risks with cattle around. Seven o'clock,' he said, 'give or take a couple of minutes.'

But this didn't fit in. Not with Shackleton's story nor with the observations made at the scene of the crime. Aaron had not left the farmhouse that morning, headed towards the field and returned, with or without the killer, removed one wellington boot and left the other on. He had not whistled for the cows to come in. He had never got that far. Because he had already been dead.

This was not how they had pictured the morning of July 7th.

None of it made sense.

So yet again she questioned Shackleton. 'You're absolutely sure? You definitely heard the farmer whistle?'

'Look, love,' Stone said, 'I tell you. I know the sound. I've heard it before. Lots of times.'

Mike interrupted. 'Did you *see* Mr Summers?'

Stone shook his head. 'I keep a low profile where that bloke's concerned. He's none too keen on dogs loose on his land. I mean I'd keep Nathan on a lead but a big dog like that needs exercise, doesn't he?'

And a swift study of Stone's dumpling physique told Joanna that tied to his master Nathan might not get much in the way of exercise.

She stared at Stone and wondered why he was lying. Or was it Shackleton who was lying? Had he seen Stone walk his dog in the vicinity on *other* occasions and decided to *invent* his presence later on that morning?

'Do you know Dave Shackleton?'

Stone wrinkled up his face. 'Who?'

'The tanker driver.'

'Nah. At least, I suppose I've seen him passing. Must 'ave. But I've never spoken to him.'

She watched his face closely to ask the next question. 'Tell me, Mr Stone, if you were in the vicinity of Hardacre at seven a.m. did you hear the shots?'

Again Stone looked blank and shook his head.

And now Joanna was confused. According to Stone's story Aaron had been alive at seven o'clock on the morning of the murders. That did not fit in with Matthew's forensic evidence.

More than that the countryside was quiet. The sound of gunshots even from inside the farmhouse would make an unmistakable noise. Stone claimed not to have heard it. Yet even half an hour's walking would not have taken him far enough away to have missed it.

So as usual in this strange, frustrating case the answers only threw up more questions.

Chapter Twelve

'He could be lying when he claims that he saw Stone.' Joanna unlocked the car door.

'He didn't actually say he *saw* Stone,' Mike objected. 'He says he saw Stone's dog.'

'One dog's very like another.'

'Not to country folk,' Mike said. 'I'd put my money on Stone being the liar. Nothing he says fits in.'

'Except I can't for the life of me work out why he should say he actually *heard* Aaron whistling for the cows. It doesn't make sense. He must know that the murders happened at six a.m. and therefore Aaron *couldn't* have been alive at seven. So why stick to his story? It's been widely enough reported in the press. Mike,' she turned the key in the ignition and sparked the engine into life before finishing the sentence, 'people generally put themselves as far away from the murder scene as possible. Why did he say he was *there* when Dave Shackleton says he saw him at Hardacre at ten?'

Korpanski folded his arms behind his head and gave a loud, tired sigh. 'I haven't a bloody clue, unless he had a *very* long walk. In fact nothing so far in this damned case makes any sense.'

He sat up suddenly. 'Unless he was there twice.' He

glanced across at Joanna. 'Maybe he went back. Killers often return to the scene of the crime, don't they?'

'Usually if they've forgotten something.'

'Well maybe he hadn't forgotten anything but *thought* he had.'

'I wonder what,' she mused.

But Mike's inspiration had dried up. He shrugged. 'Search me.'

Joanna chuckled and dug him in the ribs. 'Not giving up are you, Korpanski?'

He stared out of the window. 'I'd just like something to go right for a change. Just a little break. That's all I ask.' And he raised his eyes to the brilliant blue sky. 'And I wouldn't mind working in a slightly cooler environment either. I wasn't born to slave away in the tropics.'

Joanna stretched her arms through the open window and laughed. 'Stop complaining, Mike. Something'll turn up. And the weather won't last.'

But the briefing was another disappointment. Four police officers had widened the search for Ruthie and visited every single nursing home in Cheshire and Derbyshire used by the BPAS. But what had, at first, seemed such a promising lead, had failed to bear fruit.

There was no sign of Ruthie Summers. She had completely vanished. Neither bus nor train nor car had taken her out of the area.

Joanna stared across the pretty green fields and began to wonder whether Ruthie had ever left Hardacre at all. Perhaps she was still here, somewhere.

So they worked solidly through the next couple of hours before the heat began to drain out of the day and a soft stillness crept around the farm. Pinkers had done the evening milking again and silenced the lowing cows.

6.30 p.m.

The evening was turning to old gold by the time they wandered along the path towards Brooms. Joanna had expected to find the old lady working in her garden. It was a perfect evening for it. Birdsong and humming bees and air heavy with night-scented stock. Even Joanna could imagine working in the garden on such an evening. But although the gate was ajar they passed through the garden to more stillness.

And the cottage door gaped.

Joanna knocked. 'Hello, Miss Lockley?'

She appeared as though by magic, optimism barely lifting the lines on her face.

Joanna reflected that the old lady's character had drained since the murders. When they had first met her she had seemed tough, almost mannish, decisive and strong. But each day had seemed to see her strength diminish. She stood in the doorway, shrunken, looking as though she had neither eaten nor slept since Tuesday. And not for the first time, knee-deep in a murder investigation, it hit Joanna how terrible the repercussions were of violent death in a family. Hannah grasped Joanna's hand eagerly. 'Have you heard from Ruthie yet? Have you found her?'

The action and desperation emphasized how old and vulnerable the girl's aunt had become. Her age had finally caught up with her. Before she'd seemed young – strong. Obviously her initial calm over the dual murders had been from shock and now the full implications were hitting her she was frightened. In her pale eyes Joanna read real fear. Hannah was frightened of these killings. Frightened for herself. It served to convince her that Hannah Lockley knew more than she was saying. Impulsively Joanna touched her hand. 'Would you like a WPC to stay with you for a few days?'

'That won't be necessary, my dear. Ruthie will be back soon. She can take care of me.'

Inwardly Joanna groaned. This was not helping, this self-deception. 'Look – I'm sorry,' Joanna said. 'I'm sorry. But we've heard nothing from your niece. And as each day passes . . .' Hannah Lockley's eyes widened and Joanna found she couldn't complete the sentence. It would be too cruel. So instead she asked the old lady if she would be prepared to visit Hardacre again.

As expected Ruthie's aunt resisted the idea. 'I don't understand why you want me to go back. There's nothing there. Nothing that will help us find Ruthie. She's gone away.'

Mike spoke for the first time. 'Where?'

It only added to Hannah Lockley's distress. 'I don't know,' she said. 'I don't know.'

And Joanna cursed these confidentiality laws that prevented her talking about Ruthie's pregnancy. But if Ruthie had spoken to anyone about it surely it would have been to the aunt? She scrutinized the old lady's face as she asked her again to return to the farm.

'For what?' the old lady snapped. 'Your officers have been right through the place. There's nothing there. Nothing.'

'Please.' It was all Joanna could do, to plead. 'I'm sorry. I know it must be hard, going back and I can't really be *sure* it will be of benefit but your brother-in-law and your nephew have been dead for four days, your niece missing for *at least* that amount of time and quite frankly we're no nearer finding the killer than we were on Tuesday morning. We need all the help we can get, Miss Lockley. Please.'

The old lady stared right through her and Joanna cast back in her mind for some phrase, something she must have said to give the old lady that *frozen* look but her mind drew a blank.

So she continued to coax.

'I know it's a bit of a long shot.' She tried to smile but her lips felt stiff and her mind was still occupied with the old lady's expression.

At last Hannah shrugged her shoulders and moved towards the front door, her face mask-like. This time they noted that Hannah locked the front door but she still left the key under the mat and Joanna knew it was a superstitious act. She was leaving the key out for her niece. That was when she was certain that it had been her mention of Ruthie that had upset the old lady. It had been the phrase, missing for *at least* that amount of time.

She followed the old lady as she marched down the path with something of her old spirit, as though the act of leaving the key would, somehow, conjure up her missing 'daughter'. Hannah even managed to give Korpanski a cocky smile as he closed the gate after them. 'I haven't got a telly or a video to steal, Sergeant. And that's what I believe all the burglars are after these days. So it's no use your nagging me about leaving the key out.'

It was a return of the old fighting spirit.·

Joanna tried to make conversation as they covered

the few hundred yards between the cottage and the farmhouse.

'We called round to see Dave Shackleton this morning.'

Hannah halted in her tracks. 'Whatever for?'

'We had the idea Ruthie might be with him.'

'Well you were wasting your time, Inspector Piercy. She was far too good for him. She wouldn't have gone there.'

'We have to follow lots of leads,' Mike said without emotion. 'Some of them seem long shots and then hey presto, they have some bearing on the case.'

Hannah's features sharpened as she returned Mike's comment. 'Well that was too much of a "long shot", Sergeant. She wouldn't have gone there, with that old lady keeping court in that tiny little place. No bigger than the henhouse at Hardacre. Penniless that boy is. Penniless. He would have loved to have married our Ruthie. Get his legs stuck under the table at Hardacre. Hah. He wouldn't be driving milk tankers for a living then. Ruthie was too proud . . .' she finished and moved her eyes upwards.

They had arrived.

All eyes turned on the long, low building, with its stained-glass window porch catching the evening light at an angle, throwing gleams of blue and red in bright, bizarre patterns along the side of the building.

The front door was ajar, like before.

The day was still hot with nothing more threatening than a very distant rumble of thunder. Mike mopped his forehead. Joanna knew he was still wishing the fine weather would end. With vague pleasure she watched him loosen his tie.

The dryness had filled the air with dust, red and pungent with cow dung and fertilizer, pollens chased by dandelion clocks in the very lightest of breezes. It was as though the entire panorama thirsted. It was so bone dry. And now even Joanna could join Mike and yearn for a return to damp, cool normality. Not the tropics but the Moorlands.

Hannah Lockley stumbled on the steps, falling heavily on her hands. Mike picked her up and dusted her down.

She was nervous.

The porch was filled with swarms of black, noisy flies, buzzing around the coloured glass, a hot parody of the cool, pure interior of a church. The flies seemed a symbol of pollution, of evil. Of decay. It was a relief to leave it for the dark shade of the farmhouse.

But on the threshold Hannah seemed to halt again and she grappled behind her, perhaps to reassure herself that the two police officers were still there. That she was not alone.

Once in she exhaled in a noisy spurt. 'It all looks so ordinary,' she said, grimly smiling. 'Nothing here at all.'

Now she seemed to have regained her confidence she moved quickly around the room, muttering to herself and touching pieces of furniture. A chair back, the dusty ledge on the corner of the dresser, a finger trailing along the cheap print of a vase of silk flowers. She opened a cupboard or two and found nothing but crockery and yellowing newspapers. She picked one out and turned to face them both, holding it loosely in her hands. 'I don't understand,' she said. 'This is just paper for lighting the fire. What exactly is it that you *want* me to find?'

'Anything,' Joanna said. 'Anything. Just comb through the house and use your eyes. You must have known Hardacre Farm over the years. If you see anything changed, even an ornament in the wrong place, an object missing, however insignificant, we want you to tell us.'

Hannah's pale eyes moved away from Joanna's face. 'You expect too much from me,' she murmured.

But she did wander around the room more slowly now and as she touched the back of one of the armchairs her face suddenly went chalk white. 'This was Aaron's chair,' she said, fighting to keep her voice steady. 'He always sat here. At the end of a long evening he would rest,' her fingers were plucking the antimacassar, 'quiet like. No great talker was our Aaron.'

Her eyes dropped to a small, cane covered stool a huge cushion smothering the top. 'And this was where Jack would sit, near the fire, hugging his knees.' She gave a dry laugh. 'Fond of the fire was Jack.' She gave a long sigh.

Mike cleared his throat noisily.

Hannah took no notice but stood, swaying, in the centre of the room, her eyes half closed, as though she was dreaming the family were all still here, sitting round the fire as they must have done on numerous occasions, night after night, for years, the three of them, each in their particular seat. Joanna glanced at the small, pink armchair with a woollen, patchwork blanket draped over it. No need to ask who had sat there.

She waited for the old lady to resume her activity.

Hannah approached the black, lead grate, her

hands outstretched, as though a fire was still lit and she too glanced across at the pink chair. 'Before it was Ruthie's,' she said softly, 'it used to belong to Paulette, my sister. She sat in there. The night before she died,' she said, 'my sister was sat there.'

Then her face grew sharp as she glanced across the floor. 'A rug is missing,' she said briskly. Joanna was tempted to comfort the old woman, loop her arm around her shoulders. Maybe this was too cruel, to drag the old woman back to Hardacre, to the scene of happiness, contentment, domesticity – and then murder. 'There was a burn on the rug,' she said finally, 'we sent it for forensic analysis.'

The old lady nodded as though she understood it all, the thorough procedures of the police investigation as well as Joanna's own, personal reaction to it. 'Jack,' she said without further explanation. She sank down on the shabbier of the two chairs. 'There's nothing of them left, is there? I mean I don't believe in ghosts. But no presence at all? I can't feel them here. They've gone.'

Joanna shook her head and the old lady continued. 'Nothing – of – them – left.' She spoke the words slowly, deliberately, as though to convince herself of the truth that lay behind them.

'Miss Lockley . . .' Joanna hesitated, hating to push the old lady further but Hannah seemed to understand. 'You want me to carry on?'

'Please.' Joanna led the way towards the kitchen. 'Everywhere, Miss Lockley, in your own time.' It was a polite phrase.

So Hannah Lockley browsed through the kitchen now, muttering to herself as she opened cupboards, closing doors. Her pale eyes bored into the darkest corners, her face twitching with all the nervousness of a mouse. Eventually she stopped right in front of Joanna. 'There's nothing here, Inspector,' she said steadily. 'Whatever you thought might hold some clue, there's nothing here. All is as it was. Apart from the fact that they've whitewashed a wall in the pantry.'

Joanna's eyes swept around the room but she was forced to agree. It was simply a shabby old farmhouse. There was no clue to the tragedy that had so recently taken place. Nothing.

She held her hand out. 'Upstairs?'

Obediently Hannah Lockley opened the door that led to the dark, narrow staircase, Mike and Joanna following closely behind. She moved quickly from room to room, deftly searching the cupboards, the drawers, beneath the beds. It was only when she entered Ruthie Summers' room that she displayed any emotion.

She sank down on the bed, overcome. And Joanna realized that out of the three close relatives who had lived here Hannah had only *really* cared for Ruthie. The murders had affected her less than the disappearance of her niece.

Hannah's hands were across her face. 'What an awful thing,' she said. 'If my poor sister had known it would all come to this.' Her pale eyes met Joanna's through her fingers. 'I'm so glad she didn't,' she said simply.

She scanned the shabby interior before speaking again. 'Where on earth can the girl be?' And her face looked even more strained, but hurt too, confused and deeply puzzled. But when she stood up a moment later she left the room without a backwards glance as though the empty bedroom represented too much pain.

The three of them rattled back down the stairs and returned to the living room, Hannah standing at the foot of the stairs, her back against the door, almost on the exact spot where Jack Summers had died. Joanna glanced around hopelessly and for the first time took careful note of the room.

Four doors led from this room. The first was the front door from where the killer had fired the two fatal shots. The second led to the staircase, the third to the kitchen. But there was a fourth door. Joanna knew it led to a tiny, cold pantry, stone-flagged floor, lined with shelves stacked with aged tins of outdated food and rows of empty jars. But still she opened the door and peered inside. The wind whistled through a few airbricks and there was a faint, musty smell of old food never quite cleaned away. In here there were signs of Ruthie's industry, jars of pickles and jams, a few pots and pans, more yellowing newspapers. And yet it was not so dusty or so dirty. Hannah Lockley was right. The back wall had been freshly whitewashed, recently. It struck her as odd that this was the only decorating that had been done in the entire farmhouse, probably in the last ten years. Maybe even longer. Possibly not even since the mistress of the house had died and her role had been filled by her six-year-old daughter, with such tragic results.

And the longer Joanna stood there and stared at the wall the more bizarre this particular piece of decorating seemed.

The back wall of the pantry?

No one had touched the other two walls. They were

marked, painted cream, showing obvious signs of damp and age. There was dust on the floor.

Brick dust, cement.

Mike was standing so close behind her she could feel his breath on her neck. And he too was staring at the wall. And she knew they were both thinking the same thought. She turned to meet his eyes, and caught his mood.

Almost in a dream she put her hand out and gently tapped the whitewashed bricks.

Hollow.

Hannah was framed in the doorway. 'This is just the . . .' Then she too was staring at the wall. 'That's funny,' she said faintly. 'That's very funny.'

But she did not share the two police officers' suspicions.

'Get her out of here,' Joanna murmured over her shoulder. 'Get *her* out and a couple of strong officers with a lump hammer *in.*'

But now Hannah must have heard – or sensed – something. She reached past Mike to pull at Joanna's arm. 'What are you doing?' There was rising panic in her voice. 'What are you doing? You won't find anything in here.' She made an attempt at a laugh. 'This is a larder. Jams, pickles.' Even she did not believe that there was nothing in there.

'I'm sorry,' Joanna said. 'But you'll have to leave now. Please. Someone will take you back to your cottage.'

The old lady stood stone still, and stared at the whited wall.

*

Ten minutes later the shelves had been cleared, the jam jars neatly stacked along the kitchen formica. Joanna grabbed the lump hammer from Police Constable David Timmis and smashed it hard against the wall, loosening the first brick. Then she used it to tap. Hollow here, dull there. Flies buzzed around the pantry as though sensing a new source of nutrient. Joanna waved her arms around her head, oppressed by the rising sense of foreboding, claustrophobia, the irritating insects.

Mike had stopped tapping and was watching her with incredulous, wide eyes. There was no need for either of them to speak.

His face was very close to hers. It was a very confined space. A few whitened bricks between them. All his strength was displayed as he swung his lump hammer and the bricks jumped. A shower of dry cement powdered both their faces. His fingers scrabbled to remove the first brick.

There was a space behind the true wall, a space created by the building of a false wall. Dust settled on both their faces, their hair, their skin, their hands. Silently Timmis handed them both a mask and they continued bashing at the wall.

Behind them they heard Hannah Lockley in the living room. 'I'm staying,' she was saying. 'I'm going nowhere. You brought me here. I've a right to . . .'

Arms swung.

The blows were delivered with all the grim determination of prize boxers in the ring. Joanna and Mike removed more bricks until there was room for her to put her hand inside and grapple with something dry and boney . . . She sucked in a long breath.

She had found Ruthie Summers.

Korpanski flashed his torch inside the gap. Wrapped in a black plastic sheet, one hand resting against her hiding place, dried skin, almost leathery parchment. A strange scent, flies. Black clouds of flies.

She left the tiny larder to gulp fresher air from the sitting room, stared out through the glass porch to the embers of the summer sun.

How could anything so horrible have happened here, in this rural heaven?

It took her a few minutes to recover her composure. She must now reassemble a second SOCO team and summon Matthew again to the farmhouse.

She sat down and waited in the sitting room, facing the sole survivor of the family. Neither said a word. Hannah sat, motionless.

She knew.

Mike stood and blocked the larder door. The heap of damaged bricks bore testament to what lay behind it.

Matthew arrived at almost the same time as Sergeant Barraclough. He looked fresh and clean in a blue laundered shirt that showed a pleasing expanse of muscular brown arm. He gave her a quizzical, twisted smile before entering the pantry.

By now the two PCs had removed enough bricks to uncover the entire plastic bag and once WPC Dawn

Critchlow had forcibly removed Hannah Lockley to the Incident caravan and Barra had taken photographs of the body in its tomb they carried it into the sitting room and laid it on the floor.

The plastic had formed a winding sheet from which one hand had escaped. It had been this which Joanna must have touched. She shuddered and watched Matthew finger the rope that had been knotted around the mummy shape. 'It looks like baling twine,' he observed quietly, before slicing through it.

'We might just get a couple of good palm prints from the plastic.' Barra spoke steadily. He was, as always, in full control.

Matthew slit open the bag and clouds of bluebottles buzzed out noisily, angry at being disturbed in their perpetuation of the species. Lazy white grubs crawled from beneath beige, parchment skin.

Whatever Ruthie Summers *had* been, a small, slim, pretty girl, *singing as she herded the cows, singing as she took aim to shoot the crows*, now she was advancing in putrefaction, an object of revulsion.

Joanna muttered a swift, silent apology. This girl had not earned her suspicion. It had not been she who had fired at her father and brother. It could not have been. She was innocent of the crime, a victim herself. She must have been dead for the entire month of her disappearance. Joanna struggled to avert her eyes from the mummy shape, but it was hard. The object repulsed yet drew the gaze. Even when she was staring across the room she was conscious of it. Mike was studiously staring out of the window and she knew his emotions were the same as hers. Only Matthew showed no revulsion, yet, only fascination as he busied himself with his work, studying the hands, the hair, the face. Joanna almost vomited. *The face.*

He must have sensed her feelings because he looked up with a trace of sympathy in his eyes.

'Never did have a strong stomach, did you, Jo?'

She shook her head, not trusting herself to speak one word.

He touched the corpse's thick, dark hair. 'I take it this will be your missing suspect?'

'Almost certainly.' She was amazed at the steadiness of her voice.

'Well, she didn't die last Tuesday morning.'

'When?'

'Round about a month ago. There are . . .' Apologetically he prodded at the heaving mass of grubs.

'So I see.'

He was touching the hands, paying particular attention to the nails. And there was a grimness in his face she had never seen before.

She felt a sudden panic. 'Matthew?'

He was calm. 'It's all right. I was a bit concerned she might have been bricked up still alive.' He was smiling now. 'But panic over. Nothing under the fingernails. What I think must have happened was the arm escaped as rigor mortis wore off.'

'Thank God,' she breathed. 'So what did she die of?'

'I hate guesswork, Jo, and there's nothing too obvious besides the state of the body, but I'd lay a bet that whoever murdered this little lady came back later to finish the job. Put it like this. Someone really had it in for this family.'

'Murder?'

'She didn't brick herself in there.'

Chapter Thirteen

Saturday, July 11th, 8 a.m.

'I don't know why post mortems are always so early in the morning. And on a Saturday too.' Joanna was grumbling as Sergeant Barraclough laced her into an attendant's gown. Barra grinned. He knew her complaints were an attempt to hide her nervousness at a post mortem. He had watched her through too many before, green faced, staring at anywhere but the body. For himself he was proud of his wooden detachment from the proceedings. He coped by concentrating on efficient collection of specimens.

They were all tense as the mortuary attendant unzipped the body bag and released a powerful scent of fly spray.

Even Matthew made a face as he began his superficial examination. 'Not a pretty sight, Jo. It's possible large portions of the brain might have been destroyed by the larvae.' His eyes moved along the corpse. 'Although the abdominal organs seem in a reasonable state surprisingly.' His green eyes were almost luminous. 'It's even possible we might have a problem determining the cause of death.'

'Meaning?'

'Well, as I said last night she didn't brick herself up in there,' Matthew commented drily. 'And considering what happened to the rest of her family I'm tempted to make a connection between the deaths. Aren't you?'

'Just wait a minute.' Joanna stopped him. All night she had not slept but had pondered this one point. '*Only* Aaron or Jack would have been in a position to build that wall. They'd hardly have stood by and watched a complete stranger breezeblock Ruthie in at the back of their larder, would they? So if Ruthie was murdered it was either her father or her brother who did it. And the other must have colluded with them in concealing her body.'

Matthew said nothing but his eyes were gleaming as he continued the preliminary examination. It was a few minutes before he spoke. 'So were they murdered as a result of Ruthie's death?'

She glanced at the scalpel poised in his hand. 'I suppose it depends what she died of.'

But already her mind was working it out. Jack had been unpredictable. Jack had been mentally deranged. He had been violent on more than one occasion. What if he had lashed out at his sister?

Matthew was still busy recording his observations. 'Large portion of the brain completely destroyed. Cranium undamaged and complete.' He gave Joanna a meaningful glance. 'That knocks off my favourite cause of violent death, a head injury.' His hands moved deftly through the soft tissue. 'In fact I'm not too optimistic I will be able to ascertain a cause of death.'

'Just do your best,' Joanna muttered from the far end. Over the years she thought she had grown used to the precise nature of Matthew's work, of the butcher's shop scene of a corpse laid open to yield its secrets. No one knew better than she that it could be disgusting, horrible, gory. As a police officer she had a healthy regard for the truths that could be exposed when he wielded his scalpel. But this degradation of life was today particularly disgusting to her because of the idealized picture she had held of the farmer's daughter, a young woman who collected eggs from the henhouse, someone who sang as she led the cows into the parlour for milking, someone who had cared for her brother. But the image had been cruelly shattered. So she stood at the far end of the mortuary, beneath the air exchange while Matthew delved in Ruth Summers' abdomen, handling organs.

'They're in good condition,' he was muttering. 'Surprisingly so, considering. But then . . .' He was muttering to himself. 'I suppose the warm air whistling through the air brick must have dried the body. Mummified it to some extent.' He used his shoulder to scratch an ear, push his hair away from his face. His gloved hands were never used – sacred objects – smeared with death and decay. He was working methodically, according to the text book, using classic post-mortem techniques, a rigid set of manoeuvres learnt over the years with a few deft procedures of his own, silently slicing through tissue with his scalpel.

And all Joanna could think of, at the far end, feeling the fresh, clean air blow across her face, was this vision she had clung to, the girl, pretty, slim, dark and small, singing as she herded the cows in for their milking. *That* girl and this object could *not* be one and the same person.

Matthew was getting more excited. 'This,' he was saying, 'is really interesting. I can't believe it.'

Reluctantly she watched him finger something. 'The deeper pelvic organs are really in quite good nick.'

Suddenly he gave an exclamation and bent forwards. The police recognized the signs and moved closer with him. They forgot their repugnance at the procedure in their eagerness to know something. At last he looked up. 'Did you know your girl was pregnant?'

She nodded. 'But people don't die of . . .'

Matthew was holding up a small, tomato object, held between two sets of forceps. 'They do if it lodges inside their fallopian tubes. Your girl,' he said triumphantly, 'died of natural causes.'

'Natural causes?' She stared at the piece of tissue held between the pincer grip of the forceps.

'Natural causes? You're sure?'

'I'm sure all right. I've done a few too many corpses in this state to miss this particular diagnosis. She died of a ruptured ectopic pregnancy and I'm prepared to stand up in court and swear that under oath. There is absolutely no sign of trauma. She would have died suddenly and in great pain but no one murdered her.' He gave one of his twisted smiles. 'Unless you want to count the foetus.'

Joanna couldn't help staring at the cherry tomato object and shook her head thoughtfully. 'Or the man who made her pregnant,' she said.

Barraclough turned to object. 'But the murders?'

Matthew shrugged and dropped the object into a formalin pot while she was left floundering with the medical facts and the circumstances that had led to their discovery of the girl's body. She knew she must delve a little deeper. 'Matthew, please, in words of one syllable or less, explain so we understand exactly what happened. What was the sequence of events?' And because her head was reeling with the terrible fact that Ruthie's corpse had been bricked up and no one had confessed that she was dead, somehow the rest of her family had been slaughtered. Why? What could possibly be the reason, the connection?

Like a flash it burst through her brain.

It had to be revenge.

'OK. I'll explain.' For a moment Matthew turned his back on the body to address the police officers. 'Ruth Summers became pregnant. But instead of the little embryo lodging against the wall of her womb it got stuck in the fallopian tubes. What happens then is that the embryo grows so big . . .' His fingers moved towards the ball of tissue, no bigger than a golf ball. 'The poor girl gets ill with abdominal cramps which get steadily worse until she goes to a doctor who with a bit of luck makes the correct diagnosis and pops her into hospital where they excise both tube and baby.'

'Only in this case she didn't,' Joanna inserted drily.

Matthew misunderstood her. 'Oh I don't think many doctors would miss this diagnosis,' he said. 'It's real medical student stuff.'

Joanna shook her head. 'Ruthie Summers never visited her doctor about this pregnancy. She merely sent a urine sample off which came back as positive. He knew she was pregnant but she didn't consult him.'

Matthew's answer was a deep sigh. 'I see.'

There was a small three-legged stool in the corner of the mortuary. In her early days Joanna had spent many post mortems sitting on this stool, her head firmly rammed between her knees, the mortuary attendant keeping a watchful eye on her. She sank down on it now.

'Are you all right, Jo?' Matthew glanced across.

She nodded. She had sat here today *not* because she was feeling faint but because she badly needed to think.

Ruthie may have died of natural causes but Joanna still had a double murder to solve. No one would call shotgun blasts to the chest natural causes and now she had lost her chief suspect the field lay wide open except that Ruthie's death must be a pointer like a spinning bottle towards her father and brother's killer.

And yet part of her felt nothing but relief that Ruthie was innocent so she repeated the phrase to herself.

'Not Ruthie.'

But if not Ruthie, who? If the murders were nothing to do with Ruthie then who?

And slowly the facts began to untangle themselves. Ruthie Summers' child had a father. What if he had wondered where she was? What if he had come to Hardacre to challenge her father and brother? What if he had grown suspicious at the evasive response and believed they were keeping her from him. Then what if he had jumped to the same conclusion that she initially had?

That Ruthie had quarrelled with her brother. Her brother had struck her, killing her. What if he then had killed Aaron and Jack through frustration or revenge?

Early on Tuesday morning at around six o'clock he had called one last time at Hardacre Farm in search for Ruthie. Maybe they had told him the truth, or part of it, that she was dead. Perhaps Aaron had even confided his suspicion to him. Perhaps the gun had initially been meant to force them to reveal her whereabouts and when they had told him what they had understood to be the truth – that Ruthie had died from natural causes – he had not believed them. So he had fired. Only without the benefit of Matthew's skill they had all been wrong. Ruthie had not been murdered. She had died of natural causes. But neither Aaron nor Jack could have known that or they would not have hidden her. Probably Aaron had suspected Jack of a crime while Jack had merely failed to understand – anything. Again the vision of the poor, bemused face, staring down at the bloodstained hands swam through Joanna's mind.

So she watched Matthew drop the samples into the formalin pots with an awful feeling of waste. It had all been so unnecessary. Two murders through a misconception. Literally. And now to trap the killer she knew there was something else she must ask.

It was connected with Ruthie's child. Or more precisely, with Ruthie's child's father.

'Matthew,' she began.

He looked up, fine tweezers held in his hand like a pen. 'Yes?'

'The uummm.'

He smiled, his face warm, open, friendly. Her heart did a quick flip.

Her eyes moved from his face to the tomato-like object in the formalin pot. 'The baby is in there?'

He nodded. 'Well – an embryo. Not really a baby.' It was medical pedantry.

'Could a test give us the paternity of the child?'

'DNA profiling, you mean?'

She nodded, hardly daring to hope. This one break, this one, vital answer would surely tell them everything.

'Yes, in a couple of weeks.'

She breathed.

But as usual Matthew had a proviso. 'As long as we have a sample from the father to compare it with. Preferably blood.'

Her glance travelled along the floor towards the ante room where the fridges were. And as usual Matthew read her thoughts.

'Yes we do have blood samples from both the deceased. But.'

'Let's start with the family,' she said baldly, concealing her anxiety. That Ruthie's baby was the result of incest? It was a possibility that could not be ignored. 'Thanks,' she said.

Their job done the SOCO team were dispersing already, leaving her alone with Matthew.

'How are you enjoying your break with Eloise?' she asked diffidently.

He turned, his eyes narrowing as he read her thoughts. He knew just how much she longed to be rid of the girl. 'Very much.'

She gave a curt nod and excused herself to drive back to the Incident Room.

'The question is, Mike, where do we start?'

10.30 a.m.

The assembled team showed their shock plainly when she gave them the results of the post mortem. She watched the puzzlement creep across their faces.

'I trust you'll realize this does, in some ways, make

our job a little easier. We do know more. We know that Ruthie Summers was already dead at the time of the shootings. So she's off our suspect list. And she was not a murder victim as were the rest of her family.' She smiled.

'Excuse me, ma'am.' DC Alan King had been seconded from Birmingham, a bright, shrewd officer with wiry, brown hair and an optimistic nature. Joanna would like to keep him here, in Leek, permanently. 'What's the connection?'

'We don't know. We don't even know there is one. But three sudden deaths in one family in a couple of months. Korpanski and I don't believe in coincidence. So let's think about it.' She perched herself on a chair and the waiting officers relaxed. 'What about this? Ruthie Summers finds herself pregnant. She tells her lover. And then she disappears. Lover comes sniffing around the farm. No sign of his darling. Asks brother, or father, who deny any knowledge. Lover comes back, threatens them. They still deny all knowledge. Lover shoots.'

The officers were all staring at her. 'Well at least it gives us a motive,' she said savagely. 'And it connects what we already know. It fits the facts.'

Strangely enough it was Mike who, frowning, spoke first. 'Revenge? You think the killings were done as revenge for the suspected murder of Ruthie Summers?'

She kept her eyes trained steadily on him as she nodded.

Timmis' slow, Moorlands voice piped up from the back. 'Why did they wall her up?'

For this she had no *logical* answer. 'We may never know.' She glanced helplessly at Mike. 'I can only surmise that her brother alone was present when she died and that the father assumed he had killed her. Otherwise the only reason I can think of was that just maybe they knew she was pregnant and felt some social stigma.'

But she knew this was wrong. Two rough farmers would not have recognized a six to eight week pregnancy. Would Ruthie have told them?

Something else was tugging at her memory.

Hannah Lockley had told her, Aaron Summers had had a fear of hospitals, blaming them for much of his suffering. So what if Aaron had felt guilt because his daughter had been in obvious pain and he had dissuaded her from seeking medical help. Was it possible that his guilt might have led to the concealment of his daughter's body? Or was the dark hint of incest the true reason why it had been necessary for Ruthie's pregnancy to be concealed? She visualized Aaron's emaciated corpse and Jack's stolid face and mentally shook her head. That was not the answer.

She turned back to face the officers. 'So let's run through the list of Ruthie's potential lovers.' On the blackboard she boldly wrote four names.

Dave Shackleton
Titus Mothershaw
Neil Rowan
Lewis Stone.

'You don't need me to tell you that Dave Shackleton is the tanker driver, a long-standing friend of the family. He admits he fancied Ruthie although he denies having a relationship with her. It was he who

233

found the bodies.' She paused, reading the name through twice before adding her own thoughts. 'I suppose one of the things that points in his favour is that both Aaron and Jack were familiar enough with him to invite him into their home without worrying. Also he would have known that the gun habitually stood in the front porch and had the opportunity to load it.'

She turned back to the board and read out the second name reluctantly.

'Titus Mothershaw is a sculptor who rented property from the Summers. We have no evidence of his ever having had a relationship with Ruthie although he admits they were friends. And he quite openly says he handled the shotgun.'

Again there was something there. Something she was not quite comfortable with. It was connected with the Tree Man statue, the malevolence hidden in Jack Summers' face. It was a pointer to the murders but like a blank signpost Joanna could not read where it was directing her.

Mothershaw had seen something in the Summers family that *she* had missed. The point was would he share it with her if she asked? Somehow she doubted it. It was something he felt he had to conceal. Why? It was possible that he was not even consciously aware of it himself. But Joanna knew it was something he had picked up from one of them. Perhaps his artist's instincts made him susceptible to hidden character. Or maybe as he had carved Jack's face he had seen something. What? She sighed, became aware of the watching faces and moved on.

'Neil Rowan owns a neighbouring farm where

Ruthie Summers cleaned. He must have been one of the few men she had much contact with.' She recalled Arabella Rowan's words accusing her husband.

'*Philanderer.*'

Arabella Rowan knew her husband well. She suspected him of 'trying it on with her.' But she had continued to be fond of Ruthie. There had been no mistaking her genuine concern at the girl's disappearance. And while Arabella had no reason to shoot the father and brother of the missing girl Joanna couldn't imagine Neil Rowan really caring either way. He had been a philanderer. Not really blessed or cursed with deep emotion. Again there was no motive. Yet although mentally she discounted Neil Rowan she did not rub his name from the board but shared her and Mike's thoughts with the rest of the team. 'We've a suspicion that he might have made a pass at the dead girl and . . .' It was lame and she sensed her colleagues were as anxious as she to move on.

'Lewis Stone?' Timmis squinted up at the name.

'He's a man who walked his dog past the farm on numerous occasions, the missing rambler.'

'He *said* he was there around Hardacre at seven o'clock on the morning of the murders. But Dave Shackleton claims he saw his dog there at ten. I know . . . conflicting statements unless of course either Stone took two walks or went for one very long one. But his statement poses one very large problem. Namely, if Lewis Stone was in the vicinity of the murders between seven and seven thirty on the morning of the killings how is it he claims to have heard Aaron Summers whistling for the cows? How come he says he *didn't* hear a shot? Doctor Levin's forensic evidence is quite clear. Aaron was dead before seven a.m. Therefore Stone must be lying. But why when he clearly tells us he was in the vicinity of the farmhouse at precisely the time of the shootings?' She ran her fingers through her hair and grimaced. 'It doesn't make sense. But it will – in the end.' Something of her iron character asserted itself. 'It will have to.'

Her speech sent a ripple around the room. Faces relaxed, smiles broadened. And as they filed past her one or two grinned.

She wished she shared their confidence.

She kept Timmis and McBrine back. She had a job for them to do.

'I want you to visit the Saturday market and take statements from the people who usually bought eggs from Ruthie Summers.'

It was with a feeling of relief that she had at last understood the full significance of the eggs lying around, trodden into the floor of the henhouse.

This was not a wealthy family but a family who had to realize every tiny source of income. Eggs were precious. They were both food and money. Ruthie had not been around to gather the eggs and sell them at market because *she had already been dead*. And Aaron and Jack had been too distressed to think about something that would have been Ruthie's work, gathering eggs.

So the messy henhouse had been a symbol of neglect and distraction, a tangible sign that Ruthie had not been working for a month *before* the shootings. She had already been dead, her body concealed from prying eyes. She forced her mind away from the emotional factors back to the more practical ones. 'And

I suppose you might even look into an order of breeze block and cement made around a month ago although it's possible they were just lying around the farm anyway.' Timmis nodded.

Joanna gave them both an encouraging smile. 'I'm sort of hoping you'll be able to pin down the exact date when Ruthie was last seen. We know it was sometime in the middle of June but it would be helpful if we knew precisely.'

'Couldn't Doctor Levin work it out?'

She had to remind herself, Timmis had not seen Ruthie's corpse. If he had he would have known anything exact could not be extracted from this decay. Therefore . . . 'Not exactly. He thinks about a month but it could be up to a couple of weeks either way. The weather's been hot, the conditions very dry in there. There was . . .' She drew in a deep breath to combat the nausea, 'decomposition.'

Again that sickening vision, the desiccated, dry-bone hand touching hers. She shuddered.

'What about Pinkers?' Mike reminded her. 'Is he out of the picture?'

She shook her head. 'Not really but I can't see where he fits in. It's not possible that he was the father of Ruthie's child.'

Mike narrowed his eyes. 'Unless he raped her,' he said baldly. 'And he does have two sons. Joanna,' he said, troubled, 'shouldn't we be throwing our nets a bit wider?'

She had the awful feeling he might be right. 'Where exactly?'

'I don't know. I just hope we're not cutting anybody out who might have . . .'

'Mike,' she exploded. 'For what motive? Why would anybody else have shot those two farmers? Nothing was taken and I think we're both agreed that homicidal maniacs live more in the pages of novels than in newspapers. And if we aren't too fond of coincidence do you think it probable that a homicidal maniac blasted two rural farmers barely a month after they'd bricked up the only female member of the family? The murders *have* to be connected with Ruthie's death. Therefore surely the obvious prime suspect has to be Ruthie's lover. I admit it is possible she was raped but I don't think so. And the killer is someone from their immediate circle. He *knew* that gun was there. And he *knew* it was loaded because he'd put the shotgun pellets in sometime before he stopped Aaron from fetching the cows in for milking and shot him before turning the barrel on Jack. Someone did that. Someone with more than just hatred in their heart. They must have had a reason. This was not opportunistic killing but planned murder.'

'But the evidence of the wellington? One on, one off.'

'The *evidence* of Lewis Stone. He *heard* Aaron or someone whistling for the cows and it must have been that that made them force the gate open. Dead men don't whistle, Mike. And who would want to fetch the cows in but the farmer?'

'You're relying too much on Stone's statement.'

'Because there would be no point in his lying.'

'If he's to be trusted.'

'Who is,' she said, despairing. 'Who is?'

Mike clapped his hand on her shoulder. 'Nobody except me,' he said, half jovially. 'And at least I'm here all the time.' She smiled. But behind his words there was more than a grain of truth. Matthew was occupied with Eloise and this was a case requiring plenty of work. She needed someone.

'Look, Mike,' she said finally. 'If you're so suspicious of Stone let's start by going to talk to him.'

11.45 a.m.

But luck was not with her. As she stepped outside the Incident caravan Colclough's car pulled up, raising a cloud of pale dust.

She spent almost half an hour trying to explain how they had overlooked Ruthie Summers' body for almost a week and secondly why there was not even the *likelihood* of an early arrest. There was no one even in the frame.

His bulldog face looked fierce. 'Surely you must have some idea, Piercy,' he said tetchily.

'No, sir.' It was always best to come clean when Colclough was asking his awkward questions.

His eyebrows met in the middle when he was very angry – or worried. And yet she knew he had deemed it an insignificant case. So why the change of heart? In a flash she knew what had made the difference. In headlines, in capital letters.

MISSING GIRL FOUND WALLED
UP IN MURDER FARMHOUSE

And she felt enormous sympathy for Colclough trying vainly to protect the reputation of the Staffordshire Police. On the other hand there was no point deluding her boss only to be forced to come clean in a day or two when the Interview Rooms and the cells were still vacant. She offered him a small sop. 'We need to do some more investigations, sir.'

'What's your reasoning so far?'

Swiftly she outlined the theory of the earlier briefing. 'Ruthie was pregnant. Someone, probably the boyfriend, had been wondering what had happened to her.' She put in the theory that Aaron and Jack couldn't have known that Ruthie had died from natural causes and this must have been why they had concealed her body. 'I think this lover must have challenged Aaron and Jack. Maybe they told him she *was* dead. Maybe not. Whatever they did say it didn't impress the father of Ruthie's child. He came back to let fly with a couple of shotgun pellets.'

Colclough leant forward heavily, on his elbows, his eyes dark and questioning. 'Let me get this straight,' he said. 'Did you say Doctor Levin took a sample from this . . .'

She knew exactly what he meant. 'Foetus, sir. Ruthie's unborn baby.'

'And that DNA profiling could give us the name of the father?'

'If we collect blood samples from the suspects and provided he is one of them.' She was almost tempted to smile. Surely their list had encompassed all Ruthie's potential lovers. Surely?

'Right.' Colclough was smiling. Fist slammed palm. 'We've got him then.'

'Yes, sir.'

Colclough had small, intelligent eyes. Sometimes blue, sometimes grey. Sometimes dark, sometimes pale. Now they were lightening. 'So it's in the bag then, Piercy?' He paused. 'Why aren't you jumping up and down?'

With typical Colclough perception he had put his finger right on it. 'Because,' she said, 'it all seems a little too obvious.'

Colclough regarded her for a few moments before speaking again. 'Never reject the obvious,' he barked. 'This isn't ruddy fiction.' Then he leant far back in *her* chair. 'I hear your place is coming on the market.'

She nodded.

His eyes were cool grey now. 'Be careful, Piercy,' he warned. 'Keep your personal life clean.' His next question was a bolt from the blue. 'Planning on getting married, are you?'

She shook her head. 'No, sir.'

He stood up then, a well-known sign for dismissal. '*Your* future, Piercy,' he said. '*Your* future.'

Mike's eyes were on her as she walked back outside into the blazing sunshine. He waited until they were out of Colclough's earshot before speaking. 'I can't stand a long face.'

She climbed into the car, slammed the door and waited for him to skirt round the other side.

'I'm coming to the conclusion,' she said sulkily, 'that the police force is prudish, old-fashioned and anachronistic.'

'Hmm.'

'And thank you for your support, Korpanski.'

He was mystified. 'Support for what?'

'Nothing.'

She was silent for a moment. The car was stifling, even with the windows open. She closed her eyes and forced herself to ignore the heat.

'What do you most want to know about the case, Mike?'

'Who pulled the bloody trigger, of course.'

Her eyes were still closed. 'For my money,' she said dreamily, 'I would prefer to know who was the father of Ruthie's baby.' Even without opening her eyes she knew Mike was wondering whether the heat had touched her brain.

She smiled.

Chapter Fourteen

1.30 p.m.

Lewis Stone looked surprised to see them a second time.

'I didn't think you'd be back.' His hand tightened on the Alsatian's choke chain. 'I've told you everything I know. I can't help you. Sorry.'

'Can we go over your story again?' Joanna asked pleasantly.

'What?' Stone was wary.

'The events of Tuesday morning. Please.'

He was even more on his guard, his head nervously bouncing from Joanna to Korpanski – and back to Joanna again. 'Hoping I'll *slip up*, are you?'

'One or two facts just don't add up.' Joanna's foot was on the bottom step.

Immediately Stone knew what the problem was. 'I wasn't wearing a watch,' he said. 'I can't be exact on times.'

'No but you must have a vague idea. I mean – even someone not wearing a watch would know the difference between say seven o'clock in the morning and ten o'clock.'

Stone stared at her. 'You what?'

'You said you were at Hardacre at around seven a.m.,' Joanna said.

'Yeah. That's right.' Stone glanced nervously along the alleyway. 'You might as well come up.'

Joanna waited until they were all settled in Stone's clean little flat before continuing with the questions. 'You *said* you heard the farmer whistle the cows in.'

Stone nodded, his face visibly nervous now. He licked his lips. 'That's right.'

'The pathologist says Aaron and Jack were already dead by then.'

'He must be wrong. He *has* to be. I *heard* him. It's an unmistakable whistle. The cows knew it too. They were restless. He can't have been dead.'

'He was.' Mike dropped the words into the room like a couple of bricks.

Stone swivelled his head around to stare at him. 'Then who the hell was it whistling that morning?'

The three of them stared at one another. None of them could answer the question.

'There's another problem,' Joanna continued. 'Dave Shackleton saw your dog at ten o'clock, outside Hardacre.'

Stone's head jerked back to her. Immediately Stone relaxed. 'I was with him,' he said. 'We were just coming back from our walk.'

'A three hour walk?' Mike asked incredulously.

Stone grinned, shrugged and nodded.

'Nathan's a big, energetic animal,' he said. 'Causes trouble if he doesn't get plenty of energy walked off.'

As though in answer they heard a deep growl at the foot of the steps.

'OK,' Joanna said. 'So what else did you see?'

'Just the usual. Pinkers bringing the cows in.'

'At what time?'

'As I passed. Seven-ish.'

Joanna gave Mike a swift glance. 'You're sure about that?'

Stone nodded, surprised. 'I saw him quite clearly, as I came across the field. It takes a good five or ten minutes even walking fast. I got to the stile by Hardacre and heard old Summers whistling to the cows.'

Mike interrupted. 'Did you *see* either Aaron or Jack?'

Stone thought for a moment before shaking his head. 'No,' he said firmly. 'I didn't.' He grinned. 'But then Nathan was barking fit to wake the dead.'

Joanna stiffened. *Fit to wake the dead? But Aaron had not been dead. He had been alive and whistling. He must have been, whatever Matthew said. But in her heart she acknowledged the truth. Science was precise. And Matthew was not wrong.*

Stone had not noticed the lapse of concentration but continued. 'The cows were rattling against the gate. Then I thought I heard them come out. So I hurried on. See Nathan and cows don't mix. He chases them.' He paused for a brief moment before adding, 'It's led to problems with one or two of the local farmers.'

'The Summers?'

'Them and others.'

Joanna was frankly puzzled. Stone *seemed* honest. And there seemed no point in his version of events unless they were the truth. There was no reason for him to alter his story and yet it didn't hang together. But the truth remained. The cows had *not been* let out. They had pushed against the gate until the hasp had broken.

'And are you sure you didn't hear a shot?'

245

'No.' Stone shook his head, his bright eyes looking fearlessly into hers. 'I didn't hear any shooting. Nothing.'

And Joanna believed him.

But a shot is a noisy thing, reverberating through the countryside. Even if Stone had walked a further mile he would *still* have heard the shot. So Stone's story *couldn't* possibly be the truth or both Aaron and Jack must still have been alive at eight o'clock. Possibly even eight thirty. And Matthew had stated categorically that both had been dead at around six a.m.

So Stone must be lying.

She barely managed to keep the suspicion out of her voice as she asked her next question.

'Then what?'

'I carried on up the lane.'

'Towards the wood?'

'No,' he said. 'Past the end, towards the cottage. I don't walk through the wood. I never do. Too spooky by half. Especially when it's getting dark. Those statues, creepy. If you ask me the man's touched. And that great big thing in the middle. Shouldn't be allowed. I don't blame Jack Summers for putting a match to it.'

'You knew about that?'

'It was me shouted the alarm,' Stone said. 'Luckily I saw the light from the lane. Bloody Jack. Standing there with such a blank look on that great big, stupid face of his.' His face changed and it was at that precise moment that Joanna realized Lewis Stone had disliked Jack Summers. No, she thought hastily. Not disliked. So what was the word?

Despised?

Why? Because he was brain damaged?

Stone must have sensed her curiosity because he gave Joanna a shrewd glance of appraisal.

'I don't suppose you ever knew Jack alive, did you?'

She shook her head.

'Stupid he was,' Stone said. 'Not a glimmer of sense. As stupid as an ox.' There was a note of irritation in his voice. He gave a short exclamation. 'Half the time I'd wonder if the cows had more intelligence than he did. Anyway – we digress.' He spluttered a swift giggle. 'As the actress said to the bishop.'

'I hadn't realized you knew the family so intimately, Mr Stone.'

Immediately Stone looked wary. 'Now look here, Inspector.'

'So how well *did* you know the family?'

'I only knew Jack. He was fond of dogs. Especially Alsatians. Sometimes he'd tag along on my walk. Just for companionship, you understand.' Stone's face looked older, bleaker. 'I'll miss the stupid old blighter,' he said, 'for all he was thick.'

Some vague shadow flashed across his face and Joanna was forced to change her mind. She had been wrong about the relationship between Stone and Jack Summers. Stone had held some affection for the boy. So perhaps it had been the rest of the family he had had no time for.

Yet it had been Jack as well as Aaron who had been murdered.

She tucked the conundrum away for a later time. There would be an answer. She was sure.

Eventually she would have *all* the answers.

'So then what?'

'I carried on past the old lady's cottage and across

the moors towards Longnor. It's a good walk. A fair few miles. But I go most days.'

'With Nathan?'

Mike spoke for the first time. 'Haven't you got a job, Mr Stone?'

Stone's gaze swept over Mike's face with a touch of wry humour. 'Unemployed,' he said. 'You want to try it, Sergeant. It gives you time. Time to do everything. Time to enjoy things. Time to do things slowly. Because all you really got to do is keep yourself clean and tidy and fed and sign on once a week. Not bad, eh?'

Mike frowned and said nothing.

It gave Joanna the chance to ask her question. 'How well did you know Jack's father and sister?'

'Not that well.'

'But you didn't like them?'

Stone looked wary. 'I didn't *say* that.'

Joanna waited.

And Stone answered, eventually.

'Madam Ruthie,' he said, 'thought she was a cut above me. Never spoke, disapproved of Jack coming with me on my walks. And I was the only friend he had, outside the family.'

Again some of the claustrophobia of the father, son and daughter reached Joanna. Had their close relationship been to the exclusion of other friends then? And had this feeling of isolation extended to the exclusion of *all* other relationships?

She looked enquiringly at Lewis Stone.

He flushed. 'I don't like being looked down on, Inspector. I mean who was she? Just a farmer's daughter.'

For the first time Joanna felt a creeping dislike for Lewis Stone and his peculiar brand of snobbery.

'And Jack's father?'

Stone took in a sharp breath. 'Used him. The pair of them treated Jack like a work horse. Always lifting bales or cleaning the sheds out, fetching and carrying. He never stopped, did old Jack. Always working. All day. And half the night too. And as for having a few hours off. Put it like this. They didn't like it. Always found some excuse why he couldn't come. Something to do.'

Joanna was silent. So. Had things been slightly different from the rural image she had enjoyed picturing? Had Ruthie, in fact, been a snob? And Aaron a hard taskmaster? Had Jack Summers been more of a slave than a family member? Had his lack of mental agility made him the target of their disdain?

She studied Stone carefully. He seemed jaunty enough, confident and comfortable. But if he was totally innocent why hadn't he come forward as soon as the murders had reached the local radio and newspapers? Why had he held back?

Some cynical instinct led her to ask the next question. 'Have you ever been in trouble with the law, Mr Stone?'

His attitude altered subtly. 'I'd have thought you'd have done your homework by now, Inspector.'

'Save me the trouble.'

His head jerked back. 'Bound over to keep the peace,' he snarled. 'Soliciting. I'm gay. In the past I've been short of a boyfriend. All right with you?'

Mike answered for her. 'Short of a boyfriend, were you? So you took Jack Summers on long walks.'

Stone jabbed his forefinger towards him. 'Don't you start accusing me . . .'

'But you've already told us,' Joanna said innocently. 'You and Jack went for long walks together.'

Stone plopped his mouth closed and Joanna made a mental note to ask Matthew one or two relevant questions.

Already her mind was working furiously. What if . . .?

What if Jack had been 'seduced' by Stone. And what if Aaron had found out, objected. And Stone had blasted the pair of them.

Joanna shook her head before the thoughts were even halfway complete.

Where could Ruthie have fitted into all this? Unless Stone was bisexual.

She eyed Stone dubiously and decided not even to ask him.

Instead she asked him very nicely if he would be prepared to submit to a blood test before warning him about Jack. 'The law is,' she said, 'intercourse between consenting adults. You might have a bit of trouble proving consent.'

Stone merely smiled complacently and said, 'Why don't you get stuffed.'

They clattered back down the steps, accompanied by Nathan's menacing growls. As they reached the bottom he lunged at them, in a frenzy. But the chain was too short and they passed through without harm.

Joanna waited until they were back in the car before speaking her mind. 'I can't understand his game,' she said. 'He lies, he doesn't lie. His lies are all perfectly pointless and yet they make sense. I can't think of a single logical reason why he should have murdered the two Summers and yet I can imagine him doing it. And if he's been "taking advantage" of poor old Jack where on earth does Ruthie's death fit in? The whole thing is just so . . . annoying.'

Mike grinned at her. 'I know,' he said. 'But then that's the fun of the job, isn't it, Jo?'

She shook her head. 'The real fun of the job is getting an ice cold beer in a pub where the gardens are green and the drinks cold. And I'm buying,' she said.

3 p.m.

There were two messages waiting for her back at the Incident caravan. The first was from the estate agents telling her they needed access to her cottage to measure up ready for printing the details. She shoved it right to the bottom of a sheaf of papers. She could deal with it later.

Not now.

The second was from WPC Dawn Critchlow to say that Matthew had been trying to get in touch with her all day and would she please ring the hospital. She picked up the telephone and dialled his number.

She got her questions about Jack Summers in first and in his customary fashion his answers were guarded. 'I didn't specifically look for evidence of pen-etrative sex,' he said slowly. 'But there was nothing very obvious.' He paused and Joanna visualized him stroking his mouth, frowning, thinking, thinking. 'The best thing to do, Jo, is for me to wheel him out again

251

and make absolutely sure. If it might have a bearing on the case it's pretty vital.'

'Thanks.' She too hesitated before asking him her other question.

'Matthew,' she said tentatively, 'are you certain about the time of death?'

'Six-ish,' he said.

'What if someone said they had been in the vicinity at seven to seven thirty and they'd heard Aaron Summers whistling the cows in?'

Matthew responded swiftly and with certainty. 'I'd say they were mistaken or lying.'

'And if there seemed no reason for them to lie?'

'I'd say that there *was* a reason but that I simply hadn't discovered it.'

It was a categorical answer.

Now it was Joanna's turn to wipe her mouth with her hand, to frown and be silent.

Then Matthew spoke. 'Jo.'

She waited.

'I'm sorry.' It was a large slab of humble pie. 'I was a bit hard on you earlier. I do so want it all to work well. The trouble is if Eloise is unhappy I feel so bloody guilty.'

'You think she doesn't know that, Matthew. She's manipulating your feelings. She's taking advantage of you.'

'Please, Jo. Enough.'

She *almost* felt sorry for him. He invited her for dinner. 'I'll cook,' he urged.

She declined, using the murder investigation as an excuse.

'Please,' Matthew tried again. 'Spend a bit of time getting to know Eloise. Talk to her.'

'Well maybe I would if she stopped trying to alienate me. Look.' She did take pity on him then. 'I really am up to my ears in this case. I can't keep clocking off for dinners and things. Let me concentrate on the investigation. Then we can relax – together.'

The trouble was that Matthew could read her mind perfectly. 'But Eloise will have gone home by then.'

And she felt too ashamed to express her true feelings.

At last Matthew put the phone down just as Mike walked in balancing two glasses of iced lemonade. 'I had an idea.'

She waited.

'I was thinking about Stone,' he said, settling down into the chair. 'Maybe we should take a peep into his past record before we write him off.'

'I wasn't going to write him off,' she said. 'Anyway. What line are you taking?'

'*Why* doesn't he work?'

Joanna held her hands out, palms uppermost. 'I don't know,' she said. 'Maybe he's got a bad back or something.'

'Walking all that distance every day? He didn't look like someone with back trouble to me.'

She watched him thoughtfully. 'OK then,' she said eventually. 'Let's have a look at the computer.'

It only took a few minutes.

Like his story of Tuesday morning Stone had told them half truths. Selective bits, leaving out the worst, the really unsavoury parts. He had been done more than once for soliciting. Unfortunately he had

propositioned an off duty policeman who was straight.
But he had a habit of befriending youngsters with
emotional problems. There had been a girl with
Downs. Aged twenty-four. Mental age six. There had
been a boy with brain damage so severe his mental age
had been described as being less than three. Physical
age thirty. Stone had made a friend of him too. Three
years ago he had been noticed loitering outside a
'Special school' for children with severe learning dif-
ficulties and been reported to the police who had
cautioned him.

Then for two years, Nothing.

Nothing.

The telephone startled her. Mike grabbed it, handed
it straight to her with one word. 'Levin,' he said.

'No evidence of penetrative sex,' Matthew said
without emotion. 'So whatever your suspicions I don't
think anyone was having sex with Jack.'

She took a deep breath. 'Thanks,' she said.

She put the receiver down thoughtfully and
glanced at Mike. 'Well,' she said. 'It looks as though the
relationship between Stone and Jack was innocent.'

Mike's answer was a short grunt.

'So we have yet another blind alley.'

He was leaning over her, his hand resting on her
shoulder, his face turned towards the computer screen.
But he had dropped his eyes to her dark, unruly hair
and every breath he took was filled with a light, lemony
fragrance. Not for the first time he reflected how difficult it could be, working with a woman.

She jerked away from him. 'So, Mike,' she said,
'what about Ruthie?'

'Her death could have been coincidence. Besides. I

know the police don't exactly figure high in the Master-mind competitions but even Stone must have known there was a sporting chance we'd find out who'd done the shootings. Why say he was there at all? Why persist with the story that he heard Aaron whistling when *we* keep saying he was dead by then?'

'Maybe the shootings were done in temper, on the spur of the moment and he's insisting Aaron was fetching the cows at seven just to confuse us. Having once told the story he can't change it, can he?'

Chapter Fifteen

6 p.m.

Holiday makers had just arrived at the Rowans' farm. A black Volvo piled high with a Labrador and countless children. Suitcases and boxes of food were being unloaded as the police car pulled up.

Arabella Rowan met them, frowning. 'Saturday is a busy day for us,' she said, obviously irritated. 'I don't know why you've come back at all. These murders are nothing to do with us. I hardly knew the Summers family. Ruthie simply did the cleaning here.'

Joanna glanced around her, at the wide sweep of the valley, tiny squares of fields bordered by grey drystone walls, the fields speckled with cattle. Maybe it was the extending murder investigation but the entire scene seemed a little less perfect today, a little more flawed. A little more deceitful. Nothing was as it seemed. This idyllic holiday destination. She watched the excited children exclaiming at the farm tabby cat and wondered. Would they pack up the Volvo and leave if they knew the true story behind this pretty scene? Or was it her? Had she started to examine the characters of the people in the scene too critically to be distracted by the pretty landscape. Was it she who saw evil at every turn? Evil which did not really exist? Don't be silly, she admonished herself crossly. Of course there is evil. Two people have been murdered.

She turned back to Arabella Rowan and gave the farmer's wife her full attention without prejudice.

This evening Arabella looked hassled and hot. Her lemon shirt was crumpled and there were damp patches beneath the arms. Her face shone with sweat and the imperfections made her appear less in control than previously. It could have been the arrival of another boisterous family. Bikes were being taken off the roof-rack and propped up against Magpie Cottage. There was a lot of noise. The Labrador had noticed the attention being paid to the cat and was barking frantically, trying to distract the children from their new plaything. But the cat was unperturbed, licking its lips and yawning, its tail flicking lazily.

Joanna took in other things about Arabella Rowan, her blonde hair, flattened and untidy, her hands reddened as though by hard scrubbing around the cottages. She must be missing her cleaner and on closer inspection she looked strained, her eyes reddened and puffy.

So what else was wrong?

Was it just that in this tightly knit community three sudden deaths were enough to make all the neighbours reel? Or had Arabella Rowan something to conceal? Was the furtive darting of the eyes concern for her guests or was it guilt? On her behalf or her husband's?

It had been widely reported in both the local and national press that a third body had been found at the farm but the results of the post mortem had not yet been made public. Perhaps the current desire for confidentiality had touched Joanna too. She wasn't anxious for people to know that Ruthie Summers had been pregnant – except the father of the child. To herself she could admit she still had an absurd instinct to protect the girl's reputation.

So she kept her eyes trained on Arabella Rowan while Mike led the questions. 'How long did you say that Ruth Summers had worked here?'

'A year,' Arabella snapped. 'Now can we go into the kitchen? I'm not terribly anxious for my guests to overhear my being questioned about a murder.'

They followed her into the kitchen. As soon as the door was closed Mike spoke again. 'How did you come to employ her? Did you call round to Hardacre?'

'Certainly not.' The question undoubtedly rattled Mrs Rowan. 'I've *never* been there in my entire life. We talked – in the market. She said what a struggle things were – financially. And I said how difficult it was managing the barn conversions.' Her voice became laden with sarcasm. 'Especially on a Saturday.' Laughter wafted in from outside. A scream. *'Mum, Peter hit me.'*

Arabella rolled her eyes and continued. 'People leave them in such a mess and they soon complain if they aren't perfect when they arrive. It seemed the ideal solution to take advantage of her offer,' she finished bleakly. 'She would arrive about eleven and clean the barns for a couple of hours.'

Joanna interrupted. 'She was a thorough cleaner?'

'We had a few words,' Arabella said defiantly. 'She wasn't used to being too particular around the house. I hardly think Aaron and Jack were exacting with their standards of hygiene.' Joanna visualized the rooms at Hardacre, shabby, neglected but superficially clean.

Ruthie had had her standards but they would hardly have come up to Arabella Rowan's bench mark.

'And what was the date that you last saw her?'

'Early – no mid – June.' Arabella seemed flustered. 'Perhaps the end. About a month.' Her pupils suddenly sharpened to pencil points. 'You've asked me all this before, Inspector.'

'We just want to be sure.'

There was a brief silence until Joanna spoke again. 'So the exact date please, Mrs Rowan.'

'I shall need my booking cards.'

'If you wouldn't mind.'

Arabella whisked out of the room, practically knocking her husband over just outside. He straightened up, gave an embarrassed laugh. His wife scowled at him.

Joanna addressed him. 'I'm glad to see you, Mr Rowan.'

'Well thank you, Inspector,' he replied smoothly. 'What can I do for you?'

'We noticed a barn on the left-hand side as we came up the drive.'

'I've lots of barns,' Neil Rowan said awkwardly. But there was a wary look in his eyes.

He hadn't been expecting this one.

'It has a green painted door, sir,' Mike said brusquely.

Neil Rowan didn't like Mike, but he almost managed to hide it. It showed only in the small muscle that twitched at the side of his mouth. 'I don't actually use the field with that barn in.'

But the grass had been grazed short. 'So who does?'

'I rent it out to Fallowfield. Pinkers has a use for it.'

'Ah.' In actual fact Joanna saw nothing. The question about the barn had merely been idle introduction to the business of the day but Neil Rowan's eyes held a faintly worried look now and his head moved slightly towards the window – and the tiny barn whose roof was barely visible at the bottom of the drive.

It set Joanna's mind working. The field was more than a mile from Fallowfield. And not convenient for Martin Pinkers at all. The barn was small. Not big enough for hay or secure enough to store machinery. It was stuck out, on its own, an isolated barn with not enough room to hold more than a couple of animals. Or one large one. She felt curious. It was with an effort that she diverted her mind back to the dead girl.

'What did you think of Ruthie Summers?'

Rowan knew it was a catch question but he disguised his discomfort with a loud, hearty laugh.

'She seemed a nice girl,' he said casually. 'Arabella was pleased with her. She did her work adequately.' He was beginning to bluster. 'I had hardly anything to do with her. I don't know why you ask me.'

'No?' Joanna watched his eyes slide away from hers. At least he had the decency to blush.

'Terrible what happened to her.' He left a short, probing pause. 'I assume the third body *was* hers?'

'Yes.'

He was on his guard now, a coiled spring, tense, alert. 'Murder,' he managed.

Joanna shook her head and noted his puzzlement.

'Then what . . .?'

'She was pregnant.'

The muscle began to twitch again.

'Mr Rowan,' Joanna moved her face closer to his so

she could see right to the back of his brown eyes. 'When we know who the father of Ruthie's child is we shall almost certainly know who wiped out the rest of her family.'

'You've no right to threaten my husband like that.' Arabella had returned to speak from the doorway.

Neil Rowan was a coward. Joanna watched him shrink from his wife's sharp crack of a voice. He looked frightened. His wife shot him a glance of pure disdain and then ignored him, taking up the challenge of Joanna's smoky blue eyes instead.

'So what line of questioning are you pursuing now, Inspector?'

'Well, Ruthie Summers died of natural causes, Mrs Rowan.'

Joanna could have sworn Mrs Rowan already knew that by her flat reaction. But she had not told her husband.

'She was pregnant.'

Oddly, Arabella Rowan's face displayed faint amusement. Either she knew her husband was in the clear or else she didn't care. She could throw him to the dogs, carry on with her life unimpeded by a philandering husband.

Joanna continued. 'Naturally we connect her death with the murders of her father and brother.'

'Naturally.' Maybe Arabella Rowan was extremely brave, or a good actress. Or she could see a flaw in Joanna's reasoning. It unnerved the detective.

She glanced across at Neil Rowan and realized he was relaxed now. Sit back and let the wife sort it out. Then Joanna realized. It was talk of the baby that had *relaxed* him. It was the double shootings which had *unnerved* him.

Joanna was even more confused and floundered with her questions. 'Tell me something about the workings of a farm like yours.'

The nervousness had returned. He was completely thrown off balance by the question without realizing it had been blindly asked. But then Mike too was confounded, staring at her as though she was crazy. She gave him a tiny smile meant to reassure him of her control.

'It's a good, profitable concern,' Neil Rowan said shortly. 'What else do you need to know?'

Joanna deliberately turned her face towards him to cut out Mike. She had an idea where she hoped her questions would lead. He didn't.

'Dairy or beef?' she asked idly.

'Both.' His answers were short to the point of rudeness and a flush was creeping up his neck.

'You have calves?'

'Of course.' His face was suffused now. 'All dairy herds have calves. You can't help it. They're a by-product of milk production.'

'A bull?'

To her side Mike stiffened.

'I *had* one.' His forehead was glistening now. 'Now I . . .' His wife's eyes were on him, mocking, disdainful, uncaring, disliking.

And now Joanna knew. Pinkers and Rowan had *both* helped themselves to the animals from Hardacre. They had fleeced their poverty-struck neighbour, increased his run of bad luck, reduced his livelihood to a mere scratch. His good fortune had become theirs.

So what about Ruthie? How much had she discovered? She had been the clever one, the natural
manager of the old farm. The theft of the bull as well as
the cows would have meant more to her sharp brain
than to her father who was dying of cancer and her
brother who would never be capable of managing the
farm alone. But Ruthie? It had been her livelihood too.
She had worked, selling eggs, cleaning. Hardacre had
been important to her. And Joanna knew instinctively
that it was the farm, its animals as well as its future that
had lain in Ruthie's heart rather than a man.

So how much had the girl worked out about the fate
of the missing cattle? Had she found Doric, the bull she
had so fancifully named? One morning as she walked
to work had she peered inside the barn and seen the
animal which had been stolen? And why the hell had
they kept him there, so near the road?

The answer flashed through her mind. Because
there was joint responsibility. While the Rowans had
owned the barn Pinkers had been the one to use it. So
who would she have told? Again the answer was
obvious. A woman would confide in her lover. But who
had he been? What part had he played in the looming
tragedy? And why? Had the farm been of such import-
ance to him too? Had he been someone like Shackleton
who must have seen the farm as potentially profitable?
Or had it been the delicate woman herself with her
heart-shaped face and romantic features that had
seduced the man?

In other words had it been Mothershaw? Had the
artist found a piece of rural England he had longed to
possess and keep? And with that land had come the
farmer's daughter to entice him with her singing and

her honest, country ways? Had he been seduced by the illusion of a girl collecting eggs, herding cows, singing, singing.

So what had her lover thought when she had vanished? What would he have thought of Neil Rowan's clumsy attempts to seduce such innocence? Would he have taken up the bludgeon in defence of her innocence and the stolen cattle? Joanna pictured him as she had first seen him, in yellow trousers and pale shirt and she doubted it. To Titus Mothershaw cattle would have been artistic props, rather than practical, bread and butter objects of value.

She looked helplessly at Mike. There were still too many unanswered questions and she was impatient to know who was the father of Ruthie's child.

Neil Rowan spoke. 'Where did you find her?'

For the first time she could believe he really cared. His forehead was wrinkled with earnestness and he had stopped looking at his wife with quite such apprehension.

'Behind the wall in the back of the larder.' Joanna had decided to spare neither of them. 'Her body was partly decomposed. She'd been there about a month.'

She thought Neil Rowan was about to be sick.

Even Arabella turned white. 'I wondered . . .' She had to start again. 'I wondered. She hadn't turned up. Work. I thought . . .'

'That your husband's attempted philanderings had put her off?'

Arabella Rowan nodded dumbly. She gave a loud, inelegant sniff and collapsed into the kitchen chair, her head dropped on to her folded arms. But she wasn't crying. Joanna sensed the woman felt too much anger for that.

Neil Rowan crossed the room to touch his wife's shoulder, timidly. 'It was only a bit of fun,' he said. 'Nothing serious. She was just a young woman.'

His wife raised her face. 'You fool,' she said softly, but strangely, not without some affection. 'You are such a fool, Neil.'

Then she held the bookings cards out to Joanna and her voice steadied. 'She last worked here on June 16th.'

'And did she seem all right?'

Arabella Rowan frowned. 'No,' she said. 'Not really. As far as I can remember that day she left here early. I think she said she had a stomach ache. I could see she wasn't well. We did offer her a lift home but she said it was OK, that the walk would do her good. And I saw Aaron and Jack the following Monday at market. They said she wasn't too grand and she wouldn't be in for a week or two.' It took a minute or two for the facts to sink in before she added in a small voice. 'Did she die then?'

'Almost certainly.'

Mrs Rowan ran her fingers through her hair and looked years older, control finally lost. 'How awful,' she said. 'How bloody awful.'

'Isn't it?'

But Joanna was watching Arabella Rowan very carefully. 'Didn't you wonder why she didn't come back?'

Mrs Rowan looked embarrassed. 'To be honest,' she said, 'I thought she must have said something to either Aaron or Jack about . . .' She eyed her husband. 'Well. I

265

thought she must have said that Neil was being over-friendly. I made up my mind to manage on my own in future.'

It was a clear, sad picture, a woman working hard to make a success of a business. She had help to do the work. But her husband was a Romeo. So Arabella must manage on her own.

Chapter Sixteen

7.15 p.m.

The heat was draining out of the day, leaving a cool breeze to play with the landscape, rustling trees, waving long grass, stroking the flowers with subtle movement.

Mike took the wheel and they drove down the winding lane towards the barn standing square against the road, a grey scar on the landscape. An ancient barn. Yet it was in good repair. There were no tiles missing from the roof and the door looked as though it had been freshly painted.

Mike pulled the car into a passing place and together they swung the five-barred gate open and approached the barn.

They could hear the bull bellowing as they got within five yards. He was kicking the door. They watched in fascination as it shuddered. This must be some animal, large and strong who wanted to be in the fields enjoying himself, not cooped up in such a small space.

Mike backed away. 'I'm not going in there. What's it got to do with the case anyway?'

Joanna didn't know but felt such relief at having tracked down the missing animal she couldn't resist teasing him. 'Come on, Mike,' she said briskly. 'You don't expect *me* to enter, do you? You see it might not be Doric.'

He gave her a quick, worried glance. 'I mean it, Jo,' he warned. 'It sounds dangerous to me. I'm not going in.'

But she wasn't going to let him off the hook yet. 'I'm afraid, Sergeant.'

'You must be joking.' And then he caught the gleam in her eyes and they both started to laugh.

'We can peep through the window, can't we? Give me a leg up.'

The window pane was smeared but she could still see the animal clearly, pawing the ground. Doric was enormous, pale in colour, almost cream skinned and very heavy with huge shoulders and a great bag of testicles dangling between his legs. This was where Pinkers had been early on Tuesday morning. He had got up late but the milking took less than an hour. They left the bull to graze at night. But the animal must be hidden throughout the day. And as Joanna's mind began to unblock she turned around. 'Mike,' she said, pointing. 'Look around you.'

It was the wide, green panoramic sweep of the valley. And Hardacre was clearly in view, nestling at the top end of the lane just before it curved towards Brooms and petered out in the footpath. Joanna shielded her eyes from the sinking sun. Titus Mothershaw's sculptured wood was hidden behind the house, a dark-green area with only the pinnacle of the Owl Hole visible. To the left stood Fallowfield, looking slightly ramshackle and picturesque. She could see exhaust spouting from the top of the tractor, hear a cockerel's noisy crow far in the distance, a dog somewhere far away barking wildly. She turned back towards Hardacre and thought how dead it seemed. There was no movement and no noise. Even the animals were quiet. The place looked deserted. She and Mike turned away from the barn, climbed the five-barred gate and returned to the squad car, Mike watching her enquiringly.

'We'll get the vet up,' she said finally, 'for positive identification.' She grinned at Mike. 'This is the beginning of the end, Mike.' But she couldn't resist a final tug at his leg. 'So shall we return to the safety of the station?'

She felt a strong urge to speak to Matthew as soon as they walked inside the station. She was missing his frequent calls and visits. This was the first time since he had left Jane that they had drifted so far apart and she was feeling lonely and unsettled. The insecurity was deeply disturbing and uncomfortable. She *must* speak to him. Yet the distance between them seemed so wide she felt she needed an excuse.

She finally tracked him down at home and instantly recognized the distant, guarded tone in his voice.

Yet he was polite. 'What can I do for you?'

'I wondered if you had any results back from the lab?'

'I've got the grouping but the DNA will take longer.' He paused before adding gently. 'I did tell you, Jo.'

'So what are the results of the grouping?'

'As we thought. Neither Aaron nor Jack could be the father of Ruthie's baby.'

'Anything else?'

'You've probably got a duplicate report on the rug . . .'

'Not that I've read yet.'

'Accelerants. Diesel fuel. Plenty had been splashed around it.'

'Right,' she said idly. There was a long pause before Matthew spoke in a quiet, reproachful voice. 'You don't even try with Eloise. Joanna, it isn't going to work unless you make some effort.'

'I do try.' She was instantly furious. 'Haven't you noticed how she ignores me?'

'Oh, for goodness sake,' he said irritably. 'You're like a pair of adolescents. For my sake will you try and get on with her. It's making life very difficult. She is my daughter.'

She dug her nails into her palm. 'And have you had this conversation with her?'

'Yes.' But he hesitated. 'Using slightly different words. But remember. This whole situation has come about because of our relationship. I was married to her mother.'

Suddenly her anger boiled over and she slammed the phone down, her hands shaking.

She buried her face in her arms and struggled to hold back the tears. She tried to excuse him. Perhaps it is natural always to defend your own flesh and blood. Guilt was forcing him to shovel blame on to her. She lifted her head and stared at the brick wall view from her window. Surely . . . surely he did love her, didn't he? Memories flooded through her hotly, all the times he had begged her to see him, to meet with him, to sleep with him. Something like a creeping horror took hold of her.

Surely he did still love her?

But the horror was swiftly replaced by something fierce.

She would never forgive Eloise Levin for the way she drove a wedge between her and Matthew.

Korpanski was watching her from the doorway, tossing up whether to go in, put a friendly arm around her, console her with the statement that there were plenty of men besides Levin. But something held him back and before he could reach her she looked over and caught his eye and he felt embarrassed at being caught.

She rubbed her nose with her hand. 'Yes? What is it?'

He cleared his throat awkwardly. 'You all right?'

And she couldn't hide her feelings any longer. 'I hate it when she comes.'

But his words lit the fire again.

'Well she is his daughter.'

10 p.m.

She needed to be alone, in her own, small, secure cottage, away from other people, ringing phones, intrusion. She locked the door, poured herself a glass of cold white wine and flopped into the comfortable sofa. It had been a luxury buy, goose feather filled, covered in heavy, dark red brocade with tapestry cushions lining the back. She settled into it and closed her eyes. Not for long. The temptation was always to take pleasure from the furnishings, pieces of old furniture – some procured at local auction rooms, others inherited from an aunt – and the oil paintings that warmed the walls. Two portraits of Georgian dandies and a still life of a vase of red roses. It all felt as safe and comfortable as a nest. She sat for minutes deliberately allowing her mind to think about nothing until some instinct moved her to stand in front of the glass fronted china cabinet. As though in a dream she opened the door. This was where she kept her collection of Victorian Staffordshire figures also bequeathed to her by her aunt who must have suspected where her interests and future career would lie. For the figures were of criminals mostly, criminals who had been caught, convicted and sentenced. Without even rudimentary knowledge of blood groups, DNA, fingerprint techniques and advanced communications the police had caught their killers. It made her all the more determined. So would she.

She picked one out believing it was at random before she realized what her fingers had found. Smith and Collier. Farmers from the tiny village of Froghall, Staffordshire. A sleepy hollow of the place served by the Cauldon canal. *Smith grasps the shoulder of Collier, Collier grabs back, ready to murder him after Smith has found him poaching on his land. Collier has a double barrelled shot gun. With one discharge he has killed two rabbits. With the other he shoots Smith in the head. A pair of farmers who settled an argument their way.*

Joanna had often felt that handling the tributes made by the potters of Staffordshire to their villains gave her heart. Their police had not failed then. Nor would they now. William Collier had been hanged on August 7th 1866, the last ever public execution outside Stafford Gaol. She peered even closer at the figure.

The men stand beneath an arbour. Smith stands on the

left, dressed in a round hat, a neckerchief, a long jacket, a waistcoat, breeches and gaiters. His right hand holds a revolver while his left hand apprehends Collier. Collier wears a beaver hat, a long jacket, a waistcoat and breeches. And slung from his right shoulder is the give away, a game bag. He is the poacher. And it is he who holds the long barrel of the murder weapon, a fowling piece. On the floor is further evidence, a brace of dead pheasants and a dog who attacks Collier's right leg.

And so, holding it, she used the figure of William Collier and Thomas Smith as a medium uses a crystal ball, as a focus for her mind.

It would work.

Her subconscious mind would piece together the seemingly disconnected facts of this case. While she was sleeping it would sift through statements, recall with magic perfection the faces of the witnesses as they gave their statements; whether deceitful or honest.

She closed her eyes and slowed her breathing right down.

Sunday, July 12th, 6 a.m.

She sat up in bed and hugged her knees, sensing there was something different about today almost the second she opened her eyes. Through the curtains she could see what it was. It was dull outside, dark and threatening. The weather was breaking with a noisy, crashing thunderstorm.

Her eyes moved across to the bedside table where she had carefully stood the pottery farmers in their final death-throe struggle.

And she smiled and threw the covers off. Today would bring the truth. She knew it would only take a little more concentration before her mind clarified events to crystal quality and thunderstorm or not she could not resist the cycle ride across the ridge before dropping down into the valley of the three farms and scattered cottages.

During the night her mind had unravelled something. She *knew* who Ruthie's lover had been. No, she corrected herself as she stood beneath the shower, soaping her body with the scented gel. I don't *know* who the father of Ruthie's baby was but I shall *see* something today that will tell me. And Ruthie will speak to me.

The grass had changed colour to a sickly green in reflection from the clouds, rumbling with a threat. But no lightning, yet. And no rain – yet. So Joanna pedalled across the ridge and felt this strange new wind stroke her face with the chill of a weather front. And she was glad. The hot weather had threatened to fuel her temper, drain her energy, fuddle her brain so it lost the clarity it must have to point the eventual finger.

She must know. But it was not enough just to know. She must have proof, that or a confession.

Travelling against the wind she could almost convince herself that it was not the murders of the Summers family that she must solve but the story behind the execution of William Collier. Because as far as she gazed down into both valleys she could see nothing that told her they were approaching the millennium. Victoria could still be on the throne, not Elizabeth. There was not one modern building, no pylons or visible sign of the twentieth century. Nothing but cows and fields, hedges and stone walls. As the road dipped towards the valley she flicked the gears of her bike to reach the biggest cog and the fastest speed. She felt an urgency to prove her theory.

This morning she was up before Martin Pinkers, or the Rowans, their noisy, energetic guests, the inhabitants of the Owl Hole or Brooms. There was no life stirring this morning, only her, her feet rhythmically pedalling towards the ill-fated farm.

She locked her bike around the back of the Incident Room and waited impatiently for Mike. She had learnt her lesson about interviewing suspects alone but they had taken the guard from the farmhouse and merely locked the complaining doors, stiff from standing open once too often.

8.30 a.m.

At last Mike came and she shot her questions at him.

'What do you remember about Mothershaw's place?'

He yawned and looked fed up. 'It's Sunday morning, Jo.'

'I know,' she said briskly. 'But just picture the place.'

Mike rubbed his head. 'The owl,' he ventured, 'the one I bumped my head on.'

'Go on.'

He watched her, bemused. 'It's sort of . . .'

'Yes?'

'Futuristic?'

'And?'

He shrugged, irritated. 'I don't know what you're getting at, Jo.'

'He does wood carvings,' she said urgently. 'Where?'

'Sorry?'

'Not one chisel. Not one fragment of wood shavings. Not even one chunk of wood.'

'Oh.' Mike's face cleared.

'And the Owl Hole is far too tidy and clean for him to work there. He has a workshop, Mike, which he hasn't wanted to show us. It must have been in the original report but there were so many farm buildings we didn't really notice it. And we were searching for only one thing. Ruthie's body.'

Even with the current threat of thunder Mothershaw's work had lost some of its air of mystery and was recognizable for what it was, modern art, cleverly intertwined pieces of supple stick and wood, some skilled carving. But the mystery was missing. His was work for half-lights, for mists and winter evenings, not a July thunderstorm. Without deep shadows the faces lacked expression. Except the Tree Man. He towered over them, partly shrouded by the pale leaves of a lime tree, his thick stick arms held out threateningly. Joanna pushed aside the fronds and gazed up.

And she knew.

She knew who now and more importantly she knew the *real* reason why.

Just to be certain she walked right around the figure, studied the scorched feet, partly softened by a wrapping of moss. But it was the face which gave the entire story away. It was all there, once the full facts, each and every one, was given its right place in the sequence of events. And for once even Mike seemed sensitive to the Tree Man. He too was silent, staring fixedly at the figure. 'I suppose,' he said grudgingly, 'if I *had* to live with one of them this would be the one I'd go for.'

She swivelled her head round to take in his wide jaw line and blunt features. 'Is it? You're sure about that, are you, Mike?'

'What on earth . . .?'

'What about the one he's working on at the moment?'

Mike moved his head slightly from side to side. It was an action that asked a question.

She didn't answer it.

Mothershaw blinked when he saw them. And there was something very guarded in his expression. Today, as though he mirrored the weather, he was dressed sombrely in a black polo neck and mushroom coloured trousers. His eyes were dulled and tired and he wore a dignified air of grief.

'I heard the news,' he said quietly.

And Joanna knew the full story of Ruthie's death must have broken.

She nodded matter of factly.

'I didn't really expect you back.' There was a question behind the sentence. 'I thought you'd be busy,' he continued.

'We are.'

She let the full meaning of her words sink in before continuing. 'Titus,' she ventured, 'when did you last see her?'

He didn't even ask whether she meant Ruthie. He knew. 'Middle of June,' he said. 'I don't know the exact date.' The details were to be brushed aside.

He gave a hint of a smile. 'Do you want to come in?'

But Joanna was not to be distracted. 'No – not this morning. I think it's time we sorted out a few more details. Like where is your studio, Mr Mothershaw?'

Titus looked shocked. He tugged at the black polo neck as though it was strangling him. 'I um. There's nothing there.' It was a feeble attempt to divert them.

They tramped a further half a mile along the dirt track behind the Owl Hole until they came to a small clearing in a hollow. In the centre was a wooden shed so surrounded by weeds, debris and trees as to be almost invisible. Yet it had been wired up to electricity. Mothershaw took a key from his pocket and inserted it into a padlock. But before he opened the door he half turned as though he needed to explain something. Behind him the two police officers hesitated. Joanna wanted to give him the opportunity to speak before it was forced from him. But Mothershaw lowered his eyes and said nothing, only tugging the door wide open to let in what light there was.

Joanna knew he wanted the work to explain everything.

Inside was dim, full of vague, half finished shapes. Underfoot Joanna felt the dry rasping crunch of wood shavings and knew they were in the right place. Even before Mothershaw flicked on an electric light.

'I was working on this.' He whisked a dark cloth from the central shape and turned his head away as though he could not bear to look.

She sat naked and tiny, gracefully sitting like the Little Mermaid of Copenhagen, legs tucked beneath her, her long hair partly curtaining her face. Her head was bowed in submission, her hands relaxed at her side. When the wood was polished it would be perfect. Now it was a roughly hewn beauty, unfinished. The feet were still thick wedges of wood, the features slightly blurred, the hands and buttocks not quite fined down. And Joanna had the feeling that Titus Mothershaw would always leave it like this.

She would never be finished.

The figure may have born little resemblance to the rotting carcase they had released from behind the wall at Hardacre but it perfectly fitted the image Joanna had formed of the young woman.

There was no need to ask her name. This was Ruthie.

And as Joanna had done with the Tree Man's monstrous form in the wood she did now, circumventing the graceful statue to study it from every angle.

And there was no need for her to wait for the results of the DNA testing to know for certain who the father of Ruthie's baby was. Only a man who had loved, adored, intimately, could have carved the wood into this form of his lover's body. That same body which he had destroyed. Mothershaw was leaning against the door, staring out into the wood. 'I wondered why she didn't come back,' he said bleakly. 'I thought she must be angry about something.' He drew in a deep, long sigh. 'Angry with me.'

He spread his hands out in front of him. 'I couldn't work without her,' he said. 'It was hopeless. Nothing came to life. Wood remained simply – wood.' He turned around, his face stiff with emotion and walked slowly towards the statue. Then he spread his hands on either side of the 'Little Mermaid's' legs and burrowed his head in Ruthie's lap.

'Did you know she was pregnant?'

Mothershaw's shoulders jerked.

'Did you?' Mike repeated roughly.

Mothershaw raised his face. 'No.'

And Joanna realized he didn't know his child had effectively killed Ruthie.

Mothershaw frowned. 'I don't understand.'

'She died of a ruptured pregnancy,' Joanna said woodenly. 'I assume you are the father?' Mothershaw looked stunned. 'I think I – am,' he said wonderingly. 'I must be.'

'We can prove it,' Joanna said still in that same, brisk tone, 'one way or the other by comparing samples of your blood for DNA with that of the unborn baby.'

Mothershaw stared at her.

'So if you wouldn't mind coming down to the station at some point we can arrange to take a sample of your blood.'

She and Mike left him with his head still buried in the wooden girl's lap. And as they passed through the door she could have sworn she heard a muffled sob.

10 a.m.

They called the vet at ten o'clock and arranged to meet him outside the barn. 'You understand we would like positive identification that the bull *is* Doric.'

'No problem.' Roderick Beeston's voice was grim. 'I remember that animal. One of the best pedigree Belgian Blues around. I'd followed his progress and his sale. He's fathered more offspring than the King of

Siam.' There was a crackle on the line. 'Aaron was heartbroken when Doric vanished. Heartbroken.'

Joanna resisted the temptation to badger Roderick Beeston for the hundred-dollar question. Who did he think had stolen Doric? Yet she realized the question was better left unasked because it was not only unprofessional for him to venture an opinion but if offered it could prove prejudicial in court.

At the back of her mind the fact nagged like an aching tooth. The barn which had housed the bull was used by Martin Pinkers. But it belonged to Neil Rowan.

Beeston's Landrover arrived seconds after they did and she shook his hand recalling the last time she had met him when he had anaesthetized a dog that had been threatening to bite Joanna's hand off.*

The blue eyes and black hair were the same, but his manner was much more friendly this time around. Dressed in a check shirt with olive-green jeans tucked into some wellington boots, a little shorter than she, he looked every inch the country vet. He gave them both a wide, friendly grin. 'Detective Inspector Piercy. Hello. How are you?'

There was an open warmth about him that endeared him to her. 'And Detective Sergeant Korpanski!'

Mike grinned back. 'How are you, Roderick?'

'Fine.' His eyes were sparkling at the thought of finding the missing bull.

'We think we have the bull,' Joanna said. 'But what

---

* Winding Up the Serpent.

about the cows that went missing? What chance is there of finding them?'

Beeston shook his head. 'Very little, I'm afraid. Once their tags are removed. Accreditation papers can so easily be altered and other, poorer quality cows substituted. Doric on the other hand, is quite a different kettle of fish.' He threw back his head and laughed. 'If you'll excuse the pun. I could be certain if I could trace at least some of his calves. I may even have some of his semen back at the surgery, frozen. Then it can be compared with.' He glanced at the barn.

'Oh poor old Doric,' he said. 'Such a small barn for such a hefty animal.'

'We should be able to get a watertight case against Pinkers.'

Beeston looked surprised. 'It's his barn? I thought it belonged to the Rowans.' His eyes roamed the valley. 'Hardacre was well named,' he said steadily. 'I never knew anyone have such a struggle for survival as did Aaron Summers. Life was bad enough without some bastard like Pinkers stealing their cattle.'

'I wondered if Neil Rowan might have something to do with it.'

Roderick Beeston's face was instantly alert. 'With the murders?'

'I don't know. He isn't the sort. He didn't have the necessary . . .' and she recalled the conversation she had had with Mike. 'Desperation.'

The vet's eyebrows rose. 'Desperation?'

She studied his face, craggy and tanned from the constant outdoor life. His features lacked Matthew's sensitivity. This was a more practical man, not handsome either like Matthew but with piercing blue eyes

282

and very dark hair. Idly she wondered whether he was married, had children. A daughter?

They started across the field towards the barn. 'You see the cows were stolen first, a bit of a trial run. When they got away with that they went for the real thing, Doric.'

Beeston peered in through the window. 'Well,' he said. 'I never thought I'd see him again.' He dropped back down to the grass. 'That's him all right. That's Doric. The question is, how did he get here?'

But Joanna's mind was working in a different direction. Titus Mothershaw had come to live in the Owl Hole. With the money he had paid in rent Aaron had bought a bull, Doric. Doric had been stolen. Titus Mothershaw had then plundered the farmer of his daughter, made her pregnant. She had died. He had brought havoc in his wake, merely by taking up residence here, in the sleepy and private valley. Like the Ancient Mariner he had brought bad luck. His very presence had been a forewarning of ill fortune.

'So what happens to Doric now?'

'I can take him from here,' the vet said. 'There's a farm I use, a few miles away. It's safe and secure. They'll look after Doric until it's decided what to do with him.'

'Thank you.' Joanna gave him a warm smile.

He held her hand for a fraction of a second longer than was needed. 'My pleasure, Inspector. My pleasure. I hope I see more of you, soon.'

Chapter Seventeen

1 p.m.

Although the day was humid, hot and heavy with the threat of stormy weather making the insects bite, as Joanna and Mike cornered the lane towards Fallowfield they caught the scent of a Sunday roast wafting on the air.

'Obviously the murders haven't affected their appetites,' Joanna remarked drily.

They barged in on the family halfway through their meal, Pinkers and his two sons concentrating on forking great heaps of food into their mouths. It was Mrs Pinkers who looked up first.

'Hello.' She gave an uncertain glance towards her husband.

Pinkers himself didn't even try to be polite. 'It's you, is it? What do you want?'

Joanna settled herself in a shabby armchair. 'I thought you'd be pleased to know, Mr Pinkers, that the missing bull has turned up.'

Pinkers eyed her warily. 'Where?'

'In one of your barns.' Mike stepped forward.

Pinkers stood up, pushed his chair back. 'Now look here.'

'No, you look here,' Joanna said sharply. 'We've arranged for the vet to come and give your herd the once over. But before he comes perhaps you'll tell us exactly what you did see on Tuesday morning.'

But Pinkers knew the drill. 'I'll have my solicitor here first,' he said sullenly.

They all filed outside into the yard just as Beeston's Landrover came into view. One of Pinkers' sons had finished his dinner. He was standing in the corner, blasting at some crows roosting in a huge chestnut tree.

Beeston watched him.

'Do you know, Inspector,' he said to Joanna. 'I read somewhere that in China when a man is disillusioned with life and the political system he goes fishing. Here, in rural England, a man takes a shotgun and blasts away at crows. Now which do you think is the mark of a civilized society?'

Joanna winced as the lad discharged both barrels into the air. 'Neither.'

'Exactly.' The vet watched her with amusement. 'So let's take a peep at Pinkers' stock, shall we?'

Twenty minutes later Roderick Beeston was scratching his head. 'Is this all your stock, Pinkers?'

Pinkers nodded. 'That's the lot.'

'Then I'm surprised you don't have a problem meeting your milk quotas. They look a poor lot to me.'

'The dry weather,' Pinkers murmured.

The vet smiled. 'Yes. Of course. No real health problems I'm glad to say. Couple of good calves though.' He stuck his hands deep in his pockets. 'Nice looking calves these Belgian Blues give. Big though. I'll lay a bet your younger cows have real trouble giving birth, don't they?'

So even the rolling eyes and anguished groans of the animal giving birth in Pinkers' barn should have directed her towards the truth.

Pinkers scowled and started fiddling with the tractors. A spanner in his hand, he was tightening wheel nuts. Out of earshot Beeston spoke to him. 'Why the hell didn't you come to some agreement with your neighbour? He would have let you borrow Doric.'

'For a price,' Pinkers muttered.

'Fair's fair, man.'

Pinkers face blackened as Joanna moved nearer. 'The cattle missing from Hardacre?'

'Aren't here,' the vet said. 'I can promise you that.'

He walked with her and Mike in the direction of Hardacre and the Incident Room.

'I suppose you knew the Summers family well.'

Beeston gave a short laugh. 'Not that well. They called me as little as possible. A farm like that.' His gaze moved across the stony fields and the bare, overgrazed grass. 'They couldn't afford vet's bills. But they were hard working, all three of them. For every penny they earned they sweated. They were decent people who didn't deserve such an end.'

And somehow she had to combine the vet's opinion with the fact that when one of their number had been ill they had failed to take her to a doctor or a hospital which might have saved her life. And when Ruthie had died they had not involved the authorities or given her a Christian funeral but had done something pagan and ignorant. They bricked her up behind a wall.

She was frowning as she thanked Beeston for his help.

He grinned back at her. 'Any time, Inspector,' he said cheerfully. 'It's a shame our paths don't cross a little more frequently.'

She met his eyes with a touch of amusement. 'Well considering there's invariably an ugly crime somewhere in my wake, Mr Beeston, I think you should be grateful our paths don't cross too often. I'm afraid I'm bad news.'

'An ugly job for a woman like you,' he said and waved goodbye abandoning her to an unwelcome vision of Matthew's pained expression and Eloise's triumphant one. The images crowded her mind as she watched Roderick Beeston stride back towards Martin Pinkers' farm.

She sighed and turned back to Mike. 'Let's talk,' she said steadily. 'Let's just talk.'

The rain was just starting, heavy, drenching, cooling and welcome. The verges would soon be green again, the fields damp, the streams and rivers full. All would be well. England would be England again soon, not some mock-up of Southern Spain.

Mike was waiting expectantly.

'I don't see where Pinkers fits in,' Joanna began. 'Did he get up early on Tuesday morning? And if he did, did he visit the bull in the shed? And if he did. Mike,' she said urgently. 'You saw the view from up there. He *could* have seen something, someone. He didn't start milking until round about ten. He wasn't quite ready for Dave Shackleton, was he? Even if he got up late – for a farmer – what was he doing that morning? Where was he and what does it have to do

287

with our case?' She didn't let him speak but hurried on, softly speaking her thoughts out loud. 'I had assumed that the father of Ruthie's baby would be our killer.'

Mike didn't speak.

'Well, I am certain that Titus Mothershaw is the father of Ruthie's unborn baby. But I can't see him shooting Aaron and Jack. So was my assumption wrong? Or my judgement?'

Mike's eyes flickered.

'Go on then,' she exploded. 'Speak.'

'You're doing the usual thing,' Mike said angrily. 'Just because you *like* someone you're assuming he couldn't have killed.'

'Then do you think he did shoot them?'

Mike ran his fingers through the cropped, black hair. 'I don't know what to think,' he said.

As abruptly as it had started the rain stopped. The sky was blue and the lane steaming with evaporating puddles. The colours looked fresher and greener than Joanna could ever have imagined.

4 p.m.

It was nearly two hours later when Joanna spoke again. 'Let's go for a walk.'

For a few minutes they stood in the yard, watching the rain evaporating on the walls of the old, stone farmhouse. Normally they would have sheltered from the rain or dressed in stormproof clothing. But it was still hot. Then Joanna turned away suddenly. Something was wrong.

A low grumble of thunder blasted through the quiet.

She looked around for clues to her feeling of sudden panic.

There was nothing. The cows were peacefully grazing, a few made uneasy by the threatening weather were clustered beneath the spread of the wide chestnut tree towards the middle of the field. One or two stopped grazing and lifted their heads. Almost in a dream, Joanna moved towards the gate.

More cows were lifting their heads; one or two stood up, lowing gently. They began walking towards the gate.

One ran.

Joanna clutched Mike's arm. 'For goodness sake,' she said, 'what was that?'

Through the gloom came the unmistakable sound of a farmer's whistle. Piercing, loud. A distinctive summons.

The cows knew that sound. They stood up and jostled against the gate.

Joanna hardly dared glance back along the lane towards the farmhouse. She knew what she would see and hear. The slap of wellington boots, the farmer, come to collect his cows. Aaron? Jack? Ruthie?

She turned her head.

There was nothing. Nothing. The lane was empty. There was no one there. No Aaron. No Jack and no Ruthie.

Then came the whistle again. Pure, clear, piercing. Summoning.

And the cows knew it too.

Even Mike was nervous. 'What's the game?' he said.

'Where's the farmer? Joanna who is it?' And then the whistle came closer and Joanna found its source. Sitting in the hawthorn hedge was a starling. She recognized its small, speckled body and watched while it opened its beak and whistled again and Joanna realized how Lewis Stone had heard the farmer whistle an hour after he was dead.

Not the farmer but this mischievous bird.

She leant across the gate and began to think.

That was when she recalled Matthew's grumbling statement to her when he had wanted to buy just such a farmhouse. Isolated, traditional, old fashioned.

'Let's go and share a cup of tea with Hannah Lockley,' she said.

Chapter Eighteen

They stood outside underneath the dripping slates of the porch. *Hymns of Praise* was playing on the radio. And Joanna was instantly transported back to her childhood, Sunday teas with a tablecloth, cakes, sandwiches and jelly. A brief moment of peace between services.

She didn't bother to knock.

Hannah Lockley was in the sitting room, crumpled in a chair, staring ahead and seeing nothing.

Nothing.

Joanna sat opposite her and spoke slowly, not quite sure the old lady would take it all in. She began with a blindingly obvious statement.

'It must have meant a lot to you, knowing Ruthie would take care of the farm?'

Hannah nodded.

'After your sister had entrusted it to you?'

Again that sightless nod.

'You knew Aaron was dying.' Another statement.

Again a nod without any real connection.

'And Jack . . .?'

It provoked a response.

Hannah looked up, suddenly fierce but still a shadow of the woman Joanna had first met less than one week ago. 'He wasn't capable of running a farm.'

There was a bleakness in the old lady's entire demeanour.

Then Joanna asked the significant question. 'And Ruthie?'

Then Hannah Lockley stared at Joanna as though she was seeing right through her.

Joanna tried to help by supplying the words. 'You knew she was pregnant?'

A tiny nod.

'And you thought they were excluding her from the farm because of that?'

For the first time the old lady was coherent and offered some new information. 'I heard Aaron talking to Jack. I thought . . . Ruthie would have kept the farm going.' She turned an agonized face towards Joanna. 'There was no point,' she said. 'I thought it was the only way but there was no point. I shot them but Ruthie was already dead!' She buried her face in her hands. 'My poor, beautiful Ruthie.'

Her sobs were genuine. For Ruthie, for Aaron, for Jack. The horror of what she had done had at last come home to the old woman. 'I loved them all,' she said.

And now Joanna understood everything. A misunderstanding, a terrible mistake which had led to a misguided dual murder. But she kept the triumph out of her voice, keeping her tone deceptively calm and gentle. 'I'm sincerely sorry,' she said. 'You'll have to come with us to the station.'

The old lady closed her eyes. 'What does it matter?' she asked.

And there was no answer.

Chapter Nineteen

Monday, July 13th, 7.30 a.m.

She had used her car this morning. There would be lots of paperwork. Paperwork she could use to buy time. But first of all she must see Matthew – and inevitably Eloise.

Eloise was sulky, opening the door, tall and thin, now thirteen years old. She had Jane's pinched face, the pale hair, the sliding eyes.

'May I come in, Eloise?'

The girl didn't dare refuse. Especially when Matthew appeared at the door, his face lathered for shaving. He looked surprised to see her but grinned, ignoring Eloise to plant a soapy kiss on Joanna's cheek.

Joanna laughed, suddenly and inexcusably happy. 'I just wanted to thank you,' she said when her mouth was free.

Matthew's eyes looked bright and green and very friendly. 'Whatever for?' He gave Eloise a look of mock dismay. 'Now what have I done?'

The girl disappeared back along the hallway and again Matthew ignored her.

'The kettle's on,' he said cheerfully before planting another soapy kiss on her other cheek. He took hold of her hand. 'It's so good to see you, Jo. You don't know just how good.' He gave a deep sigh. 'I'd forgotten just how nice you can look this early in the morning. Now what is this *thing* I am supposed to have done?'

She waited until they were both perched on bar stools in the tiny kitchen and mugs of coffee in their hands. 'Before I knew about the murders,' she began, 'right at the beginning, on that first day you gave me the motive.'

'I did?'

'Yes.' She drank some of the strong coffee. 'You handed it to me on a plate.'

Matthew wiped the soap from his face with a towel and aimed it at the towel rail.

'I did?'

She nodded. 'You explained the rural attitude to property.'

He looked even more confused. 'But I don't remember saying anything.'

'Yes.' She touched his hand briefly. 'You told me the families hang on to their land for generations. Handed down from father to son, you said. Now do you remember?'

'Vaguely. But what on earth . . .?'

'Never let go of property or land.'

Matthew shrugged. 'Don't tell me that's why those two poor sods were blasted. It's a terrible reason.'

'I know.' Joanna nodded. 'And all because,' she said. 'All because Paulette Summers died. All because her daughter was given charge of looking after her brother, Jack. All because she accidentally tipped him out of the pushchair. And he was brain damaged from that day on. Then Titus Mothershaw moved to Owl Hole and he and Ruthie had a love affair. But her father had contracted stomach cancer and was dying. And tragically

Ruthie Summers died too and poor old Aaron believed Jack would *have* to be the one to manage the farm. But Hannah Lockley heard him talking. Her understanding was that her beloved niece was being cut out of the inheritance because she was pregnant so she shot both her brother-in-law and her nephew in the belief that Ruthie would *have* to inherit.

But Ruthie was already dead.'

Matthew said nothing for a while then he bent forward and kissed her again. 'Strong family ties,' he said. 'And inheritance. And all that . . .' He fell silent. 'All those consequences of events. Falling in love.' He was looking directly at her. 'So when all this is over we can make an offer on that house in Waterfall. And then we can make a dynasty of our own.'

Joanna's eyes slid away towards the floor. Was there no end to the deceit practised between herself and Matthew Levin?

From the corner of the room Eloise was watching silently and knowingly.

9 a.m.

Mike was waiting for her back at the station. A sobered, shell-shocked Mike. The solution had shocked the entire team. The scene of bloodshed at Hardacre, the discovery of Ruthie's body. These had been scenes none of them would ever forget. The Incident caravan would be towed away but the memories would be triggered every time any of them were called to an isolated, outlying farm.

Joanna sat at her desk and rolled a pencil to and

fro between her fingers. 'Do you know when I *really* knew?'

'No.' Mike was in sober mood. Even though the case had been solved relatively quickly. 'I only know,' he added, 'that it was something to do with that ruddy statue, the Tree Man.'

Joanna nodded. 'We all saw the resemblance to Jack Summers. But Jack was stupid. He didn't have the necessary fanaticism nor the brains nor the evil disregard for life. He could *never* have put property, inheritance, before a life. He had neither the intellect nor the direction. But somehow Mothershaw picked up something he *thought* he had seen in Jack's face. But it wasn't there. What he had picked up on was the family resemblance. And it was in the face of the aunt, Hannah Lockley. It was a sort of amoral determination, a putting of the farm above the lives of the people who inhabited it. Or more precisely putting safe inheritance over the lives of the farmer and his son. The trouble was, she was wrong.'

Mike stared moodily into the distance.

He left her at lunchtime to join the others for a cel-ebratory drink. She didn't go. The solution had been almost worse than the crime. Instead of pleasure she felt depressed and knew it was more than work that had depressed her.

For how long could she pull the wool over Matthew's eyes? She would never want a family. Never.

And he did.

When the phone rang she was glad of the interrup-tion and the estate agent's smooth voice. 'If you don't mind, Miss Piercy, we do have to gain entry to the property.' He had a nasal voice, a vague, London twang. 'Without measuring up we cannot print your details. Without details we have very little hope of selling your delightful little cottage. And without selling your most lovely place that super little place in Waterfall is going to slip right through your fingers.'

'That's right,' she said.

'And I do have other interested parties.'

'Yes,' she said and put the phone down.